FIRST KISS BEFORE FROST

JENNIFER BERNARD

ONE

Usually, Tristan Del Rey slept better on his boat than anywhere on land, including his own bed. Something about the way the waves gently cradled the *Desperado* made him drop off to sleep like a thirty-pound anchor. He and his boat had been through so much together—storms, accidents, breakdowns. He trusted his steel-hulled, thirty-five-foot Hansen more than he trusted most people.

By the same token, the slightest shift in the wind or the currents could bring him wide awake in no time. That was *his* part of the bargain. His boat kept him safe and he kept his boat safe. It was a perfect relationship. Nothing and no one could come between him and the *Desperado*.

But tonight, something was off. He kept tossing and turning on the narrow bunk where he usually slept so soundly. The familiar harbor night sounds—the lap of water against the floats, the sleepy cries of the occasional seagull, the clank of rigging—weren't lulling him to sleep. It was too still, maybe that was the problem. Not a single breath of wind stirred in the harbor. Flat calm, it was. The *Desperado* might as well have been in dry dock.

Or maybe the problem was the damn cruise ship docking overnight in Lost Harbor. Especially this one. The *Northern Princess* always brought trouble, at least according to local superstition. Last time it had stopped in Lost Harbor, a 6.2 earthquake had struck. The time before that, a summer storm had blown the roof off the Eagle's Nest Resort.

Generally, the cruise ships didn't even stay overnight. They used the nighttime hours to make their way to their next stop, like illuminated cities gliding across the dark ocean. He'd crossed paths with them occasionally, catching the sounds of music and parties drifting across the water as the *Desperado* chugged to the deepwater fishing grounds.

But tonight, the *Northern Princess* was waiting out a storm in the Gulf, which meant Lost Harbor was a sitting duck for whatever cursed trouble it might cause. The ship temporarily increased the population of Lost Harbor by almost one third. What if a bunch of the passengers decided to leave their own parties and descend on Lost Harbor's tiny collection of restaurants and bars? Under normal circumstances, that would be great, but with the *Northern Princess*, who knew?

Giving up on sleep, he rolled out of his bunk and dragged his ass into the immaculate galley of his boat. He prided himself on how orderly he kept the *Desperado*. Most fishermen were like that; while you were busy hauling in a net in thirty-foot seas, you needed to know exactly where everything was. If the weather got nasty and you had to batten down the hatches, same thing. One improperly stowed line could trip you up and send you sliding off the icy decks into the lethally cold water.

Not that any of that was going to happen on a peaceful September night in the harbor.

He put on the kettle to make himself a cup of tea. His last girlfriend had left a selection of loose herbal teas onboard, stowed in double Ziploc bags. One of them was supposed to help her sleep. He rummaged through the selection of plastic bags until he found the one with all the Zzzz's written on it.

Thank you, Mandy.

And then, as he scooped tea leaves into the tea ball, *Sorry it didn't work out. I warned you I was a bad bet.*

As he waited for the water to boil, he tuned into the other noises. He was so connected to his boat that a kind of sixth sense usually alerted him to any problems. But everything sounded normal. Was something going on outside, in the harbor? Or was he fucking losing it?

He touched the side of his head, under his bandana, where the hair was still growing out. What if his surgery had changed something about his brain? Made him hear things that weren't there? Worry about things that didn't exist?

Dr. Ian Finnegan had assured him that it wasn't possible. Actually, he'd said "highly unlikely," and Tristan had noted the distinction.

"In medicine, we can never say anything as an absolute," Ian had said. "Especially in neurology. The human brain, and humans in general, are too complex."

"I'm not. I'm a simple fisherman."

"Chrissie disagrees."

Yeah, he didn't *love* the fact that his brain surgeon was engaged to his high school girlfriend. But he'd gotten used to it.

"At any rate, it's not the point," Ian had continued. "All brains are complex, and of course there's an emotional and psychological component too. Have you been going to the support group meetings?"

At that point, Tristan had quickly ended the appointment. He had gone to a few meetings, but when he tried to talk, everything got jumbled up in his mind. The accident. The surgery. Divorce. So on and so forth. Why should he dump all that onto a bunch of other Lost Harbor residents who'd known him all his life? He was Tristan Del Rey, son of Victor Gammelgaard, the most respected fisherman in Misty Bay. He didn't want to reflect badly on his father. Best to keep everyone out of his business.

The whistle of the teakettle startled him out of his reverie. He poured boiling water into his favorite onboard mug—the one with the wide felted base and handle shaped like a whale tail—and headed for the deck. Three stair steps separated the belowdecks from the working deck, but he was able to take them in one long stride.

On deck, mug in hand, he surveyed the quiet harbor, seeking out the source of the strange off-kilter something that was keeping him awake at three in the morning. This late in the season, the harbor was only half full. The summer crowd had hauled their boats out of the water. Some of the fishermen had already ended their seasons. Their boats were either at the boatyard where they could work on them over the winter, or tucked under protective tarps in their yards.

Some hardcore sailors lived on their boats year-round. Tristan spotted a puff of smoke from Pedro Davila's boat. Two ramps away, a few night owls were having a beer and a smoke on the deck of the *Maggie Mae*. He inhaled the light scent of tobacco, which he loved smelling on the water, but despised in close quarters.

So far, he noticed nothing out of the ordinary. The nearly full moon gave the boats and the water a silvery glow. Up on the boardwalk, tall lampposts marched the length of the harbor. They shed light on a smooching couple behind the Olde Salt and a dog sniffing at something next to a garbage can.

Was that Fidget, Lucas' dog? Yup.

Tristan gave a soft whistle. The Irish setter lifted its head, recognizing his call. The harbormaster's dog was getting old; it wouldn't do for him to wander loose in the harbor all night. He'd take him onboard the *Desperado* and bring him to Lucas in the morning.

After setting down his mug inside the wheelhouse, he climbed over the railing and jumped onto the float where the *Desperado* was tied up. No need to bother with the boarding ladder that hung over the side. He could climb on and off this boat with his eyes closed.

He loped up the long ramp that led to the boardwalk. The aluminum squeaked with each of his steps. The tide was nearly high, meaning the ramp was almost level with the boardwalk.

"Here boy," he called as he reached the boardwalk. But the dog had decided to be cagey, and dodged behind a dumpster.

Tristan grumbled as he followed after him. "Don't be a pill. You know me, Fidget. You know I have treats for you. Have I ever let you down?"

He quieted his steps, hoping to surprise the dog.

In the silence, he thought he heard the sound of footsteps. He whirled around, but the boardwalk was deserted. He couldn't see anything on the float other than shadows. Touching the side of his head, he shook it off. He'd probably just heard a mouse scurry across the boardwalk. Not everything was a sign of impending doom inside his brain.

Behind the dumpster, he found Fidget panting softly and gazing at him with moist pleading eyes.

"It's three in the morning, buddy. I can't wake up Lucas and Megan. I can't let you roam around loose, either. You're coming with me, like it or not. I bet you'll like it, though. I have salmon."

Like any self-respecting Lost Harbor pup, Fidget recognized the word "salmon." His ears perked up.

"That's right. You know what I'm talking about." Tristan crouched down to rub the dog's ears. "Where's your collar? Did Ruby give you a bath and forget to put it back on?"

His ears twitched again at the mention of Ruby, Lucas' ten-year-old stepdaughter. "That's right, I'm a friend of Ruby. That means you can trust me. You do already, so just get over it, bub."

Was that the sound of aluminum creaking? He cocked his head, listening, but he didn't hear it again. Anyway, the ramps creaked all the time. It was one of the soothing harbor sounds that usually put him to sleep.

Tristan rose to his feet and patted his thigh. "Come on, boy. Salmon. Ruby. What more do you need to hear?"

Nothing, apparently, because Fidget followed him from behind the dumpster, onto the open boardwalk. There, he stopped and sniffed the air.

"Let me guess," said Tristan drily. "You smell fish."

The dog looked at him alertly, then trotted toward the head of the ramp.

"Good boy. You know where we're going, looks like. Smart dog."

Indeed, Fidget went right to the ramp and set one paw onto its corrugated surface. He shot Tristan a pained glance. None of the dogs liked the new ramps because they were built almost like cheese graters. The idea was to make them non-skid, so that even in icy conditions they'd be safe to walk on. For that, they worked great.

For dog paws, they were less than ideal.

Maybe he should include something about that in his mayoral platform. *"Vote Del Rey, Give Dogs a Say."*

Chuckling at the thought, he nudged Fidget onto the ramp. "You oughta be used to it by now. What kind of harbormaster's dog are you?"

When he still resisted, Tristan knelt next to him and coaxed him to give up a paw. In the haze of light shed by the tall lamp-post, he caught a glimpse of glass embedded in the pad of the dog's paw. "Aw buddy. You're injured. That'll teach you to poke around behind dumpsters. Now I really have to get you onto my boat. We need to get that glass out of your paw."

He gently settled his arms under Fidget's body and lifted him off the ground. The pup wriggled in surprise, but didn't fight him. Maybe he was happy to get a ride down the hated ramp, even from someone who wasn't Lucas or Megan or Ruby.

Tristan carried the warm bundle of dog fur down the ramp toward the *Desperado*. He had a complete medical kit onboard and could treat anything from broken bones to hypothermia. His EMT training had come in handy many times during countless fishing trips. When Jacob Volkov had gotten a fish hook embedded in the flesh of his shoulder, Tristan had managed to surgically remove it with nothing but whiskey and a fish knife. He would have left it in until they'd reached the Dutch Harbor clinic, but he couldn't take the chance since the fish hook had come out of the guts of a halibut and carried who knew what bacteria. These days, Jacob liked to proudly show off his scar, though he still couldn't drink whiskey without gagging.

Getting a piece of glass out of a dog's paw would be simple enough. "I got you, buddy," he whispered as he reached the side of the *Desperado*. "But first I have to get you onboard. Don't be afraid. I'll be right behind you."

Just because he could climb the *Desperado*'s boarding ladder didn't mean a dog could. He lifted the squirming canine over his head and nudged him forward. "Jump, Fidget. Go get that salmon."

In the next moment, Fidget disappeared over the edge. A loud thump followed, along with a squeal that did not sound remotely dog-like. It sounded like...a woman.

TWO

The world was taking its sweet time putting itself in order. And to be honest, the pieces Lulu recognized so far made no sense. Why was there a dog licking her face? Why was the ground kind of rocking back and forth? And why was there a strange man scowling at her? Why did he look like a pirate, with a bandana tied around his head?

Oh my God, had the *Northern Princess* been taken over by pirates?

No, she'd left the *Northern Princess*. She remembered that much. She'd had to. She wasn't safe on the cruise ship anymore, and neither was...

More details came rushing back. The kitchen staff had been loading up supplies from a late-arriving semi truck—the perfect opportunity to steal away from the ship.

A gigantic pallet of liquor bottles made a great place to hide. Then a pile of buoys. Dark alleys between weathered shacks. She'd worn all of her black clothing, whether it was weather-appropriate or not. After a long tense trip from one shadowed nook to another, the *Northern Princess* had receded into the distance, replaced by the smaller boats of the sleepy main harbor. Here there were only a few late-partying wanderers, oblivious to the presence of strangers.

Until that dog had poked his head behind the dumpster.

Same dog that was now enthusiastically licking her face.

She spluttered and turned her face away from its fishy breath. "Can you get your dog off me?"

The pirate looked offended by that request. "He's not my dog and you're in no position to be making demands. What are you doing on my boat?"

Oh. Apparently *she* was the pirate, not him.

She glanced around the deck quickly, but didn't see anyone else. Was that good or bad? She felt for her backpack; still there. Until she knew what was going on, she needed to be careful about what she said to this stranger.

"Sorry, I didn't know it was your boat."

"Whose boat did you think it was?"

She'd had no idea whose boat it was, of course. She was just looking for a good hiding spot. It had been the first boat at the foot of the ramp, and there had been a ladder. Temporary solution. Much more temporary than she'd hoped.

"John's," she said. "I thought it was John's boat. My mistake."

John was a common name. There were probably at least five Johns who owned boats in this harbor.

"John Smith or John Jones?" the pirate asked wryly.

The dog took a break from licking her face and sat back on its haunches. It lifted one drooping paw and gave a pathetic whimper.

The non-pirate stopped glaring at her and turned his attention to the dog. With a gentleness that shocked her—he was a big guy with quite the frown—he stroked the dog's coat. "Nobody go anywhere," he said. "I have to get my med kit."

He rose to his feet, graceful as a giant cat. *Very strong, much muscles,* she thought. And also—*Brilliant, this'll give me a chance to figure out what's going on.*

Pausing, he gazed down at her. "How's your head?"

Her hand flew to the back of her head, where a lump was rising. When the dog had knocked her over, she'd hit her head as she fell. Briefly, she'd seen stars dancing in the dark, and flashes of light exploding at the edges of her vision.

"Seems to still be attached."

"You're lucky you didn't hit the fish hold or the boom."

She had no idea which pieces of equipment he might be referring to; the boat practically bristled with gear and buoys and cables and rope.

"I have to get that glass out of his paw," he told her. "And I'll bring you an ice pack and a Tylenol if you want."

"You sure know how to show a girl a good time."

Her cheeky comment made one of his eyebrows rise, but didn't make him smile.

"Stay here," he commanded. "And keep hold of Fidget. He might try to follow me and I don't want him tracking blood on my deck."

She got the feeling he cared more about the dog than his gruff statement suggested. It was his eyes, she realized. The moonlight gave them an opalescent shine. She couldn't tell what color they were, maybe gray or blue or green, or some combination. But they held light in a way that was, well, kind of beautiful.

In her time performing on cruise ships, she'd learned to read people pretty quickly. This pirate didn't scare her, no matter how much he scowled.

"Aye, Captain."

He narrowed his eyes at her, almost as if he knew she meant that sarcastically and didn't acknowledge him as an authority in her life in any sense. She wasn't a member of his crew, after all. She was just a trespasser. Could you trespass on a boat? Was the technical term "stowaway"? Or did it have to be moving to make her a stowaway?

"Stay put," he repeated sternly, then disappeared down some stairs.

Lulu sat up and stared at the dog, who gazed pathetically after the pirate. He made a move to follow, but she grabbed onto the scruff of his neck.

"He's cute, I'll give him that, but you should stay here with me. Unless I go. Should I go?"

Silly question. Of course she couldn't go. She couldn't go anywhere until she'd determined one very, very important piece of information.

Besides, where would she go? She glanced at the boardwalk and the motley assortment of buildings lining the walkway. None of them were open for business at this hour. And what if someone came looking for her? What if *he* came? Mr. Bad Guy? She needed to stay out of sight until the *Northern Princess* had left this little port. She couldn't even remember its name, that was how shaken she was by everything that had happened.

All things considered, she was probably better off on this fishing boat than anywhere on land. Mr. Bad Guy wouldn't be able to search inside all these boats. He wouldn't *dare*. Boats were private property.

Soft footfalls brought her attention back to the deck of the boat. The pirate carried a white metal case with a red cross on it. He knelt next to her and the dog.

"What's your name?" she asked him as he opened the kit.

"Tristan. What's yours?" He drew out a silicone ice pack and cracked it to activate the cold. He handed it to her and she cradled it against her aching head.

Should she even tell him her real name? If someone did come looking for her, maybe a fake name would throw them off. But she was tired and her head hurt and she couldn't gather her thoughts enough to think of a good name.

"Lulu."

No last name. For either of them. Maybe that would be enough anonymity to keep her safe.

"What's your boat's name? Just so I know where I am."

"Not sure why it matters, but you're on the deck of the *F/V Desperado*."

"The *Desperado*?" She gave a short, delighted laugh. Was there ever a more perfectly named hiding place? No one was more "desperado" than her at this particular point in time. "Must be destiny."

"What's that supposed to mean?"

But just then, a sound from the shore caught her attention. Someone was walking down the boardwalk, playing a powerful flashlight among the fishing boats.

She flattened herself on the deck and put her finger to her mouth in a shushing gesture.

Tristan frowned, then lifted his head as a voice rang out across the harbor.

"Hey. You there. Seen anyone out here that doesn't belong?"

THREE

Tristan looked down at the woman plastered on the deck of his boat. Not a local, that was for sure. He would have known her, especially with that British accent. Probably not a tourist, either. Most of the visitors who came through Lost Harbor came prepared with fleece vests and mud boots. Or if they didn't, they quickly adapted and added a few layers. The boardwalk in particular, the way it extended into Misty Bay, could be windswept and chilly, especially at this point in the season.

But this woman wore black fishnet stockings and half-boots with a heel. Also, her jacket contained no fleece whatsoever. It looked like a black shag rug in the form of a hoodie. Her eyes were dark too, and they seemed to take up half her face as she silently pleaded with him not to give her up.

She could have saved her damsel-in-distress face. Of course he wasn't going to hand a woman over to some stranger with a flashlight. Any woman. No matter what face they made.

"Haven't seen a soul until you came through," he called. "What's going on?"

"Someone's missing from the *Northern Princess*."

"Maybe they drank a little too much and lost track of time."

The woman—Lulu? Seriously?—made a comical face at him. She had a face made for comedy, he realized. Expressive eyes, a mouth made for laughs, a dimple, a tiny nose. Everything about her features was just a little bit exaggerated.

"If you see anyone, contact security over at the cruise ship, would you?"

"Will do, sir."

He looked down at Lulu, whose smile had dropped completely. The moonlight leeched the color from her face. Or was she white with fear? Maybe she thought he was serious about contacting security. Maybe it wouldn't hurt to make her think so.

He kept quiet until the security guard, or whoever he was, had moved out of earshot.

"C'mon," he said quietly. "Let's get out of sight."

"Wait," she hissed back. "How do I know it's not out of the frying pan into the fire? I don't think I should go inside with you."

Huh. Good point. His sister Toni was an all-around badass, but she'd had a scarring encounter as a teenager in this very harbor. He hadn't known about it, and it had come as a shock when she'd told him. Since then, he'd questioned a lot of things he never had before. The way his crew sometimes talked about women, for instance. He used to tune it out, but lately he'd been calling guys out when they veered over the line.

He was absolutely no threat to this woman, but just because he knew that didn't mean she could assume that. She *shouldn't* assume that. The world was a long way from how it ought to be.

But if he tried to convince her that he was a good guy, he'd just come off as an ass. The only way you could really prove it was over time.

Besides, he had no need to prove anything to a trespasser. No matter how long her legs were and how intriguing she was.

Shit, he shouldn't even be looking at her legs. He had a dog to take care of.

In the end, he shrugged. "Up to you. If you leave, be careful on that ladder. You might be dizzy for a little while."

After taking a bandage out of the med kit, he wrapped it around Fidget's paw. He'd go after that bit of glass inside the cabin, where he'd have better light.

He bundled Fidget into his arms and got to his feet. Looking down at his unexpected guest, he saw that she still held the ice pack to her head. She looked scared, but he had no idea if he was the cause, or that security guard.

It occurred to him that he could be reading this situation all wrong. What if she'd stolen something from the cruise ship? What if *she* was the bad guy here? Seemed kind of sexist to assume that she was the victim in this scenario.

"Quick question," he said in a low voice, in case the security guard could somehow still overhear. "Are you a threat to my boat in any way?"

"What?" She blinked those long eyelashes at him. "Like how?"

He didn't want to give her any ideas. "Theft?"

"No."

"Destruction?"

"No."

"Vandalism?"

"No."

"Okay. I had to ask, because local superstition says the *Northern Princess* always brings disaster." He eyed her one more time, taking in her all-black clothing. Either she'd dressed for on-the-run chic or she had an emo-goth bent. With that quirky offbeat smile of hers, he had to go with on-the-run. "Good luck to you, whether you stay or go. Keep the ice pack."

SOMEHOW LULU HAD FORGOTTEN that her head was turning into a block of ice because of that cold pack. She shivered and peeled it away from her head. A breath of wind danced across the water and gave her another chill.

Carrying the dog and the med kit, Tristan moved around toward the hatchway that led to the lower deck of the boat. She'd spent enough time on cruise ships that she knew basic nautical terminology. Hatch. Line. Port. Starboard. As in, she'd been staying in a starboard berth. But she knew nothing about this kind of boat, though she assumed it was meant for fishing.

Okay. That meant the tall man was a fisherman. What else did she know? He was kind to dogs. He hadn't given her up to the man who said he was a security guard. He'd been irritated to find someone on his boat, but he hadn't kicked her off. Nor had he leered at her, despite her black fishnets, which were part of her Can-Can act but also the only black stockings she had.

As a cruise ship performer, she'd fended off more than her share of come-ons. Even when she was doing puppet shows for the kids, there was always that one randy single dad who slipped her his cabin number. Sometimes they weren't even single. Honestly, sometimes she thought her time as a dancer had given her a warped view of humanity.

But this man, so far, hadn't set off any red flags. Her choices were:

1. Stay on deck and freeze.

2. Leave the boat and find another dumpster to hide behind. With a bonus of possibly running into that "security guard."

3. Go inside a cozy boat cabin and help a hot guy bandage a dog's paw.

And then there was the other factor. The entire reason for this escape. She couldn't go anywhere until she figured that out.

If he was going belowdecks, she should go too and do some *Desperado* reconnaissance.

"Wait. You might need help with Fidget."

"I got it, don't you worry your frozen head about it."

"I worked for a dog groomer for a short time. It's much easier with two people."

He shrugged those wide shoulders. "Suit yourself."

She sniffed the air as another gust came through the harbor. Was that chamomile tea she smelled?

That did it. Some hot tea would be fabulous right now.

She came into a low squat and, keeping her head down, waddled across the deck like a duck. Mr. Bad Guy could have binoculars for all she knew. She couldn't risk standing up; she had to keep out of sight.

She didn't straighten up until she reached the bottom of the short stairway that led into a strictly functional galley. Tristan had spread a towel across a table that was bolted to the floor. Fidget lay on top of it like a king who was kindly allowing his paw to be tended to.

Shooting a quick glance around the galley, she spotted nothing out of the ordinary. Then again, if something was out of place, how would she know?

"What are you, a gymnast?" he asked as she stepped to the other side of the table. "That was quite a move you just did."

He must have been keeping an eye on her progress across the deck.

"I'm a dancer," she said with some pride. "Well, for now. Actually, maybe not anymore, since it seems that I've left my current place of employment."

"You've been working on that cruise ship?"

"Yes. It's my second stint on a cruise ship, but my first trip to Alaska. I always wanted to be a dancer, but to be honest, my career is probably over now."

"Hard to get good references when you leave your job in the middle of the night?"

"That too. But I'm thirty and all too familiar with these." She brandished the cold pack. "Thank you, by the way. My head feels a little better."

He fished a pair of tweezers from his first-aid case.

"Want me to do that? My hands are smaller than yours."

Not that she was paying any attention to his hands, with their gentle movements and big knuckles. She'd always been a sucker for a man's hands. In her opinion, they could tell you a lot about a guy. From her observation of Tristan's hands, she'd guess that he was strong, steady and cool under pressure.

And the fact that he handed her the tweezers spoke well of him too. He wasn't afraid to let a woman take the lead.

She bent over Fidget's paw while he kept a firm grip on the dog's coat. "Is there a vet in this town? With glass it's best to get a professional."

"Yes, we have a veterinary clinic, but I don't want to wake Doctor Vivian up at this hour. She has a new baby."

"If the glass is deep enough, it could hit something important. We don't want to simply yank it out."

He absorbed her words in a thoughtful way that she appreciated. People didn't always take dancers seriously, especially ones like her. She was no graceful ballerina; she was the comic relief. "I suppose we could just leave it until morning, but I hate to see him suffer."

She liked that he used the word "we," as if he accepted her help with this situation.

"Here, let me see if I can get an idea of how big the piece of glass is."

"The Olde Salt is pretty good about keeping the area clean. It's probably a small sliver that got overlooked."

"The Olde Salt?"

"Local watering hole. Fisherman hangout. Bottles have been broken, I'm not going to lie. But like I said, they're meticulous about keeping it clean. I know because my sister used to tend bar there. And because I've logged some time there myself."

"I don't drink much," she murmured as she bent closer to the piece of glass. Blood dried on the dark pad of Fidget's paw.

"I don't either," he said in a surprised tone. "I have an alcohol allergy."

"I have an allergy to sobbing on random shoulders, which happens after about one sip of anything alcoholic. The strongest thing I drink is a mocha latte. I don't suppose you have a cappuccino machine on board?"

"Of course we have one. It's right next to our massage chair, to the right of the hot stones," he deadpanned.

She broke out into a wide grin. "You're funny."

That drew nothing but a scowl from him. "Focus on Fidget, if you don't mind. What do you see in there?"

"It looks pretty small to me. Can you move that light closer?"

He picked up an electric lantern and held it over the dog. They both huddled over the Irish setter, who seemed delighted by all the attention. Carefully, she used the tweezers to get some purchase on the piece of glass. When she had a firm grip, she gently drew it out.

With a sigh of relief, she saw that it wasn't big enough to have hit any major veins.

"Surgery complete." She adopted an authoritative doctor-ish voice. "Nurse, you can go ahead and close."

Tristan didn't seem to mind playing the nurse. "Nice job, Doc."

He squeezed drops of blood from the pad of Fidget's paw, then blotted it with a clean antiseptic wipe. The dog whimpered, but despite his name, didn't fidget too much. Once Tristan had finished cleaning it, he wrapped a bandage around the paw and swatted Fidget on the rump. "You're good to go, buddy. Come on now. Want a treat?"

"You have dog treats onboard?"

"I promised him salmon and I could never break a promise like that. Salmon is a sacred trust." He crossed the galley and opened the half-size refrigerator. On the door, she saw an erasable magnetic whiteboard with a grid of chores marked out on it. *Clean the head. Make dinner. Swab the floor.* That sort of thing. All the spaces were blank, which she assumed meant that he was doing all those chores himself.

He drew out a dish covered with plastic wrap, then with the other hand whipped a plastic bowl off a shelf. All the shelves had pieces of wood nailed across them. In case of stormy weather, she imagined. The galley had a cozy, workmanlike feel to it. A chess set sat in a corner nook, with a box of paperbacks next to it.

Tristan set the bowl, now containing a ruby-red filet of salmon, onto the floor. That did it. Fidget leaped off the table and practically attacked the fish.

Lulu's stomach growled. She'd been too anxious to eat dinner in the crew quarters after their night's performances. She'd stuffed some water biscuits and wrapped Godiva chocolates into her jacket pockets—emergency rations, she figured. Would it be rude to whip those out now?

Did most trespassers worry about rudeness?

Digging into her pocket, she withdrew a handful of chocolates. "Would you like a little midnight snack?"

Casting her an odd look, he shook his head.

"Please tell me you don't have a chocolate allergy too. That would be altogether too grim."

"No, I love chocolate. But I get the impression that's all the food you have and I'm not about to take it from you."

"Not true." She reached into her other pocket and withdrew the packages of Saltines. "Midnight snack of champions."

He laughed for the first time and all of a sudden he didn't look like a stern boat captain but like a playful, very fit surfer. Between the sun-streaked hair and his rugged bone structure, he sure was a looker when he laughed.

And when he didn't, to be honest. Even when frowning at her, he was a good-looking man, and she'd seen her share as she traveled the world. But when he laughed, he looked like boat-loads of fun. No pun intended.

"Are you hungry?" he asked. "I can fry up some salmon for you. Little thank you for taking care of Fidget so well."

"Goodness, are you always this nice to trespassers? I'll have to leave a review on Yelp. 'When looking for a boat to hide out on, you can't go wrong with the *Desperado*. Generous host, decent accommodations. Word to the wise, bring your own cappuccino.'"

He snorted as he moved to the small galley stove. With each movement an efficient symphony of coordination, he whipped out a cast-iron frying pan, flung some olive oil in it, tossed in a salmon filet and shook some kind of spice mixture over the whole thing.

An instant later, a divine fragrance filled the air. Even Fidget lifted his head to sniff. Her mouth watered and her stomach growled again. By the time he plopped a plate on the table before her, he'd added some cold fried potatoes and a pickle.

She gazed up at him, speechless.

"Water? Tea? Ginger ale?" he asked her. "That's about all I have onboard right now."

"Some hot tea would be wonderful." Even though the galley was cozy, the chill from her midnight escape hadn't left her.

He brought her a box filled with Ziploc bags with labels on them. She sorted through the selection. Very feminine writing filled each label. *For sleeping,* with some zzzz's on it. *For when you miss me,* with a heart.

Wife? Girlfriend?

She shot a covert glance at Tristan's left hand, but saw no ring. That didn't mean much, though. Not all married men wore rings. Surgeons, for instance. Mechanics. Cheaters.

She selected some ginger tea, which had a drawing of ocean waves on it. "For seasickness?" she asked.

"Supposedly. I couldn't say, since I've never been seasick a day in my life."

"Neither have I. Everyone warned me I would when I took the job on the cruise ship. But I never did. Half the time it barely felt like we were at sea. It was like a floating shopping center. A mall, as you would say."

He filled the teakettle from a water cooler, then put it on the stove. "Are you going to tell me why you left this magical floating mall?"

She hadn't decided yet. He seemed trustworthy enough, but was there any benefit to telling him? Best to keep her cards close to her vest for now.

"Does it matter? I'm not exactly seeing this as a long-term relationship," she quipped. "If it were, we'd both have to share some deep dark secrets."

"Is that how it works?" Amusement rippled through his voice. "What if I don't have any?"

She eyed him up and down for an extended moment. He was one tall drink of water. Seawater, you could say. He carried himself with confidence and strength. And yet there was a shadow behind those eyes, which she now saw were an extremely attractive shade of gray with a smudge of blue. Her overall impression, based on her limited time on the *Desperado* and her many years of reading people, was that he had plenty of deep dark secrets.

"If you don't have any, I recommend you find yourself some," she said lightly. "Deep dark secrets make any man five times more attractive, depending on the secrets, of course. They should actually make an aftershave for it. Notes of woodsmoke and hidden wounds."

He was watching her so closely that the whistle of the teakettle made him jump. Moving back to the stove, he poured boiling water into a mug and handed it to her.

Fishing is the New Sexy, it proclaimed in flowing script. At the moment, she couldn't disagree. What could be sexier than a man who hid you from a bad guy, then made you salmon and seasickness tea?

FOUR

She blew on the tea to cool it down, and caught Tristan taking a quick look at her mouth. Her lower belly tightened. Oh dear, she knew that feeling. Early warning sign of attraction.

Ignoring it, because it didn't suit the needs of her current situation—which were to get very far away from Alaska as quickly as possible—she lifted the mug.

"Cheers," she said. "Here's to a full recovery for Fidget."

He leaned against the counter and folded his arms across his chest. "Fidget will be fine. He's tough. And he doesn't have a strange man with a flashlight searching for him at three in the morning."

"Surely it must be almost four by now."

A smile tugged at the corner of his mouth. Then he gestured with his chin at her plate of food. "Maybe some fish will get you talking. Go ahead, try that salmon. I caught it yesterday."

"Well then, I don't want its suffering to be in vain." She dug her fork into the succulent tender fish.

"Fish don't suffer in the way we think of it. They don't have nervous systems. Anyway, this salmon was at the end of its life."

"How would you know that?"

"Because that's their lifecycle. They come back to the place where they were spawned to release their eggs and reproduce. After that, they die. So eat up."

"That's either romantic or bleak, I can't decide which." Laughing, she picked up the fork and took a bite of the salmon. It slid down her throat like butter. Her eyes closed as she savored the delicate flavor. She barely had to chew, that was how tender it was. It was the best thing she'd ever tasted. And she'd been halfway around the world.

"How about neither? You're putting human qualities onto a damn fish. That's anthropomorphizing. That's one thing you learn being a fisherman. Fish are fish. Mermaids, on the other hand, well, they can be a handful."

Her head shot up. She searched his face for signs of teasing, but saw none. Utterly deadpan. Or utterly serious? Had she landed herself into the lair of a crazy man who believed in mermaids?

Or...were mermaids...*real*? Ever since the cruise ship had entered Alaskan waters, she'd sensed a kind of magic in the air. The silent, stately mountains, the secret gullies with their endless waterfalls. Talk about deep dark secrets.

Finally, a smile broke across his face, as if he couldn't keep it in anymore.

"*You.*" She tossed a piece of potato at him, but he snagged it before it hit him. "Well done, you had me going."

"Which direction? Were you starting to believe in mermaids or ready to call the psych ward?"

"Bit of both, actually. But I've always wanted to believe that mermaids existed."

"Then you should come out to sea with me sometime. I've seen things on the open ocean that I can't completely explain.

You stare at the waves enough, keep night watch enough, you start to believe that anything's possible."

His deep voice wove a spell around her. For a flash of a moment, she wished she *could* go to sea with him and witness these magical things he spoke of.

But she could quickly erase that possibility from her mind. She needed to get some distance from this place as soon as possible. If only she were a mermaid, and could simply dive into the harbor and swim until she reached safety.

"Well, maybe someday I'll come back to Lust Harbor and you can show me what you mean."

The expression on his face made her draw back. What had she said wrong?

"What did you say?"

"I said maybe I'll come back someday. I'm going to need to be moving along soon, as I'm sure you can understand. The bloke with the flashlight and all. But maybe in the future—"

"No, I mean what did you call this place?"

"Nothing." She frowned at him, mystified. "I called it by its name. Lust Harbor."

After another stunned moment, he threw his head back in a long, raucous laugh. "Let me get this straight. You got off your cruise ship to hide out in a town you think is called Lust Harbor? What were you on, the Love Boat?"

She blinked at him, not understanding the problem.

"It's *Lost* Harbor, lady. Lost, as in you've lost your keys, or you've lost your mind."

Really? She hadn't paid much attention to the itinerary after everything that had happened onboard. She'd been entirely focused on getting off that ship. And actually, she wouldn't be surprised if it had been misspelled in the information the cruise director had sent her.

"Apologies. I'm sorry to offend you. *Lost* Harbor. But ultimately it doesn't much matter. I still need to leave as soon as I can arrange it. I don't suppose you're taking this boat anywhere anytime soon?"

"Nope. I'm staying in port for now. Got other fish to fry, so to speak."

Haha. Funny play on words. But it didn't help her situation at all. She put down her fork, having lost her appetite as reality came flooding back. All she had with her was credit cards and some tip money she'd accumulated on the ship. She'd stuffed her backpack with a few changes of clothing, her phone, her laptop, and that was it. She knew no one in Lust—oops, Lost—Harbor, except Tristan the fisherman. And she had a criminal after her. And someone depending on her.

Honestly, diving overboard might be her best option right about now.

"Which other fish?" she asked in a last-ditch effort.

"Excuse me?"

"You said you had other fish to fry. Which other fish? Maybe I could make it worth your while to change your plans."

He shrugged and picked up his own mug, from which drifted the fragrant scent of chamomile. "I don't see how."

"Bribery? I can pay you rather well." *Rather* was a vague word, fortunately.

"It's not about money. I had a good season, after a rocky start. Now I've got something else I'm doing."

She stared at him in frustration. What could he be doing that compared to running for your life? Then again, he didn't know that was what she was doing. *She* wasn't even sure of that. Maybe that criminal would carry on with his cruise after he came up empty in his search of the harbor.

But she couldn't count on that, now, could she?

"If I fill you in on my situation, will you consider helping me?"

"I'm sorry, Lulu. I'm a helpful guy, in general. I don't mind helping you. But I need to be here in Lost Harbor right now."

A woman's voice calling from the deck made her jump about a foot into the air. "Hello in there. Anyone home? Burning the midnight oil while you face the inevitability of your defeat?"

In the next moment, a sprite of a woman danced through the hatchway. Her black hair was twisted into a ponytail and she wore a sparkly dress and mud boots.

She stopped in surprise when she saw Lulu. "Oh. Sorry to interrupt." She shot a glance at Tristan that Lulu couldn't read. Were they lovers? Friends? Rivals? Some weird combination of all of the above?

Tristan met Lulu's gaze, clearly sending her some kind of message. A "play along" sort of message, as best she could determine.

"Trixie, meet Lulu. Lulu is...uh, my new campaign manager. Lulu, this is Trixie Tran. Trixie is one of my competitors in the mayor's race. She thinks she has it all wrapped up, but she doesn't know I have a secret weapon." He repeated the "play along" look.

Mayor's race? *Campaign manager?* How the heck was she supposed to play along with that?

But he'd been kind to her, and she didn't want to muck things up for him in case Trixie was a romantic interest as well as a campaign rival.

"That's right. Tristan for Mayor! Rah rah. Nothing but the best for Lust Harbor!"

FIVE

Tristan winced as Lulu made her first mistake as his unofficial and very temporary campaign manager.

It was the only cover story he could think of this late at night. Trixie would never buy some kind of one-night-stand story. She knew he hadn't dated anyone since his surgery, and didn't want to. He and Trixie had a funny kind of off-and-on friendship that veered into flirtation sometimes, and even a long-ago one-night stand.

Which was enough to tell both of them they had no business being together.

Then they'd both decided to run for mayor, and things had been a little tense since then. Best to keep Trixie on a need-to-know basis when it came to the mysterious Lulu.

"She's still getting the hang of the job," he told Trixie. "This is our first meeting. She arrived late tonight and wanted to get right to work."

"That's right, lots to do, no time to waste." Lulu straightened her spine in what was probably a doomed effort to look more professional. At least she was wearing black, though fishnets and a fur jacket didn't exactly scream campaign manager.

Or maybe they did. Come to think of it, she was probably perfectly dressed to be *Trixie's* campaign manager. The two of them looked like they could have shared a wardrobe if Lulu hadn't been about a foot taller than Trixie, all of it in her legs. Long-legged Lulu. Was Lulu even her real name? Was that a name people had in England?

"Are you up early or out late, Trix?" Tristan asked. "Either way, you want some tea?"

"I'm out late, of course. Have you ever known me to get up early? I'm an insomniac," she explained to Lulu. "In case you're doing oppo research."

"Of course she isn't. We agreed to run a clean campaign, remember?"

"That was before you hired a campaign manager. We didn't agree to that."

"You have Ruthie Malone. I have to even the scales somehow."

"You have Toni." Trixie turned to Lulu. "His sister. She has a lot of influence in Lust Harbor."

Tristan choked back a laugh at how quickly Trixie had jumped on Lulu's error. Truly, she was a worthy adversary. "Actually, Toni says she's staying neutral."

"Really?" Trixie burst into laughter. "I have Ruthie to thank for that, don't I?"

"Probably."

Toni and Ruthie both worked at the new Lighthouse Brewery. The whole crew out there was tight. Ruthie Malone was the reason there was a campaign for mayor to begin with. She'd unearthed some long-lost Lost Harbor secrets that had driven the former mayor to resign. Obviously, her opinion held a lot of weight.

"Well, I guess I'll see you at the debate, Del Rey." Trixie gave Lulu one last curious glance before twirling around to head back on deck. Then she paused. "You. Campaign manager. Best prepare for a loss because this debate is going to be lit. It's not just me and Tristan running for mayor. Three other humans and a rooster are on the ballot."

Tristan groaned. "Cockles is running again?"

"Every time. One of these years he might even win." She turned back to Lulu, who was listening with an expression of fascination. "What issue do you think will be most prominent?"

Tristan wished he could telepathically throw some ideas at Lulu. Why hadn't he come up with a more believable cover story on the fly? Like, for instance, that she was his new housesitter or a dog sitter for the dog he didn't have.

But Lulu rose to the occasion. "Fish," she said.

"Fish?"

"Fish are the lifeblood of a community like this, no? Unless you want the cruise ships to be the main attraction. And we all know about cruise ships." Lulu rolled her eyes, as if she'd lived in Lost Harbor forever and knew what it was like when the cruise ships came to town.

On cue, a long horn sounded from the deep end of the harbor, where the *Northern Princess* was waiting out the storm.

Lulu's gaze flew to meet Tristan's. That was it. Her home, her place of employment, her ride back to wherever she came from—leaving port. He watched her swallow hard as an expression close to panic came across her face. No doubt, she was in some kind of trouble. And now, because of some weird cosmic serendipity, he was right in the middle of it.

With a new campaign manager.

"Thank the ancestors that ship is leaving port!" Trixie exclaimed. "It always brings a disaster with it." She eyed Lulu from under raised eyebrows. "I wonder what catastrophe it caused this time?"

"Cut the superstitious crap." Tristan scowled at her. "It's just a cruise ship."

One that had dumped a very bizarro situation on his deck. Where was this going to lead?

"Like you aren't just as superstitious as every other fisherman around here. The *Northern Princess* is trouble and we all know it."

Trixie left right after that, announcing her intention to get at least forty-five minutes of sleep before opening up her ice cream shop for the day.

Since Lulu looked like she was about to fall over on her feet, he offered her his bunk for the night.

"What about you?" she asked with a yawn.

"I'm going to keep watch on deck. Besides, I can sleep anywhere. I'm used to it. When you're fishing you grab sleep whenever you can. I'll take a sleeping bag and my pillow. You can use a life jacket." He showed her the bunk and set her up with his cushiest personal flotation device and a blanket. He noticed her gaze darting into every corner of the living quarters, almost as if she was searching for something.

He had nothing to hide. Did she?

Fidget jumped onto the bunk and flopped alongside her. Apparently Lulu had won his trust somewhere along the way.

Not wanting to watch her stretch out those endless legs in a lying-down position, he turned to go.

"Wait," she said. He turned to find her gazing at him seriously, arms wrapped around her blanket-draped legs. "Thank you."

"You can thank me by bringing me up to speed on what's going on."

"Or..." She smiled at him. "I can help you prepare for your debate. When is it?"

"Tomorrow night. The whole town will be there. You sure you want that kind of exposure?"

She twisted her mouth to one side, as if considering. Then she shrugged. "What better way to get to know Lust Harbor?"

With a wink, she lay flat and snuggled under his blanket, while he wrestled back a laugh. And a pulse of arousal.

Lust Harbor wasn't a bad name, come to think of it.

***

TRISTAN BARELY SLEPT the rest of the night. He sat on deck, his back propped against a crate, and watched the *Northern Princess* glide out of the harbor until its running lights disappeared from view. Hopefully the cruise ship was taking its curse along with it.

It did look like a floating mall making its way across the water. Lulu had a funny way of phrasing things. She was a funny girl. Kind of comedic, as if she told jokes for a living. Maybe it was part of her cruise ship job, along with dancing and wearing fishnet stockings.

He kept an eye out for the return of the stranger with the flashlight. Presumably he was back onboard the *Northern Princess,* having failed to track down the runaway passenger he was searching for. He hoped so, because Tristan hadn't liked the look or sound of him. He'd come across as almost menacing, with the blinding beam of his flashlight and the rough edge in his question about "someone that doesn't belong."

He was the one who didn't belong, and Tristan hoped he was long gone.

After all, if he became mayor, it would be his problem if unsavory characters were roaming around Lost Harbor.

Did he really want to be mayor?

The pit in his stomach told him *no*. But how could he disappoint the fishermen who had cornered him one night at the Olde Salt?

"No one else is going to look out for us like you will," Pedro Davila had said. "It's your legacy, man."

"S'right. It's time us fishermen got the credit we deserve for keeping this place on the map. We've never had a fisherman be mayor." Bennie Thompson had poured him another non-alcoholic beer, even though the expression on his face said he'd rather pour piss in his glass.

"That's because fishermen aren't cut out to be mayor," Tristan had pointed out. "We're gone all summer long, sometimes longer. We work too hard."

"And then we drink hard," said Pedro. "But you're different. You don't even drink."

That part was true enough, but it didn't seem enough to qualify for mayor. *Vote Del Rey! He doesn't drink, eh!*

"You're smart and you can represent us good," said Deke Armstrong.

"Well," he'd corrected. "I can represent us *well*."

"Glad you agree." With a wink, Deke toasted him with a shot of rum. Tristan groaned because he'd fallen into such a dumb trap.

"Shipp was a welder before he ran for mayor. Why not a fisherman?"

"He was a retired welder. He had time on his hands. I don't."

"Everyone's busy in the summer. With the internet and cell phones, you can do everything remotely during fishing season." That was Ralphie Reed's comment. He represented the younger crew of deckhands, the ones who posted TikToks of their biggest catches.

"I get why it's important for a fisherman to have a turn at mayor, but why me? Ask someone else."

They'd all shaken their heads in refusal. "We all talked about it, and you're the only one that could pull it off. You're a Del Rey. With ol' Victor retired and gone, you gotta step up, Tristan."

What the hell did being a Del Rey have to do with it? Just because his father had won everyone's respect with his mere presence, that didn't mean Tristan had the same ability. He wasn't that kind of leader. Leaders didn't doubt themselves the way he did. They didn't berate themselves over their accidents and brain surgery and divorce.

In the end, he'd given in and agreed to run for mayor. Trixie had done the same, God help him. So had a few other people in town. Six candidates in all, including a rooster, were vying for the right to lead Lost Harbor.

Now that he'd committed, goddamn it, he was going to give it his best. For the fishing community. They'd put their faith in him and apparently didn't realize that was a bad play. He wasn't himself lately, not since the accident. Nothing felt right. Even being at sea didn't help. He'd lost his zing, his sense of fun.

As the sun crested the mountains of Lost Souls Wilderness, creating a rim of vibrant light along the jagged peaks, for a moment it came back. He forgot himself and his troubles, and gazed in awe at the spectacle of the sunrise. The fresh air whispered across his face. For one short moment, he felt alive and whole again.

And then he touched the side of his head and the darkness closed back in. He'd been medevacked off his own boat. Flown to Anchorage for swelling on his brain. Just like Julie had always warned him during their marriage. *Someday you're going to regret spending your entire life on that damn boat. You're going to wish you'd paid more attention to actual real live people like your wife.*

A failure. That's what he was. Not only when it came to his

marriage, but now as a boat captain. Which pretty much covered all parts of his life.

Fidget trotted up from the open hatchway and licked him vigorously on the cheek. At least he'd helped Lucas' dog, so there was that. In Fidget's eyes, he was a hero.

He'd helped a strange woman, too. It almost felt like a dream. Like, was it really possible that a dancer in fishnets had snuck onto his boat and was currently curled up in his bunk?

"Where's the girl, Fidget? Still sleeping?"

At that moment, Fidget decided to live up to his name and trotted to the side of the boat, where he whimpered pathetically until Tristan hauled himself to his feet.

"All right, boy. You go find Lucas. Don't mention our stowaway, though."

He lifted Fidget over the side of the *Desperado* and set him on the float. The dog shook himself off and loped toward the ramp that would lead him to the harbormaster's office.

Tristan took out his phone and texted Lucas that Fidget had spent the night on his boat. Then, thinking it over, he added, *Got a situation on the Desp.*

Just in case Lulu Long-Legs wasn't on the level, he figured he ought to alert someone. Even if she was, the harbormaster deserved to know that a sketchy dude had prowled around the harbor last night.

SIX

"No no, not like that. You look like a goose on stilts, darling! Don't laugh, I'm being serious. One more time, Louise. Aim for graceful, if you can."

She didn't aim for graceful. She never did. Instead, she aimed for funny.

Nothing entertained Mum more than helping Lulu learn new dance steps. And if there was one thing Lulu was committed to, one hundred percent, it was making her mother smile. She kept a mental scoreboard of smiles versus grimaces of pain. If the smiles outpaced the grimaces on any given day, she considered it a good day.

She tried the step again, jump, extend, twirl.

"Better, Mum?"

"Not even a tiny bit."

They both laughed and Lulu propped herself against the wall for a short break. Mum was getting tired, she could tell. It was the way her eyes got glassy and her skin gray.

"I've come to the conclusion that the Royal Ballet is unlikely to want me," she declared, wiping some perspiration off her forehead.

"I'm afraid you're right, darling." Lulu's mother never fudged the truth. She always faced it head on. "Perhaps a Charlie Chaplin bit, or Fred Astaire."

"Like this?"

Lulu picked up a floor lamp and whirled it around the room, then stumbled as the cord caught in the outlet. She pretended to rescue the lamp, as if it was a damsel in distress, then rained kisses on the lampshade.

Her mother laughed until a twist of pain caught up with her. She rolled to her side because she hated showing Lulu how much she hurt.

Lulu pretended she couldn't see. That was the way they played it. Her mother hid her suffering and Lulu hid her distress. Lulu danced and her mother cheered. Every day they both knew it could be the last day.

Mum didn't want her to grieve, and so she didn't. Not in front of her, anyway. But she was on intimate terms with her pillow.

No, Mum wanted something else from her.

"Set that poor lamp down, darling. You're making it dizzy."

Lulu abandoned the lamp and hurried to the bed the hospice nurses had set up in their living room. "Do you need something, Mum? A pot of tea?"

"Lord no, I couldn't possibly bear another pot of tea. What I need, dear girl, is to think about you having some fun once this is over. I recommend some dancing and perhaps a few men. Or women, should you choose."

"Mum—"

"Or stick to men if you prefer. Somewhere out there." She flung her bone-thin arm to indicate the window. "See the world. Live your life. Leave all this behind. Take a wild leap. Dance your heart out."

Smile. She needed her mother to smile. "Didn't we already establish that the Royal Ballet would laugh me off the premises?"
"As indeed they should."

ROYAL. Princess. *Northern Princess.* Is that close enough, Mum?

Slowly, reluctantly Lulu came awake. Leaving those dreams —not so much dreams as mushed-up memories—always made her sad. Sometimes she wished that she didn't have them, but more often, she felt profoundly grateful that she did. Her mother had been gone for nearly seven months now, and these occasional dreams were all she had left of her acerbic, affectionate presence.

But she could never hang onto them for long. They evaporated in the daylight like dew on spiderwebs. Other details took over.

Her feet were cold. All night long something warm had weighed down her feet, but now her own personal blanket was gone. The other blanket—the one that belonged to the fisherman whose name she couldn't remember at the moment—had slid halfway to the floor. She sniffed her armpits. God, she needed a shower. Where did one shower on this boat? What about breakfast? What about everything else, like...staying alive, for instance?

"Psssst," she hissed. No answer. Huh. Everything had been fine last night. She'd just assume it still was this morning.

And what next?

She should contact the authorities, but which ones? Maybe the British embassy? The FBI? She swung her legs over the edge of the bunk. A piece of trim ran the length of it, formed a raised perimeter meant to keep the occupant from rolling off. Nice thought, but she had bigger problems to worry about than falling out of bed. Or into bed, for that matter.

How far was Mr. Bad Guy going to take this? Would he keep

up his pursuit or decide to cut his losses? Was he back on the *Northern Princess* or still here in Lust—Lost—Harbor?

Voices sounded from above. Probably from on deck. The fisherman—Tristan! That was his name—must be awake by now. She didn't even know what time it was. It could be so hard to tell in these Northern latitudes.

She dropped to her knees next to her backpack, which she'd stashed right next to the bunk. Rummaging though it, she found her phone, then hesitated. She'd turned it off last night because phones could be tracked, and she honestly had no idea what Mr. Bad Guy was capable of. Was it safe to turn it back on now? She had no idea, so she left it off.

She glanced around the tidy cabin. Bunks, four in all, lined the sloping aluminum walls. Each had a foam mattress covered in heavy-duty marine fabric. Underneath each bunk sat plastic storage containers. There was absolutely no privacy, but since she was the only one here, she decided not to worry about it.

Quickly she stripped off her black clothing and stuffed it into the bottom of her bag. Maybe she could find a launderette somewhere in town. She pulled on new underwear and a pair of cream dance tights, along with a sundress printed with bright tulips. Remembering that it was September in Alaska, and likely quite cold outside the cozy cabin of this fishing boat, she added a Royal Ballet hoodie that her mother had given her, sarcastically. She considered it good luck, and if ever she'd needed some of that, the time was now.

Realizing that she'd left her hairbrush behind on the ship— Could that get her in trouble? Could they collect DNA from that?—she combed her fingers through her hair, then gathered it into a braid. Braids worked well for women in dire circumstances. Just look at Katniss Everdeen.

Making a face at her own absurdity, she pulled on her trainers and shouldered her bag. Last step, the biggest beauty essential of all: paste on a smile. She knew better than most how to do that. Not only did she do it for a living every time she stepped onstage, but she'd also perfected the technique during her years taking care of her mum.

"Brilliant morning to you all!" she chirped as she stepped onto the deck. Four faces swung toward her, belonging to Tristan, another man, and two women. They were gathered on the stern deck, each holding a thermos or a takeaway cup. "Hullo everyone, I'm Lulu. I'm Tristan's campa—" She caught the slightest shake of Tristan's head. "Trespasser. I'm his trespasser."

Tristan choked back a laugh. He cleared his throat and stepped forward. "Coffee, trespasser?"

That sounded like a good idea. "Don't mind if I do. Then perhaps you could direct me to the closest hotel or inn or hovel of some kind."

"See, that's what we've been talking about," he murmured as he poured coffee from his insulated aluminum mug into a tin cup for her. It instantly warmed her hands. Even with her hoodie and her tights, the chill of the morning air made her skin prickle.

Or maybe his voice did that. Or his big body so close to hers. "Who is we?" she whispered to him. "I don't need a 'we' talking about me."

"Give them a chance," he murmured. More loudly, he went on, "Lucas Holt is the harbormaster."

Lucas lifted his thermos in acknowledgement. Dark-haired and stern-faced, he certainly looked like he was in charge. "Charmed," she told him.

"And this is Maya Badger, she's the police chief."

Oh dear. This was getting serious. The *police chief?* Maya Badger had rich brown skin and gorgeous amber eyes that seemed to perceive everything at a glance. Could she detect the bit that Lulu was keeping hidden?

Most importantly, was she to be trusted? After her experience with the "security chief" on the *Northern Princess*, Lulu couldn't assume anything.

"I'm almost entirely innocent, Madam Police Chief," she said breezily, hoping it came across as a joke instead of a nervous deflection.

Maya's eyebrows rose. "Then you're prepared to cooperate in the investigation?"

Lulu swallowed hard. There was already an investigation? She shot a smoldering glance at Tristan, who'd wasted no time at all selling her out. He shook his head slightly, a smile playing across his lips. Which were quite attractive, she noticed, firm and well-formed. Highly kissable.

"Absolutely," she assured the police chief.

In fact, Lulu would be conducting her own investigation into the local authorities, although she'd be relying on her gut instinct and talent for reading people.

"And this is my sister, Toni Del Rey," Tristan continued. "I'm not sure why she's here, except that she has a knack for being in the middle of anything interesting."

"Pleasure to meet you, Toni." Tristan's sister didn't look much like him, being dark-haired with a Spanish flair, as compared to his tawny hair and light eyes. "But I assure you all, I'm not at all interesting."

Maya was watching her steadily. Instead of a uniform, she wore snug black pants and a burgundy sweater that made her skin glow. "All sorts of things are interesting to a police chief, especially anything to do with the cursed *Northern Princess*. I want to hear more about this man Tristan spotted on the board-walk last night. Why were you hiding from him?"

"Unwanted advances. Occupational hazard for cruise ship performers." That last part was certainly true, though Mr. Bad Guy hadn't shown any interest in her until she'd gotten in his way

"Hm." Maya clearly didn't believe a word of that. "I thought cruise ships were pretty vigilant about protecting their crews."

"Generally, yes." Lulu decided to go on the offensive. "Am I in trouble, Chief Badger?"

"Haven't decided yet."

Hm, maybe going on the offensive didn't work with someone like Maya. "Well, do let me know. I'll give you my email address and you can keep in touch." She moved toward the side of the boat. Sheer bravado. She couldn't leave yet. Not alone.

But Lucas stepped in front of her. "I'd appreciate a full description of this man. I want to know if I run across him in my harbor."

That seemed fair enough. After all, it was her fault that bastard had come into the harbor. "A little under two meters, fourteen stone, age between fifty-six and fifty-eight, I'd say. Closely shaven head with a bit of salt-and-pepper at the temples. You might even call him a silver fox except his eyes are too close together to be truly attractive. Roman nose that has survived a few fistfights. Eyes the shade of my black snakeskin boots, though a bit bloodshot, but that could be due to a penchant for whiskey. I'd certainly check at the local tavern if I were you. What's it called again, the Moldy Salt?"

Tristan gave a snort that could have been either laughter or disbelief. "The Olde Salt. You're really going to have to brush up on your place names."

"But that description," said Maya. "It's very detailed."

"I have that kind of memory," Lulu explained. "I'm not much for names, but I'm very visual. Once I see a face, I can summon it up at will."

"Do you know this man's name?"

"He's registered on the ship as Sebastian Perro."

Maya picked up on her phrasing. "Are you saying that's not his real name?"

Lulu was a hundred percent sure that it wasn't, but her online research hadn't uncovered anything concrete. "I suppose you'd have to ask him. But I doubt it."

"Why is that?"

She had to tell at least some of the truth to this persistent woman. "I recognized him from a true crime program on the telly. My mum and I used to watch them. That wasn't the name they used on the show."

"Are you sure you'd remember?" Tristan asked dryly. "Names don't seem to be your strong point."

"Yes, I'm sure, because I use mnemonics to remember. *Perro* means 'dog' in Spanish, so it brings a clear image to my mind."

"And you say you're not interesting? I call bullshit." Toni spoke for the first time.

Lulu gave a little curtsy. "There you have it, my one interesting ability. May I go now?"

"That's what we want to talk about," said Tristan. "We think you should stay here in Lost Harbor for a while."

She looked around the circle of serious faces. "Why?"

"Because you're obviously in some kind of trouble. We can help to protect you here. It's a small town and we tend to look out for each other."

"But I'm not a resident of your lovely little town. I'm a stranger."

"Didn't you just get introduced to all of us?" Toni asked. "I'm Toni, in case we need to do it again."

"Lucas," said Lucas.

"Maya."

"And I'm Tristan, and of course you've already met Trixie and Fidget." Tristan gave her a faint smile. "There you go, you've already met one one-thousandth of the town."

"But..." She bit her lip, unexpectedly moved that they would actually care enough to propose that she stay. It also made her feel guilty about everything she wasn't telling them. "You don't even know the whole situation."

"That can be corrected," he pointed out. "But it doesn't matter. It's not as if you're a thief in hiding."

"How do you know?"

"I searched your bag last night." He flashed an unrepentant grin. "Basic safety precaution for all trespassers and/or stowaways."

She flushed, thinking of her red silk thong and the tiny vibrator that kept her company on her travels. "I assume I passed the inspection?"

"With flying colors."

Her own color deepened. Was he referring to the red thong?

"Sorry. I kept it quick and impersonal. I had to be sure I wasn't harboring an armed fugitive."

"I'm British," she said indignantly. "We don't carry guns around like you lot."

"Fair enough. By the way, guns aren't allowed on my boat, just for future reference, in case you're tempted at some point."

What made him think she was going to stay on his boat? That was not at all a good solution, because sooner or later he'd catch on to her big—or should she say little—secret. She was amazed that he hadn't already. She opened her mouth to say "thanks, but no thanks," when Toni spoke up.

"Here's the thing, Lulu. Leaving Lost Harbor isn't as easy as you might think. You can drive, but since you don't have a car you'd have to either buy, borrow or steal one. You can always hitchhike, which is generally safe here but possibly not in your circumstances."

"No car hires?"

"Rentals? Not here, no. You'd have to get to Anchorage for that. You could fly. We have two commercial flights a day to Anchorage. It used to be two a week, so don't complain. But the airport is tiny and very easy to monitor. If you're trying to avoid someone, you're a sitting duck there. You could also hire a helicopter or a twin-engine plane. But they all leave from the same airport, so it wouldn't make much difference."

"What about a boat?"

"Excellent question. There's a reason why smugglers are so hard to catch. Boats are the best way to sneak out of Lost Harbor. In case you haven't noticed, you're on a boat. My big brother Tristan happens to be an excellent skipper."

"That's why we think you should stay with Tristan until we've made sure your pursuer isn't still here." Lulu found Maya's practical tone more convincing than Toni's lighthearted freestyling. "If he is, well, the *Desperado* can be underway in a matter of moments."

"And as the harbormaster, I have a good read on strangers in the harbor," said Lucas.

"But why do you even *care*?" Lulu repeated. "I'm no one to you. I'm a random cruise ship dropout."

"Not true. You helped Fidget." Lucas's grin lit up his stern dark face. "Any friend to my dog is a friend to me."

Should she mention that it was her fault Fidget got hurt in the first place? He'd stepped on the glass behind the dumpster, after all.

"Also, you're on my boat, and that makes you my responsibility. It's the law of the ocean." Tristan downed his coffee in one long swig. "But of course it's up to you."

The law of the ocean? Was that a real thing?

As she gazed around the circle of faces—all basically strangers—her heart gave an unexpected twist. They truly did seem to care about her safety. Their primary concern was for their town, no doubt. She could understand that. A tiny collection of souls perched on the edge of a vast forbidding wilderness...their only chance of survival was to band together.

She, on the other hand, had been so alone since her mother died. During the years she'd spent caring for her, friends had dropped away, jobs had evaporated because she'd missed too many days. After Mum had died, she'd journeyed into a kind of wasteland of grief, a lonely wanderer trying to find her way.

The cruise ship job had satisfied her promise to her mother—there was traveling, dancing, even a few men. But she'd kept all those connections light and fun, not wanting to weigh them down with all her emotional baggage.

"How would this work?" she finally asked. "Would I still play campaign manager? I should warn you I have zero experience in that role. I convinced my postman to vote against Brexit, but that's where it ends."

"What kind of work do you usually do?" Maya asked.

"On the cruise ship, I was a dancer and a children's entertainer. Tap is my specialty. I'm especially good with kids. I do a soft-shoe clown act that they adore. I'm quite good at pantomime."

They all exchanged glances. "Not much call for tap-dancing clowns around here," said Lucas. "What did you do before you joined the cruise ship?"

"I've had many small jobs. Dog groomer, garden tender, silver polisher." Then, for some inexplicable reason, she went further. "But for the last few years I've been a full-time caregiver."

"A licensed caregiver?" asked Maya. "We could probably find—"

"No. Strictly family. So that's a no-go." Impatiently, she shook off the conversation, already regretting that she'd revealed that much. "Look, clearly I'm not suited to a life in Alaska." She gestured at her sunny outfit. "I'm like a daisy next to a clump of," she eyed the stern deck, "seaweed."

Tristan snorted and braced a hand on Lucas' shoulder. "I'm thinking we're the seaweed in that scenario."

"I like it," Lucas said. "Underestimate seaweed at your peril. A clump of the stuff can stall you out like nobody's business."

Good to know.

"Anyway, no one's suggesting you live here," Tristan continued. "Just get through the next few days until it's safe to leave."

Did she have a better plan? Not really. She'd been scrambling ever since she'd figured out what Mr. Bad Guy was up to.

"If I'm going to stay, I'll need to blend in a bit more. Can anyone direct me to a store where I can procure some Alaska clothing? Nothing with a moose on it, mind you. They terrify me. They're so large, how can they be allowed to roam around freely?"

The little group of rescuers reacted with relief and amusement.

"We got you, babe," said Toni. "We'll have you looking like an Alaska chick in no time."

SEVEN

After leaving Lulu in Toni's hands—there was talk of shopping, then toasting their shopping at the Olde Salt—Tristan drove to his house to check in on the roof repairs. The leak had started in the spring. He'd first noticed it while he was recovering from his surgery.

From his couch, he'd watched the amorphous stain on the ceiling spread and change shape. It was almost like a movie, if you didn't need characters or a plot or a setting. There was dialogue, though. Or at least a monologue.

"Way to kick a guy when he's down," he'd grumbled at the stain. "You couldn't wait until I got back on my feet? What's that face you're making? Better lose the attitude or I'll paint over you like a bitch."

Yeah, he'd come close to losing it during his recovery. If not for Bash and Toni and even Trixie, he might have.

In a more energetic moment, he'd put a bucket under the leak, then dragged his ass over to empty it when required. When he got clearance to move around more, he'd gone up on the roof and added some caulking, but really he needed a new roof. One successful fishing season later, the new roof was going on. He had the skills to do it himself, of course, but since he was running for mayor he'd hired a buddy to do it.

Also, he didn't trust his body the way he used to. Blame it on his surgery, or the toll years of fishing took on a guy...either way, he was a lot more cautious than he used to be.

His house sat on a ridge overlooking Misty Bay. He loved the way clouds of mist clung to the bluffs and surrounded his home in suspended moisture. In the off season, he sat for hours with a cup of coffee, watching the clouds and listening to music, or losing himself in a book, or kicking back with some friends. That was what he'd be doing this winter, he assumed, but the prospect didn't fill him with the usual contentment.

Maybe he should do something else. Travel, the way Trixie did. Spend some time in Chile with his parents. Adopt a dog. Learn a foreign language besides Spanish.

Of course, by this time next month, he might be mayor of Lost Harbor and have no spare time. He could be running this town. The idea filled him with nothing but dread. Why had he agreed to this cockeyed campaign?

The crew hadn't arrived for work yet. Heavy gray-bellied clouds hung overhead, which made him wonder if they weren't going to risk working on his roof today. Checking his phone, he found a text from Jon saying exactly that.

Damn. Another delay. He'd be staying on his boat just a little bit longer.

With a trespasser, no less.

He put his dirty clothes in the washing machine, then grabbed a few changes of clothing from his bedroom—extra sweaters and a set of long underwear. Then he collected the pile of paperwork he'd gathered to prepare for tonight's mayoral debate. It was mostly facts and figures about the fishing industry and what it meant to Lost Harbor. That was his platform, after all. He needed to put together a mission statement that would sum up the reason people should vote for him.

So far, he hadn't come up with much.

I can lead a fishing crew, so why not a town? Nope.

I'm a fisherman and it's our turn. Definitely not, though that seemed to be the thinking of the fishing community.

Tristan Del Rey. Born to Lead. Just like my father. Ugh. Terrible. How was he supposed to fill the shoes of someone like Victor Gammelgaard? It was impossible. He was just a guy, a fisherman who didn't take much seriously except for fishing.

He stood at his front window for a long moment and surveyed the town where he'd been born and raised. A thousand feet below his ridge, at the base of the bluffs, tiny toy houses were scattered like Legos on a green carpet. Some clung to the hillsides, others perched on the shore. Extending into the bay like a long curving arm was the boardwalk. On one side, it embraced the harbor and its bustling, bristling boats.

On the other side, rollers pounded against the breakwater that shored up the muddy spit of land. From here those waves looked like meaningless wrinkles in the water's surface, but Tristan knew they were five-foot southwest swells. Because he knew that sort of thing.

At the very end of the boardwalk sat the town's largest hotel, the Eagle's Nest Resort and Spa. Just before that was the deep harbor dock where the cruise ships tied up. It was empty, and would be for the rest of the winter, unless an oil tanker needed to come in for repairs.

With the *Northern Princess* back at sea, was there any way to check if anyone else besides Lulu had missed the departure? That might tell them if her pursuer was still in town.

He took out his phone and called Harris Badger. Maya's father was a retired Coastie and still maintained solid connections with his old shipmates.

"Tristan here," he told the man when he answered. "Is there any way to get a cruise ship to answer questions about their passenger manifest?"

"Not too likely. You'd have to get a warrant, would be my guess. They keep that information pretty tight. But it never came up when I was running the post. We never had any problem with the cruise ships. What's going on?"

"Oh, I'm sure Maya will reach out if it comes to anything."

"All right then. I'll wait for her call. How're *you* doing?"

For a moment, Tristan couldn't quite come up with an answer. "Fine, I guess. Head's doing better."

"Heard you had a good season."

"Yes, sir. Despite all odds."

"Well, don't be afraid to reach out if things are hard. It's hard coming back from an event like what happened to you. I know firsthand."

Harris had recently undergone heart surgery, so he probably did understand. Except that Harris was in his seventies, while Tristan was thirty-two and in his goddamn prime. So in that way, it was nothing alike. "Yeah. Thanks." Another thought struck him. "Mr. Badger, did you ever consider running for mayor? You were the acting police chief for a while, weren't you? And the commander of a Coast Guard station? You're an experienced leader. Why not go for mayor?"

A teasing note entered Harris' voice. "You getting cold feet, boy?"

"No." His feet had never really been *warm*, so the phrase didn't apply. "I just think you'd be a good choice."

"Maybe, but I don't need that kind of responsibility. I'm getting married, and I don't want to be the boss of my own daughter. Besides, you know what they say. Heavy lies the crown. Or the veto pen, as the case may be."

They both chuckled. "Point taken. If you change your mind, though, I'd be tempted to clear the field for you."

"Mighty kind of you, but if I change my mind, I'd be the frontrunner before you could say 'come to order.'"

Tristan laughed. "No doubt, no doubt."

He ended the call and transferred his wet laundry to the clothes dryer. Once it was dry, it could sit there until he made it back up here. Grabbing his duffel, he stuffed his paperwork inside along with his clothes, then decided to make one more call.

"Hey Toni," he said when his sister came on the line. "Are you with the trespasser?"

"If you're referring to your new campaign manager, yes."

Tristan groaned silently. Apparently they'd decided to stick with his ridiculous on-the-fly cover story. Its only real benefit was that it was consistent with what he'd told Trixie. Other than that, it was unbelievable, ridiculous, and guaranteed to be embarrassing for him. Running for mayor felt awkward enough, but now he'd have to act like he knew what he was doing.

"Is there anything she might need from the house? I'm here now but I'm about to leave."

"Let me check." Toni disappeared for a brief moment, then Lulu came on the line.

"Hullo there, Tristan."

A quick thrill when through him at the sound of her breezy voice. Even though he'd known her for less than a day, it felt oddly familiar.

"Hey, how's it going with my sister? Is she behaving herself?"

"What would be the fun in that?"

"Right. Dumb question. I'm at my house right now. Is there anything you might need from here? Toothbrush, pillow, that sort of thing?"

"You have a *house*? I thought you lived on your boat."

He pulled his phone away from his face and frowned at it,

before continuing on. "Of course I don't live on my boat. I am at the moment because...eh, doesn't matter."

"Well, don't worry about me, I've got everything I need. Toni helped me find the perfect Lost Harbor campaign manager uniform. I'm ready to get to work."

"So you decided to stick with that bonehead idea of mine?"

"Yes, for lack of a better one. We decided that if Mr. Bad Guy is asking around town about someone from the cruise ship, no one will think to mention a campaign manager."

"I suppose that's right, but that doesn't mean you have to actually *be* a campaign manager. You can fake it."

"Oh darling, I will most certainly be faking it. But I'm also going to spend some time online at the library researching how to run a good campaign. I promise I won't let you down."

"It's really not—"

But Lulu disappeared at that point and Toni came back on the phone. "We're also dying her hair. Extra safety precaution."

"Good thinking." What color was her hair? Perhaps a strawberry blond? He didn't quite remember, mostly because he'd been preoccupied with her legs in those fishnets. Not that he was about to admit that. "Well, I'll see you two later."

"Dinner with me and Bash," she said. "That's an order."

"Aye, Captain. Wait, I can't. I have the debate. Jesus, I nearly forgot. I'll just stop at the Brewery and have some of Alastair's special, whatever it is."

"Then maybe we'll see you there. I'm trying to stick to edge-of-town places, and nothing's more edge-of-town than the lighthouse."

The Lighthouse Brewery and Museum was located a few miles outside the town borders, on a historic piece of property that now belonged to Chrissie Yates, who happened to be his old high school girlfriend. He used to ride his bike out there to see her, and occasionally had taken the water route in his father's

Zodiac. Now it was no longer just a homestead, but a thriving business.

And Chrissie was no longer his girlfriend. She was now engaged to Dr. Ian Finnegan, who happened to be the neurosurgeon who had operated on Tristan.

Sometimes he wondered if the breakup with Chrissie was where his life had gone wrong. He'd rebounded into marriage, then focused on establishing himself as a fishing captain, and there went his marriage and...

He shook off the trip down memory lane.

"More good thinking. Thanks, Toni. Has she seen any sign of this mystery baddie?"

"No." From the lack of detail, he figured she couldn't really say more in front of Lulu. "But she did get a marriage proposal from Pedro Davila."

The weirdest sort of sensation shot through his chest. Was it...*jealousy*? For fuck's sake, that would be ridiculous. Not only was Lulu nothing but an inconvenience to him, but he didn't *get* jealous.

Julie had always been the jealous one—not of any woman, but of the *Desperado*.

"She could do worse," was all he said. "The man probably has marriage all figured out after four tries."

"Practice makes perfect."

"Maybe that's where I went wrong."

"Hey, no Tristan-bashing," she said sternly. "Or I'll have to bash you myself. Or send Bash to do it."

Since either she or Bash could probably kick his ass, he decided not to argue. "Are you coming to the debate?"

"Of course. Gotta cheer my girl Trixie on."

He laughed. That pretty much summed up their relationship in a nutshell. Lots of teasing, with some ride-or-die mixed in.

EIGHT

If Lulu had to write a travel site description of Lost Harbor, it would include the words charming, rough around the edges, and maybe tenacious. The people here had to be pretty tough. The town was literally situated on the edge of a vast expanse of wilderness filled with glaciers and bears and ice fields. Only one road came in from the rest of the world.

In the winter that road sometimes got blocked by an avalanche, Toni told her. The town had to be able to survive on its own. How did they do that? By helping each other out, by being "jacks of all trades"...and with a fair amount of alcohol, Toni added.

After a day in Toni's company, Lulu adored that woman. She was blunt, sarcastic and kind. Three of Lulu's favorite qualities. So far, Tristan seemed to have those same qualities, with maybe a few more, such as a nice rear end and devastating bedroom eyes.

Her debt to Tristan was piling up. After all, it was thanks to him that she'd just spent the most delightful day she could remember. Toni had taken her to Beauty by Vicki, a salon owned by the fiancée of the father of Police Chief Maya Badger. Vicki, an effervescent Native Alaskan woman, had helped her darken her hair to a muted brown that actually made her eyes a more vibrant blue.

Thus partially disguised, she'd followed Toni to a thrift store where she'd picked up some mud boots and a few hand-knit jumpers and a rain jacket with an insulated lining.

"This will get you through until October, but after that you'll need something warmer," Toni had warned her.

"I doubt that's the case, since I have every intention of being in a warm climate by then. My next cruise ship gig is to South America."

"Ohh, maybe you can visit our parents. They're in Chile. They retired there. My mother's Chilean," Toni had explained.

"Tristan's mother too?"

"Yes. I know he doesn't look it. Our father's from Denmark. We're our own little United Nations."

That explained a few things, like why Tristan had those striking looks—tawny blond hair with a hint of gold, eyes like a storm cloud with light shining through.

By the time the debate rolled around, Lulu was itching to get back to the *Desperado* and check on things. But until she found transport of her own, she had to rely on Toni. Also, she had a job to do. She might be a brand-new and completely uninformed campaign manager, but she was determined to offer Tristan her best effort.

She had to blink a few times when she saw him again at the high school auditorium, where the debate was being held. He'd ditched the ripped jumper and ratty sweats from the night before. Now he wore trousers that clung perfectly to his stellar ass, and a blazer over a collared shirt. No necktie, because such things didn't seem to exist here in Lost Harbor. His hair was combed back from his face, emphasizing the shape of his cheekbones and the playful glint in his eyes.

But what was that shorter patch of hair on one side of his head? She'd noticed it this morning, when he hadn't been wearing that bandana. She'd wanted to ask Toni about it but hadn't found a way. On the other hand, she'd heard plenty about what a standup guy he was and how Toni still harbored vaguely homicidal tendencies toward his ex-wife.

Divorce aside, Tristan oozed sex appeal, and her mouth watered as she hurried toward him.

"I've jotted down some notes for you," she whispered, handing him a folded piece of paper. "For during the debate."

"Excuse me? No." He pushed the notepaper away. "I'm good. It's just for show, remember?"

"The best show is the kind that makes you believe. I might not know about campaigning but I know about performing. It's all about the details. I came up with a few slogans and so forth. Just take it. You never know."

Reluctantly, he took the notes from her. "Please tell me you've learned the actual name of this town by now?"

"Ouch. But fair. Yes, and I also picked Toni's brain about you and Lost Harbor and fishing in general. But it's just a few ideas, of course you can take them or leave them."

He scrutinized her for a second, then nodded. "Okay then. Not at all necessary, but I appreciate the effort." He fidgeted with the fit of his jacket, and she realized he was nervous.

"Here." She reached up and adjusted the collar of his shirt so it covered the jacket lapel. "Should have steamed this jacket a bit. It looks fine now. Got the pre-show jitters?"

"I don't know. I just want to get this over with."

Oh yes. Stage fright. She knew it well. "The worst part is always right beforehand. Once you get into it the nerves will subside. If you get nervous, look my way."

"What will you do?"

"Oh, I have a few options. I could always flash you."

That got a smile out of him. "Best campaign manager ever. Did you run across your bad guy today? Any sign of him?"

"No, all clear. Another couple of days and I should be able to move on."

She couldn't see much reaction to that, either positive or negative. And why should there be? She was a random stranger who had snuck onto his boat. This odd attachment she felt must be entirely on her side, the result of being given shelter in a moment of need.

Temporary moment of need, she reminded herself. All of this was temporary. Like a weird surreal dream in which one moment she was twirling onstage in a raincoat, the next advising a smoking-hot fisherman on how to win his mayoral race.

Am I living yet, Mum?

Someone called for Tristan to come onstage. She glanced at the stage and saw that all the other folding chairs were filled, one of them with a cage containing a magnificent glossy-feathered rooster.

"Knock 'em dead," she stage-whispered as he turned to go. "But watch out for that rooster. He looks like a bruiser."

His tense expression relaxed into at least part of a smile. He hurried toward the stage. She watched him vault onto it like some kind of athlete. Maybe fishermen had to be in pretty good shape —not counting the beer bellies she spotted here and there.

She found a seat near the front, where Tristan could see her if he needed her to flash him. With a thrill, she noticed that Tristan was scanning her notes. When he gave a bark of laughter, she smiled to herself. She'd inserted a few naughty bits in there just to break things up. For example, *"On day one, I will submit a bill to change our town's name to Lust Harbor. Sex sells, after all."* In her experience, a little laughter was the best medicine for dire situations.

When the six candidates—Tristan, Trixie, three older residents, and the rooster—were all settled in their seats, the crowd quieted. Tristan sat with his long legs apart, hands on his knees, like an unruly student in the headmaster's office. Trixie wore a black tailored blazer and a red silk blouse and looked sensational. One of the other candidates wore boots adorned with a fascinating pattern of porcupine quills—the cruise ship sold similar items in the gift shop.

A young woman strode to the lectern on the edge of the stage. "Welcome to KLSW's mayoral debate. I'm Lucy Krakowski, with the *Lost Harbor Tribune*. We're going to start with a short statement from each candidate, and then I'll pose some questions that have been submitted by Lost Harbor residents. I may have a few questions of my own too, so stay on your toes, candidates. Let's start with Trixie Tran."

She brought the microphone to Trixie, then took a step back. Trixie rose to her feet, somehow looking much taller than Lulu remembered. "I'm Trixie Tran, owner and operator of Soul Satisfaction Ice Cream, one of the most successful businesses on the boardwalk. My family came here as immigrants when I was nine, and we more or less embody the American dream. I'm the next generation of that dream. Lost Harbor needs to look to the future and hear the voices of young people. We need forward-thinking leadership regarding issues like climate change. If you do me the honor of voting for me, I'll lead Lost Harbor in a new direction."

A new direction...eyeing the salt-of-the-earth citizens surrounding her, with their work boots and canvas jackets and baseball caps, Lulu wasn't sure that message would resonate.

"Next up, Malcom Crow." To the sound of polite applause for Trixie's statement, the moderator brought the microphone to the native gentleman with the porcupine quill boots.

He came to his feet. With his silvered black hair and sober expression, he radiated a kind of gravitas that even the abrupt squawk of the rooster next to him couldn't disturb. He ignored the fowl and addressed the crowd. "My fellow Lost Harborites, this is a time of reckoning and reflection. That's why our old mayor walked off the job. He didn't want to do that kind of work. Ever since we found out how this town got its start, people've been wondering what's next. I'll tell you what's next. Let a Native Alaskan lead the way. If you choose me as your mayor, I'll make sure everyone gets a chance to speak and be heard. We'll work this out. The Crow family stuck with this town when we could have left with the others. Now I'm asking you all to stick with us. Vote Crow."

Applause swept across the room, and Lulu realized that Tristan's real competition wasn't Trixie, or the rooster. It was the man in the khakis and soft-sided porcupine boots.

"And now, let's hear from Tristan Del Rey," said the moderator as she brought him the mic.

Tristan took hold of it and rose slowly to his feet, notepaper in hand. Lulu actually felt nervous on his behalf. She balled her hands into fists and silently urged him on. In for a penny, in for a pound, after all. If she was going to fake-manage a campaign, she wanted him to win.

"Thanks, Malcolm. Hard act to follow, man," he said after clearing his throat.

A ripple of laughter cascaded through the crowd.

"I'm Tristan Del Rey and I've been fishing here in Lost Harbor since I was two. Fishing is the backbone of this town. Without us fishermen, the only industry would be tourism. All those RVs and cruise ships, they come from outside. I'm running to represent the people who live and work here, who put their blood, sweat and tears into Lost Harbor."

Lulu held back a squeal of excitement. He'd used her line about blood, sweat and tears! She'd thought of it while watching a fisherman in oilskins weigh an enormous halibut on an overhead scale. The thing was heavy, and it dripped blood on his slick orange coveralls.

Tristan glanced down at the piece of notepaper in his hands, cleared his throat again, glanced at the audience, then down at his feet. *Oh no.* Something was wrong. The silence dragged on, punctuated with a few rustlings and chair-squeakings. She wished she could jump onstage and do a tap dance to distract everyone.

Suddenly, Tristan balled up her page of notes and stuck it in his pocket. "You know something? Malcolm is right." He turned to the older man, whose dark silver-streaked head tilted up in surprise. "You deserve to be mayor. I'm gonna vote for you. Just treat us fisherman right, is all I ask."

He sat down as a cascade of gasps and questions rolled through the room. Lucy took the microphone from his hand. "Are you dropping out of the mayoral race, Tristan?"

"I am. Malcolm Crow has my vote. It's about time we have a Native Alaskan be our mayor. Past time. I endorse him. Sorry, Trix."

Next to him, Trixie was glaring at him in absolute outrage.

"This is certainly bombshell news," said Lucy. "Do you have anything more to say?"

Tristan swept his gaze across the room. Lulu couldn't read the emotion in his sea-gray gaze. Maybe embarrassment? Regret? Relief? She didn't know him well enough to say.

"Sorry, I'm just a fisherman," he said finally. With a shrug of his big shoulders, he gestured toward the backstage area. "Should I—yeah. I'll get off the stage now. Thanks, everyone."

He headed offstage with that long, rolling stride. The crowd was still buzzing with speculation and the excitement of the drama. Lulu left her seat and made her way down the aisle, dodging knees and boots. She saw no need to attend the rest of the debate. Her stint as a campaign manager was over. Shortest job she'd ever had, and that was saying something.

———

OUTSIDE THE AUDITORIUM, she scanned the parking lot, absently noting the spectacular view of mountains in the background. Imagine going to school in a place where you saw that vista every day.

Finally she spotted Tristan swinging into a dusty black truck. She ran after him, glad she'd worn her new trainers instead of her boots from last night. He was already underway when she reached him, but he paused and gestured for her to get in.

"Looks like I'm going to have to let you go," he said lightly. "Campaign's over."

"Well, sorry, but you can't because I quit. There's this other candidate who really caught my eye and I have to follow my heart. Those black tail feathers, that throaty crowing...my God."

He shot her a cautiously amused look. "If you're about to give me a hard time for quitting the race, you can skip it. I'm sure I'll get shit from all sides. My sister, my crew, every single fisherman from here to Dutch Harbor."

"Why should I give you a hard time? I just left my job in the dark of night with absolutely no notice. I have no grounds to criticize anyone."

"True enough. I guess we're a couple of dropouts."

"Cheers to us. Shall we celebrate? Bottle of champagne, perhaps?"

"I don't drink," he reminded her. "But sometimes I really wish I did." They reached the main road that threaded through town. He paused, his hand on the turn signal, clearly trying to decide which direction to go.

She really needed to get back to the boat, but something told her he needed company right now. A little more time wouldn't hurt anything.

"Ice cream sundae then?"

He groaned. "Trixie will probably bar me from the premises of the ice cream shop. Man, the look on her face."

"She looked fierce, all right. But she's still at the debate." She lifted her eyebrows suggestively. "Surely she has someone else manning the shop?"

"Good point. I knew I hired you for a reason."

"Something to do with the potentially homicidal maniac pursuing me, but I take your point."

He steered the truck in the direction of the boardwalk. Signs of autumn were all over town; birch trees dropping their leaves, scrub grass turning brown, nasturtiums drooping in their planters.

Her mother had always prepared for frost by bringing in her potted herbs and mulching her perennial beds—until she grew too sick to tend to that sort of thing. Last autumn, when Lulu had her hands completely full, she'd barely gotten the pots inside before frost set in.

And now...everything was in storage and Mama's next door neighbor had taken custody of the rosemary and thyme. And Lulu was halfway around the world, stranded in a tiny town where frost would soon set in.

She shook off her moment of memory, but not before she caught Tristan giving her a curious glance.

"Everything okay?" he asked.

"Brilliant. Just admiring the scenery. Do you ever get tired of magnificent mountains and such? Do you ever just long for a strip of concrete or one of those high-rises like boxes piled on top of each other?"

He lifted an eyebrow at her, as if he didn't believe her claim of "brilliant." "Yes, actually, sometimes I just sit on the beach and stare at the breakwater. It's made of big chunks of concrete and other non-scenic slabs of rocks."

"I'm sorry, that doesn't count. Not when there's a beach involved."

"Sounds like a challenge."

Which was how, half an hour later, they ended up sitting side by side, ice cream sundaes in hand, on a giant slab of granite below the road that led to the boardwalk. The road had been shored up with rocks and blocks of concrete of all sizes—what Tristan called the "breakwater." The rumble of cars whizzing overhead echoed between the jagged rocks. She had to admit—scenic, it was not.

"You really know how to show a girl a good time, don't you?" She licked peanut butter ice cream off a pink plastic spoon.

"Yes, I generally find that bringing them to a debate where I make an ass of myself, then treating them to ice cream with a view of broken concrete gets them all revved up. Is it working?"

"Put it this way. It's not *not* working." With a quick wink, she dug her spoon back into her ice cream. For whatever reason, she wanted to keep Tristan off guard. And from the way his eyebrows shot up his forehead, it was working.

"In that case, you gonna tell me what's going on?"

NINE

Lulu shot him an outraged glance, as if he'd tricked her. "I thought we were celebrating our dropout-ness. Which, by the way, you haven't said one word about. As your now unemployed campaign manager, I think I deserve some answers."

"To clarify, you were never technically 'employed.' That would imply that I have a payroll and campaign funds, neither of which is true. Besides, I said it all at the debate."

He adjusted his position on the rocks, so his back wasn't leaning against such a sharp corner. He'd always loved this break-water, which looked as if a horde of ogres had come through and stomped on every slab they could find. But despite Lulu's suggestion, he didn't normally bring dates out here.

But this wasn't a "date" anyway. He wasn't sure how he'd categorize it, or his relationship with Lulu, but "date" wasn't even in the running.

"You think Melvin Crow would be a better mayor?" she asked.

"Malcolm. Do you have a mental block about names?"

"Yes, Triscuit, I do. But that's not the point."

He burst out laughing. He couldn't help it; something about her light touch with a quip got under his defenses in no time.

"Why do you think he'd be better?" she continued.

"It wasn't even my idea to run for mayor. The guys pressured me into it. The other fishermen."

"You didn't answer the question. Don't you think you'd be a good mayor?"

Why was she pushing this? It was over. He'd stepped aside. For all the right reasons. He wasn't cut out for anything like that.

"Malcolm Crow's a smart man and he knows this town. If I'd known he was running, I would have stayed out. What he said is right. We've always had the same type of mayors. Why not give someone else a chance?"

"And you? Aren't you a smart man?"

"The fact that I let you stay on my boat is making me question that," he grumbled. "Why the third degree? What's it to you, other than you just lost your cover story?"

She delicately twirled her tongue around a spoonful of ice cream. Her newly darkened hair lifted in the breeze off the ocean. "I may not have mentioned this before, but one of my strengths, aside from tap-dancing on cruise ships, is reading people. It started when my mother—" Stopping abruptly, she gave a cough. "And I perfected it on cruise ships. It's always good to know who's going to give you the best tips."

"After your mother what?" he asked, intrigued enough to pursue a topic that clearly made her uncomfortable.

"Got sick," she finally answered. "I dealt with a lot of doctors and I learned to read their expressions better than a patient chart."

Her expression told him to leave it at that, and he did. "So you can read people. Good skill to have. Is that why you fled the cruise ship? You read someone and got scared?"

"I wouldn't say scared...okay, terrified. Yes, more or less, that's what happened." Finally, some truth. Now if he could just get her to fill in the details. "But we're not talking about me. We're talking about you and what I read in your face when you announced you were dropping out of the race."

"Relief because I didn't have to debate Trixie over whether or not to build a new ferry terminal?"

She chuckled a bit. He liked how she laughed, as if laughter was oxygen, or drinking water—something essential to life. "No. It's not quite that specific when I read people. I thought you looked like you were proving something."

"Proving something?"

"Yes, proving something to yourself."

"That I'm a dropout?" he asked wryly, but he didn't deny her point. Maybe he was proving something. That he wasn't his father. That he wasn't a leader. That he wasn't promising anything to anyone ever again.

"Dropouts unite." She lifted her plastic spoon and clicked it against his. An odd sense of freedom drifted through him. This woman didn't expect anything from him, so he could never disappoint her. She didn't know a Del Rey from a stingray. As far as she was concerned, he was just a dude with a fishing boat. And in the end, what else was he?

A dude with a fishing boat and a divorce and a brain surgery scar and a brief encounter with town politics.

"So is this your first time dropping out?" she asked him. Clearly she didn't give up easily.

"I dropped out of marriage. But that was really my ex's choice, so I can't call that a dropout. Actually, maybe I should. She'd probably say I dropped out every time I left the harbor on a fishing trip."

Lulu's forehead wrinkled quizzically. "Didn't she know you were a fisherman when you got married?"

"She knew. But she didn't *know*. She was working at the ice cream shop—for Trixie, actually—and we had kind of a whirl-wind thing. I was in the process of buying the *Desperado* so I was in port a lot more than usual. We fell in love and man, I was on top of the world. New boat, new wife. I thought I had this thing called life *nailed.*"

He shook his head at his naive former self. In the next moment, he wondered why he was telling her about this. He didn't open up about his marriage to very many people. Maybe it was because no one could possibly be more short-term than Lulu at this point. Telling her something was like telling it to the wind.

"Were you pretty young?" she asked.

"Twenty-four. Young enough that I made a mess of it. I was just a pedal-to-the-metal fisherman. I'd stay out longer than everyone else, go out further, take crazy risks because I wanted to make my mark. Then I'd come home and she'd be furious because she'd spent the last month alone with her vibrator."

He caught himself up. He barely knew this woman and he was talking about vibrators?

But Lulu just ate another spoonful of ice cream and kept listening. So he kept talking.

"I tried to make up for it. I mean, I tried hard. And long."

"And throbbing?" she said lightly.

He snorted. "Yeah. And throbbing. We both did a lot of that. But it turns out sex isn't really enough to keep a relation-ship together. I should have stayed home more. Paid more atten-tion to her. I think she needed more of a social life than she got here. She was from Florida and she missed all her friends back there."

He felt a light touch on his knee. Great, here came the sympathy. "Tristan, to be honest, it sounds like your marriage didn't have a snowball's chance in hell."

He jerked his head around to meet her eyes. Was she laughing at him? "Huh?"

"And it absolutely doesn't count as a dropout. Sorry, you get no credit for that."

Wait...did he want credit or not want credit? He'd lost the thread here. "Do I at least get credit for a good sob story?"

"No, you do not, because a sob story implies it isn't genuine. Sorry, no sob story points either. Was it very difficult for you, the divorce? My parents went through quite a bitter breakup, though they were never married."

"My parents have an incredibly happy marriage, so I felt like a real failure, along with the broken heart. I licked my wounds for a while. One of my deckhands caught me sobbing into the fish hold once. It freaked him out so much he went belowdecks and wrote a letter to his girlfriend proposing to her. First letter he ever wrote in his life. They're still married."

Her laughter was filled with so much delight that he smiled at the sound of it. "I like your laugh."

His spontaneous declaration obviously caught her by surprise, because the laugh ended on a hiccup. "Oh. Well, I enjoy a good laugh, and I liked your story."

"The part about me sobbing or the part about Yeet's letter?"

"Yeet? That's his name?" She'd paused her ice cream consumption in order to listen. A late-season black fly buzzed near her spoon, and he waved it away before it could land.

"Nickname. His real name is something Russian that I can never pronounce right."

"So you have an international crew?"

"There's a fair-sized Russian population here in town. Some of them fish. One of my longtime crew members is from Brazil, and another from Somalia. Hell, I'm part-Chilean so any crew of mine is going to be pretty eclectic."

"And now you have a British stowaway."

"That's right. And if you don't follow captain's orders, it'll be Brexit all over again. Boom. Out."

She burst into peals of laughter. "That's a good one. I can't believe an Alaskan fisherman knows or cares about British politics."

"Of course I know. But I didn't say I cared. Y'all can do what you want. I'm just making a point about who's in charge on my boat."

"What if I hire you and your boat?"

He frowned down at her. "For what? You want a couple tons of salmon?"

"No." With a light shrug, she went back to her peanut butter ice cream. "It's just a thought."

"Go on with it. What comes next in this thought?"

"That you could take me someplace where I could disappear for a while. Like..." She waved her hand at the magnificent mountains across the bay, their jagged peaks shining stark white against the vibrant blue of the autumn sky. "Over there."

He stuck his spoon into the remaining lump of his ice cream and set the container on the rock next to him. "Over there. Do you know what that is, over there?"

"Mountains. Wilderness. A place where no one would find me." She glanced at him sideways and for the first time he caught the real fear behind her lighthearted manner.

"Oh sure. Except the bears. They might find you."

"I'll bring bear spray. I read about it. It's very effective."

Good God. She wasn't serious about this, was she? "You do know that winter's coming, don't you?"

"It's only September."

"And this is Alaska. First frost will hit any day now. Freeze-up could happen in a few weeks. First snowfall came on October fifteenth last year. You want to be in Lost Souls Wilderness for the first snow dump? Where? A tree? A tent? A hunter's cabin? What's the plan, exactly?"

When her eyes filled with tears, he cursed himself for being too rough on her. And then he worried he hadn't been rough enough.

"Then there's the old saying, 'strange things happen around Lost Souls Wilderness.' You know why that is? Because it's *wilderness*. It's not meant for people to be wandering around in it. Especially cruise ship tap-dancers with no survival training."

Her eyes flared from a cheerful blue to a stormy slate.

Ah hell, he'd gone too far with that crack. But it was too late to take it back. Before he knew what was happening, she snatched up her paper dish of ice cream and dumped it over his head. The cold sticky mess dripped down his cheeks and even into one of his ears.

He probably deserved that.

"Well, hell," he growled. "Now there's only one thing to do."

Her eyes widened and she shrank away from him. "Sorry, I don't know what got into me. It was an impulse. All the stress, you know."

He cast her a stern look as he got to his feet. "Stress is no excuse for wasting perfectly good ice cream." He stripped off his blazer—he hated the thing, but he didn't want to get ice cream on it—then unbuttoned his collared shirt and ripped off his t-shirt. Turning his back to her, he unfastened his trousers and stepped out of them.

When he was down to his navy blue briefs, he climbed off the rocks and jogged down the beach toward the ocean.

As a child, he'd spent hours in the ocean—in the harbor, in hidden coves across the bay, at the beach on warm days. He and Toni had both loved swimming but as he got older, he focused more on fishing while she remained a swimming-obsessed mermaid. But he still took a dip now and then. It was important to keep that connection to the ocean that gave him so much—freedom, peace, adventure, not to mention a living.

He dodged a long curtain of slippery kelp that lay across the pebbles like an abandoned nightgown. The tide was halfway in, rising fast. Each wave left curls of white foam on the rough sand, only for the next wave to wash them out. Perfect time for a quick dive, then he could ride the current back in.

Perfect, that is, if you didn't mind getting an all-body ice bath. Steeling himself for the shock, he waded into the fifty-degree water. His entire body went on red alert. *Danger, danger. Unacceptable conditions.* He ignored the screams of his nervous system and forged onwards. Ice cream dripped from his hair onto his shoulders. He wasn't sure which was colder, but he knew which was stickier.

Hauling in one last breath, he consigned his soul to the Lord above and quickly crossed himself. He wasn't especially religious, but like many fishermen, he was plenty superstitious.

Then he dove.

Instant brain freeze. Skin freeze. Bone freeze. Possibly inner organ freeze too. With part of his brain, he knew that blood was leaving his extremities and pumping toward his heart and lungs, the organs essential to continued life. The rest of him was basically straight-up screaming.

He surfaced and howled up at the sky. "Wooooooo!!"

Then he dove back down because the chilly air blowing off the bay cut against his skin like knives of ice. Underwater, he shook his head and ran his fingers through his hair to get the ice cream out.

And despite everything—the debate, dropping out, the cold, the shock, the possibility of hypothermia—he laughed.

TEN

"It's official," Lulu told herself. "You've put your life in the hands of an insane person."

There was no other explanation for why someone would voluntarily subject themselves to that water.

Quite possibly, this would be a good time to part ways with Tristan. She could take his keys from his pocket and borrow his truck. She could drive it back to the *Desperado* and then right to the airport. She'd leave it there for him with a nice note and maybe a cappuccino maker.

Her plans got a little foggy at that point. Perhaps find the British embassy, if there even was one in Alaska? But still, it might be a safer option than continuing to associate with a clearly deranged dude.

Even if he did look like a work of art chiseled from the finest Italian marble when he took off his clothes. She'd barely taken a breath after he'd undone the first button of his shirt. Or even blinked. She'd watched him every step of the way, savoring the flex of his thighs in those Calvin Kleins and the strong lines of his shoulders and back. His was a *working* body, with tan lines at his neck and upper arms.

Finally she'd managed to tear her gaze away and that was when it occurred to her that she could leave. Of course she could leave at any point—no one was keeping her prisoner—but without a vehicle it was more difficult.

She palmed Tristan's keys and craned her neck to look beyond the breakwater at the vehicles whizzing past on the road above. Tristan had parked in a small pullout. It wouldn't be hard to climb up there. She could be at the *Desperado* before he managed to get his clothes back on.

Sure, it would be a shitty way to repay his kindness, but this wasn't just about her. She had someone depending on her and that was more important than anything else. Tristan could take care of himself.

As she gazed up at the road, a movement in the rocks caught her eye. She couldn't see whether it was a person or an animal of some kind, but it looked furtive. What if it was Mr. Bad Guy trailing her, waiting for a moment when she was all alone?

What if she got into Tristan's truck and he followed her and ran her off the road and no one ever heard from her again?

Or...what if she managed to get away and Mr. Bad Guy went after Tristan when he was half-naked, mostly frozen, and without a vehicle?

She caught the movement again, this time with a swish of a bushy brown tail. Relief surged through her, leaving her a little lightheaded. It was a squirrel or a chipmunk or whatever little rodents lived in Alaska. It wasn't Mr. Bad Guy. She wasn't in danger, at least not immediately. Neither was Tristan. And of course she wasn't going to sneak off with his truck. That wasn't her. She was the kind who stayed until the end; if she knew nothing else about herself, she knew that.

How many times had her mother lectured her about getting on with her own life? Too many.

She grabbed Tristan's clothes and picked her way across the beach, which was strewn with piles of seaweed, long strands of kelp, and even a stranded jellyfish. Tristan's hoots and hollers got louder the closer she got to the shoreline. At least he was still breathing.

"You coming in?" he shouted to her as she reached the water's edge. A wave broke on the sand and rippled toward her. She skipped back, not wanting to get her new trainers wet.

"Absolutely not. But I have your clothes right here. Should I go hunt down a defibrillator as well?"

"I just got defibrillated. Or fibrillated, whichever one means you get an electric shock right to the heart." He swam closer to her, everything but his head staying under the surface. His eyes shone with a wild gray light. With his hair wet with seawater, his bone structure stood out more. He had bold features; prominent cheekbones, a wide jawline, a square face. Each rough plane of his face conveyed solidity and strength, and in the midst of it all, the eyes of a dreamboat.

"Are you all right? Shall I call the emergency number?"

"What for? Feels great." He lifted one hand above the surface and turned it this way and that. "Oh good, my hand is still attached. I couldn't feel it. Had to check."

"*Tristan.* Get out of there. I'm sorry I dumped my ice cream on your head. That was very childish of me."

"Yes, and we can't ever tell Trixie about that. She'd be very hurt. She takes a lot of pride in her product." He put his hand back underwater and took another stroke through the waves.

"It was fabulous," she said. "Five stars on Yelp, I promise."

He swam closer. "Sure I can't tempt you?"

Oh, he tempted her, all right. In ways she hadn't experienced in a very long time. If ever, really.

On the cruise ship she mostly spent time with other performers, who were mostly young and free-spirited partiers. Back in England, she'd been surrounded with health care professionals, who were mostly women. She'd had a secret crush on one of the male nurses, but he'd turned out to be married with a child on the way. Once in a while she'd ridden her bicycle to the butcher shop and lusted after the butcher's assistant, a young man from Turkey with the most rippling musculature she'd ever seen.

But that was all fantasy, and Tristan was very much reality. Everything about him—his blunt approach, his basic kindness, his comfort in his own skin—spoke to her on a visceral level.

But none of that meant that she was getting anywhere near that water. "You cannot," she told him. "If you want revenge for the ice cream, I'd prefer if you think in terms of running me over with a truck rather than getting me in that water."

He laughed, water streaming down his face. "Your loss. But I get it. You probably want to wait for the Polar Plunge in January."

She was about to explain that unless "Polar" and "Plunge" referred to something sex-related, she had no interest, when he rose up out of the water. Her words wound up caught in her throat, because who could speak when they were presented with a sight like a wet, nearly naked Tristan Del Rey?

Fighting to keep her eyes on his face instead of where they clamored to be—eating up every inch of his defined body—she held his clothes toward him. "Perhaps you could use the t-shirt as a trowel," she suggested. Then she heard her own words, and blushed. "A towel, that is."

"Good idea. Toss it over." He made his way out of the water, each step a symphony of slick limbs and flexing muscles. He needed a theme song. A boom-chicka kind of soundtrack. She wished she could record this moment on her phone and watch it over and over again.

She shook herself back to reality and tossed him the t-shirt.

He wiped his face first, clearing the saltwater from his eyes. Oh thank God. That gave her the chance to release the strict leash she had on her gaze. She allowed it to roam freely over his body, gathering details as she went. Wet hair swirling from his belly toward the waistband of his briefs. Navy fabric clinging to his thighs and private area. *The bulge.*

Wasn't cold water supposed to make the manly parts shrink? She spotted no shrinkage. Unless he, in fact, *had* shrunk, and this was the *shrunken version.*

She swallowed hard and dragged her gaze back up just in time for his head to emerge from behind the t-shirt. He shook the excess water from his hair, then toweled it off with the shirt. With his arms raised overhead, the width of his chest was even more striking. His skin had an undertone of coppery gold to it, especially in places where the sun hit him, like the back of his neck. Maybe that was from his Chilean side. Whatever combination of genetics had produced this man had resulted in a masterpiece.

He finished with the t-shirt and extended his hand. "Shirt, please."

With regret, she handed it over and watched him button it up over that spectacular chest. "Do you want your trousers too?"

"Not yet. My undies need to dry a bit first." He winked at her. She found his word choice adorable, along with everything else about him. "If you weren't here I'd be going commando."

"Don't let me stop you," she blurted before even thinking about it. "I mean, you probably want to be comfortable and you don't want to get a fungus."

He nearly choked on his laugh. She realized that she enjoyed making him laugh. It was something she drew pleasure from in general, but with him, even more so. "True that," he said, taking the trousers from her. "Be back in a second. Unless you want a show, I recommend watching the waves for a while."

He loped up the beach toward the tumbled rocks of the breakwater.

And if I want a show? She left that thought where it belonged, in silence. She didn't need the distraction of a sexy fisherman in her life. What she needed was a plan that would keep her safe.

Following his advice, she faced the glimmering expanse of the ocean. A tern winged across the waves, singleminded, as if it was late for an appointment. The small brown face of a sea otter popped above the surface, glanced around with curiosity, then disappeared again. A moment later, it reappeared, close enough for her to see its whiskers. She held her breath, savoring the magic of the place and the moment.

On the cruise ship, she rarely had time to pay attention to their surroundings. She had a busy schedule of kiddie performances in the day, then adult shows at night. She wondered how the others were getting on without her. Britney would have to take over the kids' shows. They'd have to eliminate the "Singing in the Rain" sketch because no one else knew how to tap dance.

They all probably either hated her by now, or were terribly worried for her. She'd love to get a message through to them that she was fine and very sorry for disappearing, but that seemed much too risky.

Or maybe it wasn't, what did she know? She had zero experience with dodging bad guys. Face it, she was in way over her head. If only she could bob with the waves like that sea otter.

The creature's eyes were so moist they seemed to be made of seawater. He was looking at her, completely unafraid. As if this was his world and she was an interesting new curiosity.

"Making friends with the wildlife?" Tristan's deep voice interrupted her reverie. He stepped next to her, fully clothed but just as potent as ever. "Never trust a sea otter, by the way. They'll steal your catch right from under you. They can eat a quarter of their body weight a day."

"Same," she said, feeling even more kinship with the creatures. "I have days like that, don't we all?"

He chuckled. "When I get home from a fishing trip, the first thing I do is go to the Burger Queen and order half the menu."

The sea otter performed a sinuous flip back under the waves.

"You scared him away." She sighed, missing the bright-eyed visitor.

"He isn't afraid of me. The sea otters can get away with anything. They're federally protected and I swear they know it. They're like the Lokis of the ocean. I love them, but they drive the crab fishermen nuts."

Sure enough, the otter popped back up a second later, now floating on his back, feasting on something.

"I like how he uses his belly as a table." She laughed, enchanted by the creature. "Like me when I watch the telly."

"Yeah, they're cute as hell." His smile dropped a little, and he looked over his left shoulder. Then his right.

She peered behind him, a feeling of dread gathering in her stomach. "What's the matter?"

"I get the feeling we're being watched. But I don't see anyone."

"I know that feeling from matinee shows on the cruise ship."

Her crack didn't draw so much as a smile from him. He shifted his shoulders uncomfortably. "Maybe we should get back to the truck."

The urge to run at top speed came over her. She wanted to flee, to hide, to burrow into safety. "Slowly, like normal? Or should we make a run for it?"

"Split the difference and make it a fast walk?"

She nodded and licked her lips nervously. He noticed and

bent to murmur in her ear, "I'm right beside you. They'll have to go through me, whoever it is, even if it's just a squirrel."

He took her hand and she had to admit it felt good, big and rough-palmed, though still a little clammy from his time in the water. They walked quickly across the beach, all the seaweed and stranded crabs nothing but a blur to her. He kept his body angled so that if any hazard came flying at them, he'd take the brunt of it.

Which was absolutely not fair, she realized. She couldn't expect this near-stranger to take a bullet for her.

A bullet. Was that what she was afraid of? This was America, after all, and guns were easy to acquire. Mr. Bad Guy probably had an entire arsenal. He could be hiding in those rocks, aiming one of those laser-dot jabberwockies at them.

Her heart pounded and adrenaline flooded her system. Fear, primitive and unreasonable, washed over her. Sweat made her hands slick.

"We got this," Tristan murmured. "See the truck? We're almost there."

And they were...the rocks of the breakwater were just a few feet away, and once they climbed that, they'd reach the guardrail, and then the truck...except something was happening to the truck. It was breaking apart...flames...metal...

Tristan slammed her to the sand at the edge of the break-water and threw his body on top of her. A percussive wave of sound passed through her. Her ears rang like a bell, then a high whine took over.

Bloody hell. Tristan's truck had just blown up.

ELEVEN

As soon as he could move again, Tristan pulled Lulu to her feet and dragged her into a crevice between two slabs of rock. She didn't resist as she stumbled after him.

They crouched underneath the rock just in time to avoid a piece of metal flying through the air. It landed on the sand mere inches from where they'd just been, then tumbled to a stop. Jesus. *A piece of metal.* From his truck. Which had just been blown to smithereens.

"What just happened?" Lulu whispered. Her eyes were enormous and nearly purple in the shadow of the breakwater.

"Shhh." He put a finger to her lips, then hugged her against him and whispered in her ear. "Listen."

She nodded, and they both went quiet. The roar and crackle of the burning truck filled the air, soon followed by the sound of sirens. Darius Boone and his crew were on their way.

That made Tristan relax. But he didn't move. Someone could still be out there. No one could clamber across these rocks without making a sound. He'd played enough hide-and-seek here to know that.

After an endless length of minutes, he released his hold on her. "I don't hear anything, do you?"

She shook her head. "Just your poor truck. I'm so sorry."

"It's insured. I'm just glad we weren't closer to it."

He felt a shudder run through her body.

Actually, he had no idea if his truck was insured against random explosion. Or intentional explosion.

"Trucks don't just explode out of nowhere, do they?" she whispered.

"Not generally."

"It must have been him. It must have been deliberate. Mr. Bad Guy blew up your truck and it's because of me." The shudders intensified. He tightened his arms around her, trying not to notice how good it felt to hold her, and how good she smelled. Like strawberries and whipped cream. "I can't believe it. I'm so sorry. I shouldn't be here, Tristan. You could have been killed."

"And you," he pointed out.

"Yes, but you have nothing to do with this. This is my fault. If I'd stayed on the ship, or picked another boat to trespass on, or simply left town..."

"Shhhh." Realizing she was on the verge of a full-blown panic attack, he ran his hands up and down her arms. He was trying to soothe her, but the gesture had the unfortunate side effect of making him notice how silky her skin felt. "Did you blow up my truck?"

"No! Of course not."

"Then stop it. This wasn't your doing."

Unless there was more to the story than he knew. Which, since he didn't know *any* of the story, was entirely possible.

He waited until her trembling had eased. The fire engine had reached the truck, but its siren was still wailing. A new noise joined the ruckus; the hiss of water dousing the flames.

"Lulu, you do realize that you're going to have to tell me what the fuck is going on now, right?"

She expelled a shaky breath as she drew away from him. "I suppose I owe you that. Or at the least a new truck."

"I'll settle for an explanation." Hell, he had two old junker trucks sitting in his yard. A few parts and some tinkering and he'd be back in business. And he'd just cleaned out his poor Chevy, so he hadn't even lost any traps or tools or gear or any of the other clutter he usually carted around. "Whenever you're ready," he prompted her.

"You mean, like now?"

"Now would be good, so I have some idea of what to say to Darius."

"Who's Darius?"

"The fire chief. I'm sure he'll be getting involved, because truck explosions don't happen every day around here. No more than once a week at most."

His silly joke worked, and her tense expression eased. "That's a relief, because tourism would really take a hit, and that would leave a big mess for the next mayor to deal with. Poor rooster, he's really going to have his hands full."

He refused to go along with her attempt to distract him.

"Any chance it was something mechanical?" she asked, almost wistfully.

"The fuck if I know, but it's a five-year old truck, which makes it essentially brand-new around here. Zero mechanical issues to this point. So I'd say no, there's not much chance of that."

She let out a long sigh and dropped her head into her hands. He wanted to stroke her hair, tell her it would be okay, and that she didn't have to say anymore if she didn't want to.

But he stopped himself, because it was time. Past fucking

time. He was flying blind here, and now he'd lost his truck and he deserved an explanation.

So he waited, and waited. What was taking so long? This should be simple. All he wanted was the truth.

Finally she spoke. "Do you have any skills that are almost like superpowers?"

"Excuse me?"

"Like...I don't know, fishing. It sounds like you're very good at it. Would you say it's your superpower?"

He thought about it briefly. "I'm good at fishing, sure. But I'm better at being a captain. Or at least I was. I'm not sure anymore."

"So your superpower was captaining a boat, but now you've lost it?"

Her curious expression made him stiffen. "We're not talking about me now. No tangents. Go on."

"Okay, sorry. But I hope you tell me about that sometime. My superpower is that I always remember faces. Not just faces, but where I saw them. I've never forgotten a face. When I was twenty-five, I recognized my babysitter from when I was two years old. I greeted her like an old friend and she had no idea who I was. It's just one of those odd quirks of how my brain works."

"So you recognized someone's face?"

"Yes. On the cruise ship, in the middle of one of my very best performances of Singing in the Rain."

"So sorry, I hope someone caught it on tape."

She blinked at him in surprise. "I never even thought of that. Maybe there's a tape sitting in someone's phone. Maybe that would..." She shrugged, changing direction. "It's a little late for that now. Anyway, part of the act is that I take my mac off—sorry, my raincoat, as you call it here—and fling it into the audience. I always aim for a man, because they love it. Women don't seem to like having garments thrown at them. So I tossed it at a man sitting alone, and right when he caught it the spotlight shone onto his face. And I recognized him instantly."

"From the true crime show, right?" he asked, impatient to get to the end of the story so he could climb up the rocks and debrief with Darius.

"Yes. As I mentioned this morning, my mum and I used to watch those shows when she was feeling blue. I recognized him as a kidnapper who's been featured on the FBI's Most Wanted list. Very dangerous, because not just anyone makes those lists, do they?"

"No, those spots are very coveted," he said dryly. "Okay, so you threw a raincoat on a criminal. Then what?"

"Unfortunately, I...you know...gasped." She demonstrated a shocked gasp. "I made it quite obvious that I recognized him. I should have been smarter, but I'm not accustomed to performing for criminals. As far as I know," she added, after thinking it over a bit. "I tried to cover it up by pretending my gasp was part of the act. I did it again, very Betty Boop, covering my mouth."

She dropped her jaw and put her hand over her mouth, exaggerating the movement.

There was something about this story that he wasn't buying, but he went along with it anyway. "Did it work?"

"No. His eyes kept drilling into me the entire remainder of my act. So I knew I couldn't just play it off."

"Scary." He put a hand on her shoulder, giving her a squeeze of sympathy that she'd crossed paths with someone so dangerous.

"Yes, it was. I knew I had to notify the authorities. I managed to take a photo of Mr. Bad Guy with my mobile phone and showed it to the ship's security head. I explained that I was sure he was a wanted criminal. He was able to match my photo with a passenger, Sebastian Perro, a father and tropical fish exporter with no criminal record. He told me I must be mistaken. But I'm absolutely sure I wasn't."

"Did he let you scan through the ID photos yourself?"

"No, he said that would be a breach of our passengers' privacy. But he said that he would check into it further."

Tristan had no idea if the privacy argument was true. Then again, so much of this seemed a little fishy. Starting with the Singing in the Rain act. "And did he?"

"He said he came up clean." A shadow of anger darkened her eyes. "He told me to 'go back to my can-can' and forget about it."

"Sounds like an asshole."

"Yes, although the proper word would be wanker. Still, I knew there was a chance I was mistaken. A photo can be misleading. My memory for faces is good, but not infallible. I tried to find the crime show online but came up empty. I had nothing more to prove my case. Until..."

Something shifted in her expression and he got the sense she was censoring this story, sifting through it to decide how much to share.

"Until..." he prompted.

"Until I took a sip of my morning coffee and ended up in the infirmary. I would have died if I hadn't been on deck at the time, and a gust of wind made me lose my grip on my cup. It went flying overboard, and the next thing I knew, I was vomiting on the deck. My friends took me to the medics, and they immediately suspected that I'd ingested something toxic. Even more toxic than the crew coffee," she added.

It was a pattern with her, wasn't it? Using light humor to cover up her fear. "Did they figure out what it was?"

"They said it would take a few days to get the results. I don't know what it was, but I do know he tried to poison me. Or someone else did."

"How many enemies do you have on the *Northern Princess?*"

She tapped her chin thoughtfully. "There was the time when one of my high-kicks went awry and bruised Angela's jaw. Maybe she tried to poison me in revenge, even after I ordered her the biggest box of Turkish delight the gift store carried. Can you imagine Turkish delight being your favorite sweets, when peppermints are *right there?*"

He had to admit, he liked the way Lulu told a story, with plenty of detours for some extra entertainment.

"What happened after that?"

She put a hand over her heart, as if testing her heartbeat. "I felt cornered. As long as I was on that ship, I didn't see how I could avoid more threats on my life. I suspected that he had at least one other person working with him—a bodyguard sort of bloke. Once again, the security head dismissed my fears, and I began to believe that perhaps Mr. Bad Guy had paid him off. I couldn't perform two shows a night with a target on my back. When they announced we were staying in port overnight, I decided it was my best chance to make my escape."

Okay, well. It was a story. A hair-raising one. Maybe it was true. But he'd bet the *Desperado* it wasn't the *whole* truth.

He heard shouts from the road, and recognized Darius Boone's deep, worried voice. Everyone knew his truck, with its *Desperado* bumper sticker. He felt a short pang of grief for his beloved black Chevy, but shoved it aside. At least it wasn't his boat. "We'd better get up there and let them know we're alive."

"Do you think it's safe?"

He met her eyes, luminous in the shadow of the rock. "I have no idea. But I'd rather be in the middle of a crew of firefighters than hiding down here."

She nodded, and put a hand on his arm. "Tristan, after this I'm leaving. It's not fair to make you suffer because of whatever this is."

Despite her brave facade, he felt the tremble of her hand. She was scared down to her bones, and he didn't blame her. Maybe it would be easier if she left. He didn't owe this woman anything.

She was a stranger who'd parachuted into his life and cost him his truck. What good could he do her anyway? He wasn't a body-guard or a police officer or an FBI agent.

But no matter how much his brain argued the point, some core part of him wouldn't—couldn't—let her face this on her own.

"Are you telling me the whole truth?" he demanded.

A muscle in her cheek twitched. "That's the gist. I can add much more detail if you like, for instance about how I executed the escape. I waited until the overnight shift change, then—"

"It's okay." He waved her off. Even if she wasn't telling the whole truth, he still felt compelled to help her. Why, exactly, he didn't know. But he was going with it.

"Then I'm coming with you."

"Coming with me? What are you talking about?"

He poked his head out of the rocks and did a careful survey of the beach and the breakwater. Nothing caught his eye, so he climbed out of their hiding place, then offered her a hand to help her out. "I think we need to get out of town."

"We?"

As soon as her sneakers touched the beach, he bundled her ahead of him.

"No, Tristan. *We* don't need to do anything. *You* need to get back to your life and *I* need to disappear."

"Shh. Don't argue with me. You owe me that much." He guided her to a shortcut over the rocks.

"I owe you some peace and quiet and lack of exploding trucks, that's what I owe you."

"And I'm holding you to that."

TWELVE

The fire chief turned out to be an imposing black-haired giant of a man who explained that without his previous experience in big city fire departments, he never would have recognized the signs of a detonation.

"Pissed anyone off lately?" he asked Tristan.

"Well, sure. I just pissed off the entire fishing community, and then there's Trixie, she's generally ticked off at me. My crew, because it took me some time to get back to fishing this summer. The rest of the Dutch Harbor fleet because even though we got started late, we kicked ass. Toni usually has some kind of beef with me."

Darius dug a hand into his hair. "Enough. Sounds like you've been pissing people off your entire life but no one's tried to blow up your truck before." He turned to Lulu, who wanted to shrink away from his penetrating gaze. "Is it safe to say you're the target here?"

"I'm sorry," she said. "I had no idea—"

"We should pull Maya into this convo," Tristan said. Lulu appreciated the way he stayed close to her, and made it clear they were a team. As much as her guilty conscience kept screaming at her to leave, it felt really good to have an ally.

In the faded yellow one-story compound that housed both the police and fire departments, she repeated the story she'd told to Tristan to Maya Badger. The look in the woman's rich brown eyes made it clear she was none too happy with the fact that Lulu hadn't told it earlier.

If only she knew the *entire* entire story.

Lulu shoved that thought to the far back corner of her mind. She didn't want any hint of secrecy showing on her face, and she really wasn't any good at hiding things.

"Why didn't you tell us about this earlier?" the police chief demanded when she was done.

"My plan was to leave Lost Harbor as soon as I could manage it. I didn't want to involve anyone here."

"We've never had a truck blow up on the boardwalk before," Maya said dryly. "I think we're involved."

Darius the fire chief propped one ankle on the opposite knee. "There was that time when that longshoreman messed with Padric Jeffers' engine a couple years ago," said Darius. "I'd just started the job here, and I remember thinking maybe I had it all wrong about a small harbor police chief being a boring job."

"I'm glad my ex-truck is adding to your entertainment." Tristan rolled his neck to work out the kinks. Swimming, truck blowing up, it was a lot. She wanted to slide her hand under his damp hair and help him.

"Sorry, man," Darius said. "You need something to drive for a while? Emma Gordon—Kate's grandmother—has some extra rigs sitting around the peony farm. She starts them every year on her birthday, so I know they all work. Might need some fluids and bodywork, but they'll serve."

"Nah, I'm good." Tristan shrugged his big shoulders. "I

wouldn't be a real Alaskan without my quota of junkers lying around. How are we going to find this guy?"

"*We* aren't." Maya folded her arms on the desk and cast a stern look at Tristan. "Not if *we* includes you. All I need from Lulu is a positive ID." She opened an iPad and swung it around so Lulu could see it. "Can you identify the man you saw on the cruise ship? I did some digging into the alias you mentioned, Sebastian Perro."

The iPad showed a grainy photo of someone who wasn't the man. "Can I..."

"Yes, scroll away."

Lulu flipped through photos until she found the one that even now gave her chills. "This is him." After giving Tristan a moment to take it in, she spun the iPad back toward Maya.

Maya read from the iPad. "His name is Seb Antonov. Lithuanian national. Kidnapping. Trafficking. Forger. Bad dude."

Lulu swallowed hard as her fear came welling back.

"What I don't understand is why he's coming after you. Just because you recognized him? It doesn't seem like enough of a reason." Maya's forehead wrinkled in a frown. "Are you sure there isn't more than that?"

Oh dear. Clearly, she was dealing with a smart police chief. After all, Maya Badger had managed to identify Mr. Bad Guy in under a day. "I went to the security head, like I told you. I assume it's because of that."

"But clearly whatever he'd done to cover his tracks worked."

Lulu ran her tongue across her suddenly dry lips. "Yes, but maybe he thought I'd keep pushing? I wasn't going to, but he didn't know that. Maybe he just didn't want to leave any loose ends at all."

Maya narrowed her eyes, still looking unconvinced. "So when you left the ship, he went after you to what, get rid of you?"

"Maybe he thought I'd go to the authorities here. Like I am now, with you all."

"But you only did that after he apparently blew up Tristan's truck. And that's another thing. He wasn't trying to kill you, in my view."

Darius was nodding along with Maya's assessment, his bulging forearms folded across his midsection. "I was thinking the same thing. If it was a remote detonator, he could have waited until you were in the truck. But he didn't. He triggered it when no one was nearby. Not a single person got hurt. It seems more like a warning."

Lulu's gorge rose, and for a moment she thought she was going to vomit. *It was a warning.* Of course it was. And she knew exactly what he was warning her about.

Should she tell these kind and capable people everything? No. Not yet. Not until she had one very important conversation. Then she would.

Maya picked up her cell phone. "I'm going to reach out to the Anchorage FBI office and let them know there's been a sighting of this fugitive. I know they'll want to talk to you, Lulu. I have a contact there, Agent Clement, who I've worked with before. I'll ask him to come down as soon as possible."

She nodded, but her stomach still roiled. How long would they take to get here? Could they be trusted? Would she be a sitting duck until they arrived? And what would happen once they did?

Tristan got to his feet, his height and broad shoulders a match for even the mighty fire chief's. "Call me when the FBI is here. It's probably not safe for Lulu to use her phone."

"She'll be with you?" Maya frowned again, shaking her head. "I'm not sure that's safe. Obviously the suspect knows you're together. I can arrange a secure place for her."

"Are you sure about that?" Tristan settled his shoulders in his jacket. "Face it, none of us here in Lost Harbor knows shit about people like this guy." He gestured at the iPad.

"Ethan James?" suggested Darius.

"Former private eye from Los Angeles," Tristan explained to Lulu.

"Ethan's out of town on a job. He won't be back until next week." Maya drummed her fingers on her desk. "Maybe Bash could step up as a bodyguard."

"Former MMA champ." More explanations from Tristan. "And my future brother-in-law."

"Of course, I met him with Toni—"

They barreled on as if she hadn't spoken. "Maybe she could stay someplace more remote, like in a yurt on the Lighthouse property," Maya mused.

"Hell, Emma Gordon has a rifle and the best eye on the peninsula. And those geese she keeps are better than any guard dog." Darius took out his phone, ready to text.

"Maybe we should think more creatively, like maybe Bethany or Ian can find an empty room at the hospital. It has lots of people, paramedics coming and going, good security."

At the thought of being stashed in a hospital, after everything she'd gone through with her mother, Lulu rebelled. She had to get back to the *Desperado*, immediately. Nothing else mattered until she did.

She bolted to her feet. "I'm sure you all have good intentions, but I'm a grown woman and you're all talking about me as if I'm not even here. This is my decision. You have no authority over me. I'm not even a citizen of this country. Am I under arrest?"

Their faces all swung toward her, showing various versions of surprise.

"Of course not," said Maya.

"Then I thank you all for your offers of help, including roping in random other Lost Harbor residents, but I'm going to leave now." She spun on her heel and marched out the door.

"I highly advise against it," Maya called after her. "This man is dangerous."

Yes, she knew that part. But she had to get back to the *Desperado*. Desperately.

Of course her dramatic exit was ruined when she took a wrong turn on the way out. She wasn't surprised when a firm hand on her elbow guided her back toward the exit.

Tristan wasn't going to be that easy to shake. In so many ways.

"You got a plan?" he said in her ear.

"More or less."

"More Lulu, less everyone else?"

"How did you guess?" They reached the back door of the compound and stepped into the parking lot. A stand of birch trees quivered in the wind and a few bright leaves drifted to the ground. This place was beautiful, even in the dying days of fall. Small comfort under the circumstances.

"Listen, let's go back to the *Desperado* and you can have a shower and a nap."

Yes! That suited her perfectly. She needed to get back to the boat. That was priority number one.

She twisted her hands together, her anxiety ratcheting up. "Do you think Mr. Bad Guy—Seb Antonov—knows your boat, and that I'm staying there?"

"Just in case, I've had it under guard since this morning."

"You have?" She glanced at him in shock as he pulled out his phone to text someone. "By who?"

"A few people. Boris Clancy's one. He's the one with his pet chicken in the basket of his bike. People assume he's harmless, but he sees everything that goes on in the harbor."

Everything? That made her a little nervous. He could have uncovered her secret.

"I offered him a year's worth of salmon skin for his chickens if he kept watch on my boat. Believe me, he's probably barely blinked since then. Lucas, the harbormaster, has been sticking close too. Bo, one of my old deckhands, has been camped out in my sister's cabin on the boardwalk. He set up a camera and a telescope and swore no one would get past him."

A camera—her worry tightened even further. On the other hand, if these watchdogs had discovered anything, surely she would have heard by now.

"You did all this today? When?"

"When you were with Toni. I figured there was a chance I didn't fool the guy last night. If he came looking, I wanted to know about it."

He finished his text and sent it with a soft *swoop.* "Ride," he explained.

"Uber? Lyft?"

He chuckled. "The Lost Harbor equivalent. A friend who owes you."

THIRTEEN

A few minutes later, Trixie pulled up in an enormous white SUV. "Hop in, Bonnie and Clyde," she grumbled.

"How are we Bonnie and Clyde?" Tristan swung into the passenger seat. "We haven't committed any crimes."

"I'm sure it's just a matter of time."

Tristan rolled his eyes, but Lulu wondered, not for the first time, what their relationship was all about. They were definitely more than friends. Ex-lovers?

Lulu got into the backseat and pulled the door closed behind her. As Trixie pulled away from the police station, Lulu gave into a wave of exhaustion. She slumped against the door, then slid down until she was half lying on the comfortable heated leather. The stress of this day had left her bone tired, knackered, emotionally spent, every nerve ending frazzled. To keep herself conscious, she focused on the conversation between Trixie and Tristan.

"How did the rest of the debate go?" he asked Trixie.

"You mean after you endorsed my fucking opponent?"

"It could have been worse. I could have gone for the rooster."

"That would have been a good choice, because I'm pretty sure Cockles won the debate."

"Oh yeah?"

"In the middle of a heated argument about sustainability, he busted out of his cage and flew into Janet Holt's lap. She already thinks her dead husband was reincarnated as a yak. Now she believes Cockles might be one of our early mayors come back to finish his work. You know how influential she is. The rest of us might as well pack it up just like you."

Tristan laughed as Trixie pulled out of the lot. "So all I had to do was jump into Janet Holt's lap and I could have walked away with this thing?"

"No, all you had to do was stay in the race. Coward."

Even from the backseat, Lulu caught the slight wince that accusation drew from Tristan.

"Not gonna argue, Trix. Just take the opportunity and run."

"Oh, I will. And boy, will you be mad when I expand the number of cruise ships coming to Lost Harbor." She made a little face at him. "Especially the *Northern Princess*. The more trouble the merrier."

He rubbed his temples. "Go Cockles."

"So, am I allowed to ask why your former campaign manager is lying down in my back seat?"

"She's had a long day."

Lulu buried her face in her elbow, laughter welling from her throat. Right behind it, she knew, were tears, so she couldn't let any of those out.

"So have you. I'm sorry about your truck. The curse of the *Northern Princess* strikes again."

"Yeah."

That one word contained a world of reaction: sadness, anger, fear. A whiff of burning rubber filtered into the SUV, and by the sudden silence up front, Lulu realized they must be passing the wreckage.

"Just drop us at the ramp. Thanks, Trix. I owe you one."

"Forget it." Trixie's chastened tone showed the sight of Tristan's destroyed truck must have had an effect on her. "If we count all the way back to high school, we're even."

Soon afterwards—Lulu might have actually dropped off for a few moments—they came to a stop and Lulu climbed out of the backseat, where Tristan met her with a shielding arm around her shoulders. They hustled past wandering tourists enjoying the last moments of the sunset. He guided her to the front steps of a dilapidated cabin perched above the boardwalk.

A kid—maybe twenty or so—sat on a glider on the porch, staring into a telescope. He pulled away as they walked up the steps and jumped to his feet. "Hey, Captain."

Tristan gave a sigh. "Not your captain anymore. Even when I was, you didn't have to—"

"I just like it. Get over it." He turned his sassy gaze to Lulu. "You're the dancer from the ship?"

"That's me." She did a little soft-shoe on the weathered boards of the porch. Amazingly, he joined in and they danced together for a joyous moment that felt like a surprise gift dropped into her lap from on high. Bo wore a zebra-patterned vest over a black shirt, along with tight velvet peg trousers. Oh, and fuzzy purple slippers. She laughed in delight as they mirrored each other's movements. God, how she loved dancing, even in the midst of the worst crisis of her life.

Well, second worst. Nothing would ever come close to watching her mother fade away.

When they finished, both with arms spread wide and big grins on their faces, Tristan gave an irritated growl. "Are you just about done?"

"Yes, Captain." Bo drew himself up straight and saluted.

Lulu swallowed her laugh as storm clouds gathered on Tristan's face. "Did you see anything?"

"Lots of things. I spotted a Caspian tern that Megan Holt got really excited about. I didn't know what it was, but Ruby told me. She hung out with me with her binoculars for a while when she got out of school. Also, I think Pedro Davila's having an affair with the receptionist at the Eagle's Nest. And the Wild North water taxi is putting more people on their boat than they're allowed."

"No suspicious strangers near my boat?"

"No one came near your boat. No one even walked past it. I even kept an eye on the water in case someone swam up to it. Nothing. No one. Guaranteed."

Lulu relaxed, relief flooding through her veins. Her heart was still beating fast, but that was probably because of the impromptu dance. "Thank you so much for keeping watch, Bo."

He swept into a bow. "Anything for Captain Del Rey. He saved my life."

At first she thought he was being dramatic, but he looked much too sincere for that to be the case. "Does that mean I can trust him with *my* life?"

"Oh yes, just don't fall in love with him. Believe me, I've seen it happen and it doesn't end well. There's a bar in Dutch Harbor with his face on a dartboard—"

"Okay okay, that's enough of that." Tristan's frown had grown even more stormy. "You can stand down, Bo. We're good. Thanks for the help."

"If there's anything else you need, just text me." He hopped off the glider and slung a feather boa around his neck. "I'm off to my new gig at the library. Story hour."

"I wouldn't mind some story hour," Lulu told him with a wink. "I'm sure that dartboard's just the tip of the iceberg, right?"

But Bo's first loyalty was obviously to Tristan, because he

made a zipping gesture across his lips, then stood at attention to salute his former captain.

Rolling his eyes, Tristan gestured for Lulu to follow him back down the rickety stairs to the weathered planks of the boardwalk.

"Was he really one of your deckhands?"

"He really was." They trotted down the ramp that led to the floats. The corrugated metal made a tinny sound with each step. She looked down into the murky harbor water and wondered how cold it was. Extremely, she imagined. "I took him on as a favor to Chrissie Yates—my ex-girlfriend. He'd never been on a boat before, but he did well when he wasn't either throwing up or filming the crew. Then we got into a bad—"

He broke off and shifted the subject with a wave of his hand. "Long story, not relevant." They reached the *Desperado*, with its black hull and red stripe at the waterline. She glanced around nervously, getting the sense that eyes were on her.

"Do you feel that? Someone watching?"

Tristan turned toward the boardwalk, then waved at someone on a bicycle. "That's Boris Clancy. Another one of our guardian harbor-rats. That's what we call people who work on the board-walk," he explained. "It's a compliment. Rats are survivors."

"I suppose I should channel my inner rat, then."

Tristan gave the scraggly-bearded man on the bicycle a thumbs up, then turned back to help Lulu climb up the ladder into the fishing boat. When they were both onboard, he did a careful survey of the deck.

"I left a camera recording as a last line of defense. If someone came onboard, I'll know." Outside the hatchway that led to the wheelhouse, he crouched next to a plastic bucket that held a coil of thick bristly rope. He pulled out a digital camera and scanned through it for a long moment.

Lulu held her breath. *Please no, please no.*

"Nothing. We're safe." He slung the little video camera over his shoulder and gestured for her to come inside.

She urged her heart to start beating again. "That's a pretty word, safe." Nothing more than a word, of course. At any moment, everything could fall apart. She knew that from personal experience.

They stepped into the cabin belowdecks. She did a rapid-fire survey of the tidy space and saw nothing out of place. Another moment of relief.

"Do you want to take a shower?" he asked. "I have to do one more thing."

"What?"

"It might be overkill, but I'm going to put on a wetsuit and some goggles and check out my hull."

She nodded as he opened a tote that held a pile of Gore-Tex gear. "I suppose you want me to turn around again while you change?"

"Or go take a shower." He rummaged through the gear, then pulled out a hooded wetsuit.

"Can we talk about this situation, because being on the run from a bad guy has very few perks. Seems as if this could be one of them."

"What could?"

"Watching you strip down to your undies again."

When he glanced over his shoulder at her, she tossed him a saucy wink. "Just a thought."

"Suit yourself." With swift motions, he stripped off all his upper layers—blazer, shirt—and bared the magnificent expanse of his torso.

That was the point at which she realized that seeing him bare-chested on a beach was a lot different than in the confined space of a fishing boat cabin. "Shower?" she squeaked.

He pointed to a narrow passageway behind her. She knew it

led to the sleeping bunks. "Door on your left. It's small and the water heater's even smaller. You have about five minutes before it gets tepid."

"That's all I need." She fled toward the little corridor. By the time she got out of the shower, Tristan would be in the water examining the hull. Hopefully, that would give her all the time she needed.

FOURTEEN

Using the last light of day, dressed in full wetsuit, hood and flippers, Tristan scoured every inch of his hull to make sure no one had attached an explosive of some kind. He found some barnacles that would need to be scraped off this winter, and an interesting clump of kelp.

But nothing that looked like an explosive. Of course his only knowledge of that sort of thing was from movies. But he was pretty sure no one had yet invented a bomb disguised as a barnacle, so he felt confident that the *Desperado* wasn't going to get blown to smithereens when they left the harbor.

Which would have sounded like such an insane statement up until a few hours ago. Someone had blown up his fucking truck! The reality of that still stunned him.

What was he doing? Why was he putting his beloved boat at risk to protect a stranger? Talk about insane. Maybe his brain surgery had done something to his common sense.

But he knew that wasn't it. He'd always had a protective side, which was why the accident that had sent him and Ralphie to the hospital had struck such a blow to his self-esteem. His bone-headed error had given Bo a concussion, Ralphie an impaled shoulder, and Tristan a brain bleed. People had gotten hurt because of him.

Which was why he should step away from this situation. Yes, that was exactly what he should do.

"Lulu, or whatever your real name is, because who the hell is named Lulu, I'll take you back to the police station and let them handle this. You don't want to be under police protection? The hell with that. I'm going to handcuff you to Maya's chair if that's what it takes. Hell, let's lock you in the holding cell. Got a problem with that? Call the British embassy. I can't keep you safe. I can try, but I can't promise anything. I can't promise anything to anybody."

New mantra, who dis?

I can't promise anything to anybody. And I'm not going to try.

Yes, that was exactly what he should tell Lulu, and yet even thinking the words left a bitter taste behind. Something about Lulu wouldn't let him be.

Maybe it was her obvious bravery. Or how she'd kept her lighthearted sense of humor throughout this entire ordeal. Laughing in the face of fear. He respected that. He admired it. Also, face it, she was cute as hell. He missed the buttery locks she'd had the first day he saw her, but the mousy brown did nothing to take away her appeal. Her mouth was still wide and generous, her eyes kind of merry and expressive, as if she was always on the edge of a laugh.

But behind that laugh lay much more than a sunny soul. He sensed that she'd been through something hard, just as he had. She'd made veiled references to being a caregiver, but hadn't gone into detail. Maybe that was one benefit of suffering a trauma; you recognized it in others.

He had a lot of questions for Lulu, and no intention of abandoning her before he got answers. That's what this was about.

She'd invaded his boat with all her drama and cost him his truck, and damnit, he deserved answers.

The fact that she made him laugh with her saucy quips and valiant smile had nothing to do with it. Neither did her loose-limbed gracefulness when she danced, or her endless legs, or her flirty teasing. Nope. All that was completely irrelevant.

With water streaming off his wetsuit, he climbed back up the ladder he'd dropped over the side. He used a freshwater hose on the deck to rinse off his suit, then peeled it down to his waist as he stepped into the cabin.

It was so quiet that a thought flashed through him—maybe Lulu had left. A kind of cold emptiness followed. It might be easier if she left, but he didn't want her to.

But when he peeked into the cabin, he saw that she was sound asleep on his bunk, curled on her side, her mouth half-open, her breath stirring his old plaid blanket that came with him on every trip. She held her cell phone in one hand, as if she'd been in the middle of checking it when she'd simply fallen asleep.

The vise around his heart loosened. Keeping as quiet as possible, he changed out of his wetsuit and into comfortable sweats. He went back on deck, then climbed the two steps into the wheelhouse and started the engine. Normally he would check in with Lucas or another fisherman to let someone know where he was headed. There were no regulations about that, but the Lost Harbor fishing fleet was tight-knit and always watched out for each other.

But this time, he didn't. He wasn't sure where he was headed, for one thing. For another, he couldn't be entirely sure who was monitoring communications.

He listened to his engines, the two powerful Volvo Pentas that could drive the *Desperado* up to speeds of almost twenty knots an hour. The Volvos were fairly new—he'd recently upgraded—and didn't need much time to warm up. In a few minutes, the initial roughness had smoothed out.

He stepped onto the deck, ready to climb down and untie the *Desperado* from the float. This was why he rarely operated the *Desp* on his own. It was a lot easier to do this kind of thing with a deckhand instead of a sleeping tap dancer.

"You forgot this."

He jumped as the voice of Lucas Holt sounded from the float. In the descending darkness, the harbormaster held up the line he'd just unwound from the cleat.

Tristan nodded to him to toss it on deck. "Thanks."

Lucas, bless him, didn't ask any more questions, just moved to the aft cleat. "I'll be monitoring the usual frequencies," he said. "You reach out if you need anything."

"You got it. Thanks."

Lucas tossed him the line, then stepped back, hands in his pockets. "One more thing. For what it's worth, I think you would have been a good mayor."

Tristan let out a snort. "Famous last words?"

"Fuck that. Of course not. See you when you get back. Oh, another thing."

Tristan paused on his way back to the wheelhouse. "Yeah?"

"Being mayor isn't the only way to lead around here."

Irritation scraped across his nerves. "I don't know what you're getting at, Lucas, but I'm not looking to lead anything. I'm just a fisherman."

"Sure. Is that where you're going? Fishing? Seems like there's something missing. Oh yeah, your crew."

Tristan flipped him a middle finger, then grinned. "Call it a cruise."

"Thought you hated cruise ships. Especially the cursed one."

"Maybe they're growing on me. Catch you on the flip side."

He went back to the wheelhouse and took the boat out of

idle. He eased away from the ramp and glided through the harbor, past the dark hulks of the other big trawlers in port today. Not all were based in Lost Harbor. He spotted Big Booty's boat out of Unalaska, and the Ryan brothers from Kodiak Island.

He didn't even stop at the gas pumps at the mouth of the harbor, because he'd fueled up a few days ago and hadn't gone anywhere since then. He didn't want to risk any more slow-downs, or have any more chats. Leaving at night like this wasn't unheard of, although usually he'd set out before dawn instead of after dusk. The fewer people who knew he was leaving the harbor, the slower word would get out.

The beauty of the night ocean took his breath away. A crescent moon already hung in the sky like something from a child's imagination. It cast a limpid trail of silver across the ripples on the surface of the water. He loved this part of a trip, when you were just setting out and unknown adventures lay ahead. All was possible out here on the open water. Wild hope flooded his heart —he didn't even know what for, just...hope.

Maybe everything would be okay. Maybe he'd manage to keep Lulu and his boat safe. Maybe he wasn't going to fuck up every single thing in his life.

"What are you doing?" The furious yell came from the lower hatchway that led to the cabin. Plexiglass windows offered him a clear view of Lulu's panicky face.

"We're getting the hell out of dodge," he called down to her.

"We can't...we can't do that!"

What was her problem? Hadn't she talked about hiding out in Lost Souls Wilderness? "I'm doing what you wanted," he shouted over the hum of his engine. Then he gestured for her to climb into the wheelhouse.

When she did so, she was practically vibrating with some combination of fear and fury. He didn't understand either one.

"Didn't you say you wanted to hide out in Lost Souls? That's what we're doing."

"Why did you just leave without telling me?" Her hair was tousled from sleep and she had a red mark on her cheek, probably left by her makeshift pillow.

"You were completely out. I didn't want to wake you. You obviously needed your sleep."

"I didn't mean to fall asleep. I need to...shit." She dropped her head into her hands, shoulders slumped. "This is bad. Very bad. We have to go back."

"Why? We're safer out here. We're halfway to Lost Souls already." He gestured at the dark outline of the mountains on the other side of the Misty Bay. "We can disappear into one of the coves over there. I know them all. No one will find us, not even an overflight could spot us. We've got supplies, a warm place to sleep on the *Desperado*. It's the perfect solution until the FBI can get Antonov into custody."

She shot him a glance full of so much panic that he threw up his hands. "Seriously, you want to go back? We can go back. But you have to tell me why. And what you want to do instead."

She chewed on her lower lip but didn't answer.

"You don't have a better plan?"

"No. I mean, this is a good plan. I know you're trying to help. It's just..."

"Just *what*?" He throttled down the engine to a rough idle. The waves pitched them from side to side, a familiar motion for him, because they often had to work at an idle while fishing.

But cruise ships didn't rock like this, because she lost her balance and stumbled forward. He caught her in his arms, a sleep-warmed bundle of long limbs and soft windblown hair.

"What's going on, Lulu?" He tilted her face up to his. "We're in this together, okay? You can tell me."

She shook her head, but at the same time leaned against him, as if wanting the strength he was offering, but unable to accept it. "I wish I could."

So there *was* something she was keeping from him. Disappointment ripped through him. He'd asked her straight up if she'd told him the truth, and she'd said yes. That wasn't just a lie, it was a lie about a lie. At least she wasn't lying about lying about lying. Or was she?

"Can you just trust me?" she whispered. "There's something I can't tell you, but it's only because I promised someone."

"Trust you?" He let out a sharp bark of laughter. "You looked me in the eye and said you told me the whole truth."

"I said it was the gist. Tristan, please." She reached up a hand to stroke his cheek. Her eyes shone with tears in the greenish light from his dashboard. Was she trying to play him? Was that why her touch felt so gentle and her body was trembling? "I wouldn't be saying any of this if it wasn't important. I'd still be sleeping on that bunk, ready for my getaway to Lost Souls Wilderness. Will you just...believe me?"

He closed his eyes for a long moment. Trust wasn't his strong suit. His trustfulness had taken its first hit when Chrissie, his high school girlfriend, had left Lost Harbor without even telling him. His divorce from Julie had given it another cutting blow. He wasn't even sure that he trusted *himself* anymore. Wasn't that why he'd dropped out of the mayor's race? Wasn't that why he'd taken forever to get back on the water after his surgery?

And now this virtual stranger was asking him to trust her after misleading him several times already?

"It's all right," came another voice, a young, scared one.

His eyes flew open. A kid stood on the deck, at the bottom of the wheelhouse steps. He was about ten or eleven, and wore a dirty pair of sweatpants and a soccer jersey.

"You can tell him, Lulu."

He spoke with a light accent, a mixture of Spanish and

proper British. The boy had curly dark hair and pale skin. South American perhaps?

"Where did you come from?" Tristan asked, utterly astonished.

"I was hiding," he said proudly. "There was something metal and many ropes."

"Why. The hell," Tristan heard the menace in his own voice, the flat-out shock that his boat had been invaded like this, "were you hiding in my anchor bay? Who are you?"

Lulu steeled her shoulders and slowly faced him. "Tristan, this is Raul. Raul, meet Tristan. Raul was on the cruise ship. He came to all my kiddie events—clown shows and puppet shows and so forth—and we became friends. He's...well, I'm helping him run away." She cleared her throat. "From a kidnapper. From Antonov."

FIFTEEN

"Oh, hell."

That was definitely not the reaction Lulu had been hoping for. This was exactly why she'd begged Raul to stay out of sight until she could scope out the situation more thoroughly. She'd wanted to trust Tristan—she *did* trust him already to some degree —but she'd wanted to be a hundred percent sure.

"Tristan, listen to me. Be mad at me all you want, but we have to protect Raul. All of this is because of him."

He threw up a hand. "Stop talking, Lulu. Just stop."

She snapped her mouth shut. He hadn't changed course yet. They were still chugging toward Lost Souls, which perhaps was for the best, after all. While Tristan had been examining the *Desperado*'s hull, she'd huddled with Raul and they'd decided to go directly back to the police station and tell everything to Maya Badger. Their plan was to wait until Tristan was back onboard, then explain it to him, then go to Maya. But she'd fallen asleep while Tristan was still in the water, then panicked when she realized they were already at sea.

But now that Raul had revealed himself to Tristan, she was glad they were heading toward the wilderness. She wished Tristan would turn on the turbojets or whatever would get them there faster. Once the FBI had arrived and it was safe, they'd go to Maya.

Tristan turned to Raul. "Explain."

Raul seemed to like the big fisherman's direct approach. "That man pretended to be my father on the ship, but he's not my father and I don't wish to stay with him. My mother was... together with him."

"He's your stepfather?"

"No, no. I don't know. My grandmother is more my mother than my mother is. I only saw my mother a few times. I was with her for a weekend but she went away and he took me with him. All I want is to go back to my grandparents in Colombia. I don't want to be here. Sorry. Your boat is nice," he added politely.

Tristan appeared to be suppressing a smile. That was a good sign, right? "Thanks. Lots of good hiding places, is that it?"

Uh oh. That sounded less promising.

"I told him to hide," Lulu said quickly. "I was going to tell you everything once I was sure it was safe."

Without looking her way, he gave her that same shushing gesture. She found it rude, but decided he held the cards in this situation.

"Have you been on my boat this whole time?"

"Si, Capitán."

"I'm not your captain. You're not a member of my crew." He shot an annoyed glance at Lulu, who'd snorted softly at the sound of the dreaded word "captain," now in Spanish.

At that point, Tristan reeled off something in Spanish that Lulu didn't understand. She'd learned some French at school, but it hadn't stuck. She only recognized a few words here and there— the word "loco," for instance, and "muchacha."

Apparently they were talking about her, the crazy lady.

Raul looked delighted at the chance to explain himself in his own language, and they rattled on until Tristan finally nodded, apparently satisfied.

"Raul, why don't you go down and get yourself a snack from the refrigerator," he told the boy. "I need to talk to Lulu."

Raul looked at her for confirmation, and she gave him the go-ahead with a nod. "It's okay. Tristan won't toss me overboard."

Her nervous joke made Tristan narrow his eyes. "Jury's out," he muttered.

Raul looked from one to the other of them, clearly trying to assess the tension. Whatever he saw seemed to satisfy him, and he skipped away belowdecks.

When they were alone in the wheelhouse, the tension between them amped up to a nearly unbearable degree. Tristan's face was unreadable. All those laugh lines looked more like fury etched across his face.

Lulu folded her arms protectively over her chest. "You're angry."

"Yes."

"I'm sorry for that, but I had to protect Raul at all costs. When he told me he was going to run away from the ship, I couldn't let him go alone. I insisted on going with him and then I couldn't be responsible for getting him into even more trouble. I had to be completely certain that you and Maya and the others are trustworthy. Please don't take it personally. I didn't know you or your friends or this place, or even this country, and with Mr. Bad Guy chasing after us like that—"

She broke off as Tristan took a long stride until they were face to face. The breath fled from her body. He reached behind her, to the hatch, and with a sudden rush of panic she thought—*he is going to toss me overboard.* Instead, he closed the door, cutting out the sounds of waves and wind.

The sudden shift in sound disoriented her. Or maybe his sudden proximity did that. He was so close she could see the ring of opal gray around his irises, the scar hiding under his hair, the slight chap of his lips.

He cupped his hand under her chin and tilted up her face. His touch was so tender that she felt tears form behind her eyes. She swallowed hard, unnamable emotions racing through her. He didn't seem to be angry with her, and yet he'd said that he was.

"Why didn't you go to the police?"

"When I tried that on the ship, it didn't go so well. I wanted to be sure."

"What about me? You could have told me." His quiet voice, like rough velvet, struck heat deep in her belly.

"I couldn't take that chance," she whispered. "Not at first." She was hypnotized by his mouth, the firm cut of his lips, the dark gold scruff surrounding it...how would it feel if she touched it with her hand, her lips?

"No. I suppose you couldn't."

Her eyes flew up to meet his, and she saw understanding there. Even...respect. And something deeper, hotter.

He lowered his head, closer and closer. The journey seemed to take forever, and yet still it took her by surprise when their lips met. Not because she didn't know they were about to kiss, but because the contact brought an explosion of sensation that made her stagger.

Sure, it might have been because the boat lurched as a swell passed under it. Perfect excuse to grab onto Tristan's arms and savor the feel of his hard muscles. She felt the power of them, of all of him, but his kiss was light and teasing. The contrast made her want him even more.

He moved his lips across hers, like a butterfly looking for the perfect place to land. She sighed under his mouth and savored the sweetness of his touch. That first kiss told you so much about a person. Were they considerate? Sensitive? Arrogant? Selfish?

From Tristan's kiss, she could do away with any thought of selfishness or arrogance. He was direct, curious, unhurried, deliberate. He didn't do anything until he was good and ready—like parting her lips with his tongue to take the kiss deeper. She welcomed him eagerly, drawing him inside and dancing her tongue to meet his.

And she got even more from his kiss—joy and sadness, two things she understood very well.

At that point, she let go of her thoughts and abandoned herself to sensations. Liquid heat traveled straight to her sex. Her nipples tingled with electric desire. The palms of her hands prickled—always a sure sign of lust with her. Her toes curled inside her trainers, and her inner thighs tightened.

Good lord, one kiss and she was ready to shag this man?

She imagined him hoisting her up on that dashboard and parting her legs. Putting his big hand between her thighs, watching her as he stroked her into a frenzy. Her heart hammered against her ribs. *She wanted him.* Oh, how she wanted him. This virtual stranger that the mysterious workings of the universe had tossed into her life like a floating clump of seaweed.

He drew out of the kiss, his tongue sliding across his lips as if he was still tasting her. His eyes dark with desire, his breath coming fast, he held her gaze and let her see how much *he* wanted her. The physical signs were there too; she felt his bulge against her hipbone. It made her dizzy with need.

Or maybe that was the fact that the boat kept tilting and rising and falling. How could she possibly keep her head under these conditions?

"You were supposed to toss me overboard," she finally managed. Go for the quip. That was her default.

"Change of plans."

Or was it? Maybe he had tossed her overboard, into a wild ocean filled with crosscurrents of lust and swells of desire.

"You aren't angry with me?"

"I'm angry with the asshole who kidnapped Raul. I got a few more details from him. His mother is from an extremely wealthy family, but he hasn't seen her much over the years. His grandparents have a lot of security, but his mother's more relaxed. That's how Seb Antonov managed to snake his way in. She has bad taste in boyfriends, apparently."

Wow. She hadn't gathered that much information from Raul in all her time with him. Impressed, she pecked a kiss onto the corner of his mouth, only to find herself pressed against his chest.

"Don't poke the bear." Half laughing, half gruff, his voice vibrated through her body.

"This is Alaska, what else are you supposed to do with the bears?"

"Avoid them. Save yourself."

She supposed that was meant to have a double meaning, but all she could think was how good it felt to be held by him. His strength, his heat, his seafarer eyes, his solid wall of hard muscle. How easily she could get drawn into his world and never want to leave.

But she had responsibilities. Or rather, one responsibility. A very important one. She still could hardly believe she'd fallen asleep before she could follow through with their plan and contact Maya Badger. Her mind and body had simply shut down from exhaustion and the ongoing stress of this situation.

Or maybe she really had trusted Tristan, and so she'd allowed herself a moment of rest.

Now part of her wanted to spend the rest of the night kissing Tristan and not worrying about anything else. But she shoved that aside. The crisis hadn't ended just because Tristan knew about Raul now. But at least she wouldn't have to deceive him anymore.

"What do you think we should do now?" she asked him.

"Carry on with the plan." Picking up on her shift in mood, he stepped away from her, back to the steering-wheel. He took the boat out of idle and they resumed their course. She couldn't tell where they were in this dark world of ocean and night, but he seemed unfazed by the lack of visibility. "We'll tuck ourselves into a cove and wait until the FBI gets to Lost Harbor. When we're sure it's safe for Raul, we'll hand him over to the appropriate law enforcement authorities."

"How are we going to know when it's safe?"

"Maya is really good at her job. I trust her. We can also hire a lawyer to represent him. My friend Kate is a lawyer and also very good at her job. Ethan James, the PI, should be back soon. He's worked with law enforcement extensively. If all of them are satisfied, I'm thinking we should be too."

Maybe. But that meant trusting Tristan's friends. She didn't know any of those people, other than Maya Badger. Maya had impressed her, but she was only one person, the young police chief of a very small town.

"What if..." She held onto a grip bar and braced her legs apart as the *Desperado* picked up speed. "What if his mother is dead? He doesn't think she is, but there's a chance. I don't know what this Seb Antonov is capable of."

"You can 'what if' all kinds of things, but there's no point until we know more. Raul says he didn't hurt him, so that's a good sign."

Silent, she gazed out the spray-flecked window of the wheelhouse. Between the scrum of sea salt on the plexiglass and the darkness of the night, she could barely see a thing. Weren't boats supposed to have lights? Maybe he'd left all the running lights off so they wouldn't be spotted.

"What if he's following us?"

"He's not following us, at least not in a boat. I have instruments here and they say we're the only craft within a five mile radius." He tapped one of the gauges on the dashboard. "You really should give the 'what if's' a rest. You can drive yourself crazy."

"Yes, Captain," she muttered.

He snorted, then turned his big body sideways and reached a hand to her. "Come here."

"Will you consider it mutiny if I don't?"

"Yes, and I'll maroon you on an island with nothing but bad coffee."

She slipped her hand in his and let him tug her to his side. "Listen, Lulu. I just wanted to say...I really respect what you did. I mean, it was nuts and probably illegal. There's international boundaries and trafficking laws and God only knows what else. And you really should have gone to Maya if you didn't trust me. But Raul thinks you're an angel sent from Heaven to watch out for him."

"I'm not an angel. But no one else was going to help Raul. That security head was probably bought off. He was all alone. I..." Emotion clogged her throat. "I know what that feels like."

He tightened his arm around her, and she let herself release some of the tension she'd carried with her from the cruise ship. She relaxed against him, giving him the weight of her body. The boat leaped over a wave, and a bit of spray splashed across the window. It was just the two of them, alone on the vast dark ocean.

Except for the runaway kidnapping victim down below.

Was that a kiss he dropped onto her head? Her mother used to do that too. For a moment, grief threatened to overwhelm her, the way it occasionally did, a wave crashing over her and turning her tear ducts into waterfalls.

"I would like some more details, if you can manage it." Tristan's deep voice steadied her. "Did you tell the security chief about Raul and that you thought he'd been kidnapped?"

"You want to know how much of what I told you on the beach is true."

"Yes."

Fair enough.

"A lot of it, but not all," she admitted. "I left out Raul. I did recognize Antonov from a crime show, just as I said, although I thought of him as Mr. Bad Guy. I went to the security head about him. He shut me down. I didn't realize at that point that Raul was connected to him. Raul came to all my shows but he always had a guard with him. I assumed he was the child of someone important. Obviously he couldn't speak freely in front of his guard. But after my Singing in the Rain performance, Raul overheard Antonov ranting about me recognizing him. So you know what he did? He *mimed* the basics of the situation story to me during my pantomime class! The guard didn't notice a thing."

"He's an amazing kid."

"He really is."

She was so grateful that Tristan saw that too, instead of assigning Raul the label of problem-to-be-solved.

"So you *didn't* tell the security chief about Raul?"

"No, because I couldn't trust him at that point. He'd already dismissed me when I told him I recognized Antonov. I suspected he was on the take."

A large swell lifted the boat, then plunged them into a valley made of dark water laced with white foam. She gasped and gripped the edge of the dashboard. "Are we okay?"

"This?" Tristan laughed. "We're getting some real ocean swells now, that's all. They get twice as big once you get past Far Point." He used his sleeve to clear a spot on the window, then gestured ahead of them, at something that apparently was land, though she wouldn't swear to that.

"That's a point?"

"Yes, it marks the end of the Lost Souls Wilderness land mass. Past that is open ocean. But don't worry, we're not going there." He moved his arm to point at another indistinguishable piece of darkness. "We're going there."

"What is it?"

"It's called Del Rey Lagoon."

She tilted her head to look up at him. His smile curled at the corners of his lips, and she got a glimpse of the playful boy he must have been once upon a time. "You have a lagoon named after you?"

"Yup. I named it myself. I used to take my little skiff all through these inlets and bays and tidal lagoons. I found one that the mapmakers missed and claimed it for myself. I know it seems impossible that there's anything on this earth that doesn't show up on maps, but you'll see for yourself tomorrow."

"You didn't notify any mapmakers, I assume, selfish boy?"

"Nope. It's literally not on any map. I'm sure I'm not the only person who's ever been there. Once I found the remains of a campfire, and figured it was a hiker who stumbled across my lagoon. I looked it up on Google Earth once and it just looks like it's part of the forest. You'll see."

She snuggled against him. "It seems I chose the right boat to trespass on."

"The *Desperado* takes care of its own." He peered ahead into the murk and made an adjustment in their direction. "Which brings me to my next question. How the hell did Raul get on the boat—and stay on it—without me knowing?"

"Well." She bit her lip, hoping this part of the story didn't ruin their newfound mutual respect. "Remember when Fidget landed on me?"

"Yes."

"Raul climbed onto your boat first and he was right next to me. I shoved him aside so whatever was coming over the side wouldn't hit him. I'd already told him to hide as soon as we got onboard, so that's what he did. He crawled into a tote. Then when we were helping Fidget, he climbed out of the tote and hid under some oilskins. He just kept hiding. I found him after you went up on deck with your sleeping bag. I got him some food and water and told him to stay hidden while we figured out what our best course of action was."

"You wanted to leave Lost Harbor."

"I did. But he refused. He kept saying he liked this boat and we should give it a chance. He swore he'd stay hidden in case Mr. Bad Guy was lurking around. After your truck blew up, I was terrified. That was a message from the kidnapper warning me to back off. At least that's how I interpreted it. I knew we had to tell the police, but first I wanted to get back and make sure Raul was still safe. I didn't want him to be alone anymore, not with that man out there. My next step was going to be tell you, then Maya Badger."

He throttled down the engine as they passed a looming dark hulk that must be an island. "I still don't understand why I didn't hear him, or the two of you talking. I always hear everything that happens on my boat."

She didn't have the answer for that, and shrugged. "If it makes any difference, during our escape from the cruise ship, we got really good at not making any sounds. He paid close attention during my pantomime classes, and that's how we initially made our connection. We kind of figured out how to communicate silently." She demonstrated with the expressive facial movements and gestures that she'd used to tell Raul to stay hidden.

"Stay out of sight or I'll kick your ass," Tristan interpreted.

"More or less." She laughed softly. "I'm sorry we invaded

your boat. It must feel strange to you, not knowing what was happening on your own turf."

"Yeah," he said, the brief word holding layers of emotion. "I'm going to have to have a chat with the old *Desperado*."

"Don't come down too hard on her. I officially love this boat now."

She couldn't quite interpret the look he gave her, but for some reason, she blushed.

SIXTEEN

Tristan dropped anchor in the dark, still waters of Del Rey Lagoon. On all sides of the lagoon, tall cottonwoods and ancient spruce trees leaned over the shoreline, as if trying to look at their reflections. Some of them had fallen during the last windstorm, he saw. He drifted as close as he dared to the edge, mindful of the tide, and hurried onto the bow to release the anchor cable.

Glancing up at the overhanging trees, he caught the barest glimpse of starlit sky beyond the canopy. That forest would keep them safe even from an overflight, he hoped.

The downside of this spot was that if anyone found them, they could get trapped here. But he had a plan for that too. He knew this lagoon like his own backyard. Better, because he spent so little time in his backyard.

And maybe, if they made things challenging enough for Seb Antonov, he'd simply give up and leave them all alone.

After he'd dropped the anchor, he joined Lulu and Raul in the galley. She'd already made some tea and peeled potatoes to fry up. She'd also repurposed some of Tristan's clothes for Raul. He wore an Olde Salt Saloon hoodie that hung almost to his knees, and a pair of fleece long underwear with a piece of rope as a belt.

"Thanks for the clothes, *Capitán*."

Tristan sighed and gave up on training yet another young person to *not* call him captain. "Glad you found something. We don't usually have kids onboard. Well, Ruby, but she's a little younger. Ten, I think. It's her dog Fidget that you met the other night."

Raul brightened. "I like that dog. I asked him not to bark at me and he didn't. Can we play with him again?"

"Sure, I'll arrange a playdate after we stop running from the dangerous kidnapper," Tristan said dryly.

Lulu shot him a scolding glance and dumped the potatoes in the frying pan. "There might be an opportunity to play with Fidget again, Raul. Maybe Ruby too."

"I thought you were dead set on getting out of Lost Harbor," he murmured to her as he pulled a salmon from a cooler filled with ice. He whipped out another pan and tossed some oil in it.

He rinsed off the filet, which he'd caught in Ninlik Cove only a couple of days ago; it seemed like another lifetime. A simpler one, in which all he had to worry about was getting a bite on the end of his line. Now he'd landed in the middle of a freaking international incident.

"That was before you discovered Raul. Things are different now," Lulu hissed.

"I didn't exactly discover him. He just got tired of hiding." The fish sizzled in the olive oil in the pan.

"He's just a kid, after all. We can't forget that. He's had such a rough time. Let him play with Fidget if he wants."

Jesus. They sounded like parents arguing over their own child. Tristan shook himself back to common sense. "Fine. He can play with Fidget when we get back to the harbor. Lord, Lulu. Are you taking this seriously?"

"What do you mean?" She turned those round blue eyes at him and for a moment he was back in the wheelhouse, kissing her as if *that* was the most important thing in this messed-up situation.

She'd gotten under his skin. He wanted her in all kinds of ways. And that bothered him.

"Do you take *anything* seriously? You're always making jokes, like it's all a game."

Something flashed behind her eyes, something deep and intimate. And off-limits. "You don't know me, Tristan. You only met me two days ago."

"It's been an intense couple of days, but you're right. I don't know you. But is it wrong, what I said?"

"That I treat everything like a game?" She cocked her head, pursed her lips, then edged closer to him. "Only the fun things."

With that, she pinched him on the rear. Then danced away, out of reach for any chance of revenge. He glanced over his shoulder and saw that Raul was completely immersed in a PS2 one of his deckhands had left behind.

Saucy freaking wench.

Not that he minded her hand on his ass. He planned to return the gesture as soon as possible.

Then Lulu sobered and propped one hip against the countertop. "Here's what I take seriously. I learned it while taking care of my mum. You have to find those moments of joy or you'll get crushed. I'm trying to keep Raul from getting crushed."

Now that...yes, he saw the wisdom of that. His respect for her inched up another notch.

"As for his safety, I've decided to put my trust in you and your Lost Harbor brigade."

"Good. I'm glad you came to the logical conclusion."

"You think I just do things on a whim and not because they're logical?" She pointed her spatula at him. "Admit it. You think I'm nothing but a ditzy dancer."

"I think..." He paused to reflect back on everything he'd learned about Lulu in the past couple of days. "I think you're pretty phenomenal."

Her mouth fell open, her eyes going wide with astonishment. Gracing her with a smug smile—see, he could catch her by surprise too—he brought the frying pan to the table and dished out the salmon onto three plastic plates.

Now that he'd left Lulu speechless, they both sat and watched Raul devour every bit of his fish. Hadn't Lulu been feeding him?

He cast her a questioning look and she shrugged. "It was hard to scavenge food without you noticing."

Damn. It irked him that she'd been afraid to tell him about Raul. Did he really come across as someone she couldn't trust? Then again, maybe she was right. His crew had trusted him and he'd let them down. Then there was Julie. The people who trusted him ended up getting hurt. *I can't promise anything to anybody.*

Shoving aside those dismal thoughts, he focused on Raul. As he devoured his meal, Tristan managed to sneak in a question or two between bites. What town did he live in? What was his mother's name? His grandparents? Exactly how had he met Mr. Bad Guy?

By tacit agreement, they stuck to English instead of Spanish. His Spanish wasn't as good as it should be, anyway, since their parents had mostly spoken English at home.

Raul barely had an accent and his English was impressive. His grandparents must have made sure he had a good English tutor, probably a retired professor or some such. He spoke with an almost formal cadence and mostly perfect grammar.

By the end of the meal, he had a fairly good picture of Raul's situation. His mother had been a wild child who ran away from her wealthy family. Tristan got the impression drugs were involved. When she got pregnant, she went home to have the baby, then left Raul with his grandparents. They'd raised him, almost entirely. Every so often his mother would come back and visit, then get into a fight with her parents and leave again.

She'd met Sebastian Perro—Seb Antonov—very recently. He'd romanced her and swept her off her feet. She'd requested some time with Raul so that he could meet her new boyfriend. Raul hadn't liked him from the start, but he'd been polite about it. They'd all gone to a festival together, and Raul had gotten separated from the two adults.

"I was eating my churro and I looked around and couldn't see either my mother or her stupid boyfriend," Raul explained between bites of fried potatoes.

"That must have been scary."

He nodded as he chewed. "I've practiced what to do if that happens, so I also was quite excited. I went right to the nearest *polizia* that I saw. But before I could reach him, Senor Perro found me. He said to come with him and we'd find my mother. But we didn't. We got into a car and drove for a long time. I wanted to call my grandparents. He called them, but as soon as I said "Hola Tata" he pulled the phone away and got out of the car. He locked me in so I don't know what he said."

Tristan exchanged a long glance with Lulu. A ransom demand, no doubt.

"How'd you end up on the *Northern Princess?*" he asked Raul gently.

"In the morning we went to Buenaventura and got onto a big ship. A *barco mercante.*"

"A container ship?"

"Yes. Container ship. I think he paid someone for us to be on it. We had to hide."

That made sense. If their IDs didn't match, a child traveling with a lone adult could inspire some questions.

"Where did that take you?"

"To a city in America. After we arrived there, he talked to someone on the phone. A man came to meet us and give us some papers. And then we got on the cruise ship, all three of us."

"The other man was your guard on the *Northern Princess*?" Lulu asked.

"Yes. I think..." He took a break to stab a chuck of salmon into his mouth, then chewed until he could speak clearly again. "I think he wanted money to give me back to my grandparents, and he's waiting for my *abuelo* to send it to him."

Tristan glanced at Lulu to see what she thought. She was listening to his tale as if some of it was new to her. Maybe she hadn't had a chance to hear all the details before now. "What do you think, Lulu?"

"I agree. It sounds like he paid their way onto the container ship, and by the time they reached the U.S., his forged documents were ready to go. I don't know why he chose the cruise ship. Maybe for all the free babysitting?"

Even though she said it lightly, she had a point. "Taking care of a ten-year-old has its challenges. But wasn't there a risk that Raul would tell someone?" He looked again at Raul. "Did he threaten you if you told anyone?"

"*Si, Capitán.* He said he'd find my mother and kill her. I don't know if he can but he was very scary when he said it."

Lulu's face paled, the blue of her eyes like forget-me-nots against her skin. "You were very brave to trust me."

"Why did you decide to tell Lulu?" Tristan asked him gently.

"The guard was always following me, but he didn't pay attention in the pantomime class. I didn't say anything out loud. But I thought it might be safe to do the miming. I tried it and he didn't notice."

"I'm glad you did," Lulu told him. "But it was very reckless and brave."

"Also, you didn't treat me like a stupid child with an accent. I thought you would listen and maybe believe me. And then you kicked someone. I thought you were very strong."

Lulu pulled her bottom lip between her teeth, her eyes welling with laughter. "Strong is one word for it. I aimed one of my high-kicks at a customer who'd been bothering one of the other performers. Hit him right in the stomach. Of course I'd been aiming a little lower, but it worked. I apologized like the ditzy dancer I am." She made a little face at Tristan. "They docked my pay for the day, but he never tried that move again."

Tristan saluted her with a forkful of salmon. "Cheers to the ditzy dancer."

Who was clearly not nearly as ditzy as she presented herself to be. He wouldn't even use the word "ditzy," actually. In his view, her lighthearted style masked a lot of things. As if she used laughter to move beyond pain.

Maybe it was the reverse for him. He'd always been an easy-going, carefree sort of guy, until the painful things had piled up like a load of bricks on his head. Only occasionally did he see daylight through that pile. As she'd put it, maybe he was being crushed.

One thing Lulu had done, for sure, was break him out of that rut. Maybe it had taken a tap-dancing cruise ship staffer and a brave kid thousands of miles from home to wake him up. At any rate, they were on his boat now and that made them his responsibility. He would not let them down.

SEVENTEEN

Tristan assigned Lulu and Raul bunks for the night, and gathered his own sleeping gear to take on deck.

"What if it rains?" Lulu protested as he bundled up his sleeping bag and a pillow.

"Then I'll come inside. I want to keep watch as much as I can. Don't worry about me. I've slept in conditions neither of you can imagine."

He launched a story of the time the *Desperado* had gotten trapped by ice during a cold snap in Unalaska. They'd radioed for help, but while they were waiting for an ice cutter to arrive, they'd reduced their rations and hunkered down. They were all driving each other nuts in the confined space of the cabin, so he remembered a story he'd read about a baseball game among whalers in the Arctic.

He'd rigged up snowshoes out of plastic dinner plates and duct tape, and whittled a bat from a backup spar. One of his deck hands had made a ball out of old fishnet. And they'd climbed out onto the ice and played baseball until it got dark. By the end he was so exhausted that he'd taken a nap on the ice, with his head resting on Bennie Crow's right leg.

"That can't possibly be true," Lulu protested. "You're making it up."

"You can ask Bennie's right leg when we get back to Lost Harbor." He grabbed a jacket for extra warmth, then nodded to them both. "Hot tip for you. Never question a fisherman's story. Just enjoy the ride."

He winked at Lulu as he turned to leave. He could have sworn he saw some color rise in Lulu's cheeks at the word "ride." Was she imagining a different kind of ride, the kind that ought to follow a kiss like the one they'd shared? He hoped so, because he sure was.

On the deck, he chose a sheltered spot on the leeward side of the fish hold and unrolled his sleeping bag. In the darkness, he felt it before he saw it: a light coating of frost on the weathered boards of his deck.

It was here. First frost. Time was running fast through the hourglass, and before long the world would be covered in snow and the forest would sink into its deep winter slumber.

One last adventure before the season ended. One more chance to sleep on the open ocean. One first kiss before frost.

Yeah...that kiss. Man, that kiss. It had taken him for a spin, for sure. He hadn't meant it to be *that* kind of kiss, at least not at first. A quick "thank you" peck on the cheek, maybe. Or a gesture of appreciation.

But maybe that was an excuse and he'd simply given in to his curiosity about what it would feel like to hold Lulu close. He'd imagined it like capturing a butterfly, feeling its wings bat against his hands, then releasing it. He'd wanted to be close to her bright spirit, to show her that she didn't have to hide anything from him.

But quickly it had moved into different territory. Hot and

wild territory, where the two of them struck brilliant sparks of fire with every touch.

He gazed up at the stars, which appeared only in snatches between long clouds drifting overhead. His scar throbbed, the way it did sometimes. He'd asked Dr. Finnegan about that, and he'd said it meant nothing. Either it was all in his head, or it was lingering physical memory left from the surgery.

Which was probably another way of saying it was all in his head.

He couldn't get involved with a runaway tap dancer with a kidnapped kid in tow. Was he out of his mind? He had nothing to offer them other than a bunk on his boat and some salmon. A night's protection, that was all. Or two nights, if he hadn't heard from Maya by tomorrow. Three nights, if that was what it took.

After that, he was done. They deserved more. Like the FBI, for example.

As for this attraction for the long-legged, funny, surprising woman who'd leaped into his life and high-kicked him in the gut? He'd just have to shove that aside. Maybe after this was over, he'd take a trip to Anchorage and see Shawna, with whom he had an extremely mutually satisfactory no-strings relationship.

Top priority: get Lulu out of his system.

He tuned into the sounds surrounding the boat. The gentle lap of ripples against the hull. The sigh of wind in the treetops. The occasional chirp of a protective squirrel. The very low murmur of voices in the cabin, as Lulu and Raul got settled into their bunks.

Yeah, he'd protect them with everything he had—for now. Until someone better showed up. Then he'd say goodbye.

He drifted off, lulled by the knowledge that all the sounds were made by something that belonged here. The early warning radar system in his head would wake him if anything else showed up.

But it failed him. Sort of.

In the middle of the night, he felt a warm breath on his cheek and came awake instantly and fully.

"What's wrong?"

Lulu was there, shivering in the frosty air, crouching next to him. "Nothing. I'm here to relieve you. You're keeping watch, aren't you?"

"I'm sleeping."

"With one ear open. You can't get good sleep like that. Go ahead. I'll stay on deck. You go get some real sleep."

The wind played with her hair. She wore one of his watch caps, her hair tousled under the doubled-up hem. She was adorable, and worried about him, and he wanted her.

He unzipped his sleeping bag and opened it up. "I have a better idea. Crawl in here with me and we'll both keep watch."

Her eyebrows drew together. "Is there room?"

"More or less. I like a roomy sleeping bag. I don't like feeling trapped inside. I always make sure there's extra space for me to thrash around." He moved his legs to demonstrate, then reached for her hand. "Come on. You look cold out there. It's like Florida in here."

"I worked on a cruise ship out of Florida once. I danced the can-can dressed like a banana."

"There you go. Just...no high-kicks, if you don't mind."

She giggled lightly, then nodded. "Okay. Raul's conked out, but..."

"I get it. No screaming orgasms."

She gave a pout of exaggerated disappointment. "I will definitely be mentioning that in my Yelp review."

He smiled as she crawled into the sleeping bag next to him, sighing as the heat enveloped her. Gently, he settled her head into the nook between his shoulder and his biceps.

"I feel like I'm in a cradle," she murmured. "The way your boat is rocking, and how warm it is in here. Being held like this."

He gritted his back teeth together, jaw muscles flexing. He wasn't feeling the cradle vibes at all. But if that was how she wanted it, he'd keep his swelling erection to himself.

"Hey, Lulu..." he whispered.

"Hm?" She already sounded half asleep.

"What is your real name? What's Lulu a nickname for?"

A soft snore was his only answer.

So much for catching her off guard. He tucked her head under his chin and gazed across the deck of his boat at the soaring black trees. Drifting to sleep along with her, he wondered if those trees recognized the *Desperado*, if they were aware of the occasional comings and goings of humans. So much of the world was a mystery. Why had he nearly lost his crew in that midnight disaster? Why hadn't he seen how unhappy Julie was?

Who was this woman slumbering in his arms?

Sure, there was a lot he still didn't know about Lulu.

But he knew enough to want her with deep and persistent urgency.

EIGHTEEN

Lulu surfaced slowly from a dream about salmon doing the can-can. A sound was dragging her awake—a disturbed human sound. She jerked into consciousness and blinked in the dim gray pre-dawn light.

The puzzle pieces of memory fell into place. She was on the deck of the *Desperado*, tucked into a sleeping bag with Tristan Del Rey, and he was moaning in distress. Still asleep, she saw when she lifted herself onto one elbow. He must be having a nightmare.

After wrestling her heart rate back to semi-normal—hey, at least the sound wasn't from someone boarding the boat, or from Raul—she shook him lightly.

"Tristan," she hissed. "Wake up. You're having a nightmare."

His head thrashed back and forth. "No. Not him. Damn it," he muttered.

"Tristan," she said more loudly. Then, "Captain!"

Apparently that really was the best name for him. His eyes flew open, although at first she thought he was still seeing images from his dream. He stared at her blankly. "Lulu?"

"You were dreaming. It looked like a rough one. Are you okay?"

She put her hand on his heart. The rapid pounding felt like a jackhammer against her hand. He wore only a thin t-shirt, a fact she'd taken note of last night when she snuggled next to him. Now it clung to his muscles, damp with sweat.

"Yeah. Sorry." He started to sit up, then saw the sun hadn't risen yet, and sank back down. "Frost."

"What?"

"It froze last night. I can see frost on the rails. Are you warm enough?"

The blank expression in his sea-gray eyes tugged at her heart. "Yes. Don't worry about me. What were you dreaming about?"

"Nothing important."

"Really? Then why is your heart racing and your t-shirt all sweaty?" She plucked at his shirt.

"Maybe it's because I'm in bed with a beautiful woman."

That sexy growl ought to be subject to international safety protocols. "I don't see a bed," she pointed out.

"Close enough for me. Do you mind if I..." He tugged his shirt over his head and dropped it on the deck. "Sweaty fabric gets problematic when it chills down. You're better off with bare skin. Just a lil' safety tip."

"I'll keep that in mind." Her heartbeat picked up speed, preparing for something momentous. He settled back down, all broad chest and wide shoulders and heated skin.

"I can be your bed," he offered helpfully. "Just roll on up here and stretch out. I'm like a bed with a built-in heater."

"Oh no. I mean, tempting offer, but I get the idea you're trying to change the subject. I want to know what you were dreaming about."

He shifted uncomfortably, then flung an arm across his forehead. "Why? It was a bad dream. Meant nothing."

"You were saying something. It sounded important."

"What did I say?"

"Something about 'no, not him, damn it.' It sounded real, not like a dream."

She noticed the flex of muscle in his jaw. "Why do you care? You barely know me."

"I am in a sleeping bag with you," she pointed out. "We're in the middle of this crazy adventure together. Is it so strange that I'd want to know more about you? I'm trusting you with my safety, and Raul's too."

He gave a soft snort. "I don't even know your real name. I know for sure it ain't Lulu."

Right, now she remembered that he'd asked her about that right before she fell asleep. *Conveniently* fell asleep. "Lulu is my stage name."

"And when you're not onstage?"

"Louise."

"That's it? Louise?"

"I know, it's boring, right? Old-fashioned. That's why I go by Lulu. It's a better name for a dancer."

"No last name? You didn't even give Maya your whole name, I noticed. Come on, Lulu. Cough it up and I'll tell you about my dream."

She let out a long sigh. "Fine, you want the whole thing? Louise Charlotte Victoria Spencer-Bennington."

He rolled over onto his side to face her. The sleeping bag might be roomy, but right now it felt awfully crowded with those big shoulders tenting the material. "That sounds like a name for a royal baby."

"I'm not a royal baby. But my mother was fifty-third in line for the throne," she admitted quickly. "It didn't pass on to me because I was born out of wedlock. Also, she fell for a postman and more or less disgraced herself. And me by extension."

"So just to make sure I got this...you're sort of a distant member of the British royal family?"

"I suppose you could say I'm royal-adjacent. Occasionally we used to get invited to something. And I have met some of the lesser royals. But it's a very distant connection and meant absolutely nothing to me when I was growing up. Now that my mother is gone, it means even less."

Nonetheless, he was staring at her with fascination. "You're princess-adjacent."

"Stop that. I grew up in a two-room apartment. My father delivered the post for a living. My mother didn't want to saddle me with anything royal-related. That's why she didn't want to marry." Her voice caught as a visceral memory of her mother rushed back to her. *The royal family is a corrupt enterprise and you're better off far away from it.* "She was a woman of many opinions. She's why I'm here. Well, not here in this sleeping bag." Actually, Mum would be ecstatic that she was snuggled up with Tristan. "She encouraged me to leave England after she died."

In the darkness, his gaze softened. He reached for her, tucked a strand of hair back under her watch cap. "I'm sorry. I didn't mean to upset you."

The gentleness of his touch unnerved her. How could hands so big and rough land so lightly on her hair? He stroked her cheek, then cupped his hand around the curve of her neck.

"You didn't upset me. I was very close to my mother, that's all. When she died, I...I didn't know what to do. I mean that literally. I'd dropped everything to take care of her, and then she was gone. For the first few days, I'd wake up with this terrifying blankness. The day ahead of me would feel like an endless desert. I closed up Mum's apartment and I've been traveling the world on cruise ships ever since then."

"And fishing boats," he corrected. "I know it's a downgrade."

"No." On impulse, she leaned toward him and brushed a kiss

onto his mouth. "It's not a downgrade at all. I like this. Honestly, my berth on the *Northern Princess* wasn't much bigger than this sleeping bag."

He chuckled, and when she tried to pull back, he firmed his grip. She relaxed into it, letting him take all the weight of her head, of her entire being.

When he kissed her, she felt like Alice in Wonderland tumbling down the rabbit hole into a world where things didn't make sense...and yet made more sense than they ever had.

Why should a fisherman and a runaway dancer share a connection so bright and powerful? How did he know how to kiss her so thoroughly? Why did her body behave as if she'd known this man all her life?

She stretched and tangled her legs with his, seeking out heat and hardness. He helped her by scissoring one muscular leg over her and tugging her close to his hips and the glorious bulge swelling under his sleep pants. She inhaled his smell, composed of frosty spruce trees and hot man. Even the hint of sweat made her wild.

Everything inside her released, as if she'd been holding a knot inside her ever since she left the cruise ship. Or maybe even longer. Maybe since her mother died. Whatever the case, it burst like a dam under pressure, and hot lust ran through her veins. Her nipples pebbled hard. He responded by running his hand under her shirt.

She arched her back as his palm settled over her breast. Ah God, that felt good. That primitive pleasure, that joy in just being alive...it had been so long. So terribly long. Her pussy pulsed with deep need. And her clit...she wanted his hand there, on the little tingling nub.

She wanted to do this right now. Right here. Was that insane?

Pulling out of the kiss, she whispered, "I don't know what I'm doing."

He paused, going still. "Like, big picture, or right now?"

"I mean, I know what we're doing in this sleeping bag. Or at least what I hope we're going to do. But outside of that, I know nothing. I don't know where I'll be tomorrow, or the week after. I can't promise anything."

"I know the feeling," he murmured. He took her earlobe between his teeth and tugged. It felt divine. "No promises needed. I'm in the same boat. Not good at making promises, so I don't."

She giggled a little at that phrasing. "So we're two ships just passing in the night, right?"

"Just two ships tooting our horns at each other. Maybe exchanging some supplies."

"Oh God, can someone put this terrible analogy out of its misery?" she moaned.

"My pleasure." He dropped kisses along the side of her neck. She arched to give him better access. The heat of his palm on her breast drove her mad, especially when he squeezed ever so lightly, just enough to bring her nipple peaking to attention. "Lulu, how do you feel about taking some of these clothes off?" His breath warmed the skin of her collarbone.

"I'd feel really good about it, except for Raul."

He groaned softly. "He's asleep, right?"

"He was sleeping hard when I came up here. But if he wakes up and comes looking for us...I'd rather have some clothes on."

"That's all right. I can work with clothes." His head disappeared beneath the sleeping bag and a moment later she felt air on her belly and breasts. He shoved her thermal shirt above her collarbone, and covered one nipple with his mouth.

She made a squeak, which she quickly buried in the crook of her arm.

"You okay?" he murmured from the area of her chest.

"Yes. Don't stop. I'm just trying not to make too much noise."

"I want to hear your noises." He released her nipple with a soft wet pop, then circled his tongue around the achingly sensitive flesh. "Another time. If I'm lucky."

She clenched her jaw against the onslaught of sensations he was generating with his mouth and tongue. The man was magic. Staying quiet was going to be the challenge of a lifetime. She choked back another moan when he slid his hand under her waistband. For sleeping, she'd chosen a pair of sweatpants with glittery letters reading "One Hot Mama" across the rear.

Tristan sure made her feel like one.

With delicate fingers, he explored her most private area. Mound, outer folds, inner flesh, and then, so deliciously, her clit. She closed her eyes, letting the world go from the dark gray of oncoming dawn to the star-spangled black behind her eyelids. The pleasure intensified with the absence of distraction.

He moved his mouth to her other nipple and lavished it with wet strokes of his tongue. She started to cry out, then remembered and choked it back. *Be quiet. Keep it down, young lady.*

He seemed to have gotten the lay of the land between her legs, even in the dark cramped space of the sleeping bag. With total confidence, his fingers surrounded her clit and danced across it. *Oh yes, right there,* she told him mentally, hoping he'd understand. Certainly he'd understand the way her legs fell open to let him in. And the way her inner thighs trembled and strained.

As she sighed and twisted under his fondling, her right hand went on an exploratory mission of its own. Hard, flat belly. An arrow of hair pointing the way. Elastic waistband. Divots in his skin from the waistband. Moist heat and thickening curls, rough and springy. Her heart pounded in her mouth as she touched the velvety hard shaft that lay rigid against his hipbone.

She took hold of his erection and wrapped her hand lightly around it.

"Condom's in my bunk," he murmured softly. "This is all for you."

He stroked her clit with a deliberate thumb. Then pulled it from her and licked it himself. Put it back where it was and *oh God*. The added moisture nearly made her scream.

"Pull out?" she whispered. It wasn't as safe, obviously, but she trusted Tristan in so many ways, why not this one too?

He shook his head. "Not in here. Besides, safety first, princess. Just lie back and enjoy. Pretend I'm your valet or something."

Choking back a laugh, she ran her hand up and down his shaft. "Valets are for men. But you can be my lady's maid if you insist."

"As long as I get to do this, you can call me whatever you want." Still stroking her clit, he slid a finger inside her.

She squeaked again, writhed from the pleasure.

No, more than pleasure. This was something more. It was the way he touched her, both strong and sensitive, with a kind of command that told her he wasn't stopping until she reached her climax. It was the way he concentrated on her. The way his breathing sped up to match hers. The way he worked her body as if he appreciated everything about her. It all sent flames streaking across her skin and along her nerve endings.

"Can we promise each other one thing?" she gasped.

"What's that?"

"That we do this again, at least once, with a condom. I want to feel you inside me."

His voice deepened so it seemed to come from somewhere in his chest. His heart, maybe. "I can promise I want to. I can promise I'll fucking try. But that's about all I can promise, the way things are going."

He had a point, she thought through a haze of dizzy pleasure. "Yes. Me too. Oh god. Oh god."

After that, they abandoned themselves to the silent grunts and soft gasps and wet strokes and searing pleasure. She clung to his upper arms when she came, those hard muscles the only anchor as she spun into a sky filled with stars. She floated there for a timeless moment as he stayed with her. Touching her, holding her, murmuring to her.

Lulu, beautiful Lulu, brave Lulu. And, maybe most important of all, *I got you, Lulu. I got you.*

NINETEEN

Few things in life were more satisfying than watching a woman orgasm against his hand. Tristan soaked in every moment of Lulu's spectacular but silent climax. It would have to do for them both, because this situation was complicated enough without taking a risk like condom-free sex.

He didn't even mind that much, he realized with a smile. Watching Lulu—sorry, Louise Charlotte Victoria—come would give him fantasy material for a long time. And he couldn't even see her that well in this pre-dawn light.

But how she felt...her soft skin, her long limbs, her eager movements, her swollen nipples...yeah, he could come right now just thinking about those details.

That promise they'd made to each other? He'd be moving heaven and earth to keep that one. Maybe they could give the kid some headphones and a video game and take their chances.

As her eyes slowly opened, he savored their sex-dazed expression. "Feeling good, princess?" he asked, because he knew the answer to that.

"Mmmm. But I'm sorry to say that I reject that endearment. I'm not any kind of princess."

"You're my princess," he declared. "And I'm a Del Rey, so I'm royal-adjacent myself. It's right there in the name."

Apparently too satisfied to argue, she snuggled her head back into the nook between his shoulder joint and his chest. It could have been designed with her in mind, that's how perfectly her head fit there. "Now that we got that out of the way, how about we get back to the important stuff?"

"Excuse me?" He had no idea what she was talking about. What could be more important than a righteous orgasm on the deck of the *Desperado*?

"Your dream. You said you'd tell me all about it if I told you my full name. I did that, and then you started touching me and so forth. And it was all one enormous distraction. But I didn't forget." She turned her head to kiss him on the chest. "I nearly forgot my own name, but I didn't forget that."

"Your name *is* pretty damn long," he pointed out.

Her soft giggle sent a tickle of air against his skin.

"But I'm right up there with you when it comes to long names."

"Really? What's your full name?"

"Tristán Izquierdo Antonio Del Rey." He let it roll of his tongue with a little extra Chilean flair.

She laughed, the delighted sound mingling with the murmur of waves against the hull of the *Desperado*. "Now that's a name. But I thought your father was Danish."

"He was born in Denmark, but he went off to sea at a young age. He didn't get along with his family, so he and my mom decided to use her name for me and Toni. I could have been Tristan Gammelgaard, imagine that."

"I'd never have gotten into a sleeping bag with Tristan Gammelgaard."

"Is that right? Thanks, Papí. I owe you."

They both laughed, and he felt as goofy as a kid curled up in a blanket fort.

"The dream," she reminded him.

Damn, she was persistent, and he wasn't even sure why it mattered to her. "I'm working up to it. When's your birthday?"

"The thirty-first of May. What's yours?"

"February first. I'll be thirty-three."

"I'm thirty. I supposed I should figure out what I'm doing with the rest of my life one of these days." Her light tone made a joke of it, but he knew that was a shield.

"You don't want to keep dancing?"

"Dancing...well, I love it. It was the one thing always guaranteed to get a smile from my mum. But I have to be honest with myself. My position as a member of the *Northern Princess* entertainment staff was most likely the peak of my dancing career. That's as far as I can go. And I was lucky to get that gig."

He lifted a strand of her hair and tucked it back under her watch cap. "That's rough."

"Oh, I won't miss the sore feet." She tangled her feet between his. "Or the pulled muscles. Or the way my face ached from smiling all the time."

"I have a special talent you might be interested in."

"Oh, I'm very interested," she purred. Her leg slid along his, silky and warm.

"Foot rubs," he said quickly, before she got him all revved up again. "I've been told my foot rubs are second to none."

"Tristán Izquierdo Antonio Del Rey!" she exclaimed. "You've been holding out on me all this time? I've known you, what, two days and you only now mention your talent for foot rubs?"

"My other talent wasn't enough for you?" He wriggled his fingers at her with a leer.

She ran her fingers lightly across his chest, spreading warmth and pleasure. "I have no complaints about any of your talents."

"I can also dance. Bet you didn't guess that one."

Propping her head on her elbow, she lifted her eyebrows at him. "What kind of dancing?"

"I'm the guy that stands on stage and lifts the girl over my head." He caressed the hand that was still playing with his chest hair. "Trixie roped me into a performance of *The Nutcracker* one year, and every winter they hound me to do it again."

For some mysterious reason, that information made tears come into her eyes. "That's so sweet," she whispered.

"What's the matter? What did I say?" Alarmed, he rolled back onto his side and lifted her chin to examine her face. Yup—tears. One of them rolled down her cheek. What the hell had he said to upset her? "I take it back, whatever it was."

"No. It's nothing. It's not you. It's...me. And dancing. I think..." She blotted the runaway tear with the heel of her hand. "Dancing is...a way to stay connected to my mother. I used to dance for her. She loved to critique my technique. We used to fight about it, because she was quite the taskmaster. I can still hear her voice sometimes when I dance."

He was searching his mind for the right thing to say—and coming up empty because he was a fisherman, not a grief counselor—when a low sound caught his attention.

"A plane," he whispered. "Twin-engine. It's a sightseeing plane, they fly low. Might be searching for us."

She sat up and stared into the pearly sky. "What should we do?"

"Go belowdecks. I'm going to cast a line in the water. Hurry. Take the sleeping bag with you."

They scrambled out of his bag and he bundled it quickly into her arms. She disappeared through the hatchway. He raced to the wheelhouse, where his hip waders and rain gear hung on a hook.

Quickly pulled them on, grateful that he'd chosen a dark slate color instead of the standard orange or yellow.

He didn't want to draw attention, and if someone spotted them, he wanted to look like a fisherman hoping for one last salmon.

He grabbed a rod and hurried out to the deck. Cast a line and let it sink down a few feet below the surface. With quick jerks that would make the lure flash, he reeled it back in.

In this stage of their lives, the salmon weren't feeding. They wouldn't bite the lure, but they might confuse it with another salmon. The goal here was to get one to come close enough for the hook to snag it.

Actually, the goal here was just to look as if he was fishing. Good thing, because this wasn't his kind of fishing. He didn't enjoy snagging, although the soothing rhythm of casting and reeling in the line always cast a spell on him.

Trails of mist drifted across the surface of the water and clung to the treetops. Here in Lost Souls Wilderness, the clouds didn't seem far away, but close enough to feel on your face and marvel as they rolled through a valley or down a slope.

Maybe there was enough condensation in the atmosphere to obscure an overhead view of the lagoon. Maybe that plane carried guests for the Aurora Lodge, or bear-viewing tourists setting out on the adventure of their lives. Maybe he was panicking for nothing.

Not panicking. Just preparing.

He glanced up as the twin-engine plane came into view. It didn't pause as it passed over the lagoon. In case someone was looking down at him, he lifted his hand in a wave, same as he would have done if were actually fishing.

And then, damn it all, he felt a tug on his line. He reeled it in, fast and steady, steering the thrashing fish away from the hull of his boat until he could pull it over the side.

It flopped on the deck, a nice-sized late-season silver Coho salmon. Good for breakfast.

"You caught a fish!" Raul ran from the hatchway, dodging past Lulu, who tried to snag his shirt and pull him back. "He's so big!"

Tristan looked up at the plane again. Still in view, meaning *they* were still in view. But it didn't turn back or show any reaction at all.

Maybe it didn't matter. Maybe it was just a tourist flight. Even if it was Seb Antonov, that didn't mean he'd spotted Raul. The clouds, the mist, the distance, the fact that the plane had already passed by, all gave him hope that they'd escaped notice.

"It's okay," he told Lulu, who wore a horrified look as she dashed onto the deck after Raul.

"I'm so sorry. Raul was asleep, so I went to the loo and when I came out he was running out here."

"It's all right. I don't think they saw." But a knot in his stomach said otherwise. And they should probably accept that possibility, and act accordingly.

"Come on, kid. Let's put this guy out of his misery."

Fish didn't "suffer," per se, since they had no nervous systems. But gasping for air—or water—wasn't fun for any creature. He showed Raul where to strike the salmon on the back of its head so it died instantly.

"Thank you, my silver friend," he murmured to it. "I didn't mean to catch you, but I'm grateful."

Lulu was watching him strangely. "Do you always talk to the fish you catch?"

"Not always out loud. But kind of, yeah. In my head."

He'd been doing that since he was about Raul's age, actually. He didn't know why, except that as a fisherman, he felt a mix of gratitude and awe toward his catch. Maybe it was a way to honor the fish that came into his nets. Or onto his line.

"Anyone feel like salmon for breakfast?" he asked. "Raul, have you ever cleaned a fish?"

When the boy shook his head, he told him, "Let's do this, *pescadorito.*"

RIGHT THERE ON THE DECK, he showed Raul how to gut and clean the salmon, and even let him use his sharpest filet knife to try for himself.

"I want to be a fisherman," the boy announced as he tossed the guts overboard for a bright-eyed seagull bobbing expectantly off the port side. "Can I work for you?"

"Tell you what." Tristan brought out the hose and sprayed the blood off the deck. "When you're eighteen and you've graduated from high school, or whatever the equivalent is in Colombia, and you still want to be a fisherman, you give me a shout. But if you decide to go to college or something else important and exciting, I'll understand."

They brought the fish into the galley, where Lulu, looking preoccupied, was pouring water into the coffeemaker.

"We have to talk about that plane," she said to Tristan in a low voice. "It could have been Antonov."

"I know. But we need to include Raul. There's no point in hiding things from him. He's part of this."

She nodded regretfully. "I know. I've been trying to protect him, but we're probably beyond that by now. He can only hide out in the anchor bay for so long."

As he cooked up the fresh salmon, Lulu sat at the table with the boy. Pale and serious, she looked much different from the woman who'd snuggled with him on the deck, or the woman who joked her way through pain. One more Lulu layer, revealed.

"Raul, you saw the plane that passed over us, right?"

He shook his head. "I heard a plane. But I was watching *el capitán* catch the fish."

"Well, there's a chance your kidnapper was on it. I knew he might try to follow us, even all the way out here. He's awfully persistent, isn't he? So we have to assume that he found us."

Raul twisted his mouth to one side and looked down at the table. "Okay."

What bothered Tristan the most was that he accepted the news so stoically, as if he was used to his life being disrupted at a moment's notice. "The fact that the plane didn't circle back is a good sign. And you still have us, kid. We're not going to let him get you."

"No, we absolutely are not." Lulu pounded her fist on the table like a rabble-rousing politico. "We came this far, didn't we? Help is coming from law enforcement, and all we have to do is hang in there. We can do this."

"Yes. We got this." Tristan turned around to emphasize the point with his spatula. "Say it with me, kid. We got this."

Raul repeated the phrase, then frowned. "My English tutor wouldn't like that at all. It's not correct, is it?"

"The hell if I know." Tristan smiled to himself as he turned back to the frying pan. They sure made a motley crew: the runaway royal-adjacent dancer, the desperado fisherman, and the rich kid with the English tutor. "But it gets the point across and that's all I care about. I'll say it again. *We got this*."

He slid the spatula under the fish and flipped it onto a plate. Carrying it to the table, he slung one leg over the bench bolted to the floorboards. The aroma of steaming fresh fish brightened everyone's expression.

"We just have to figure out exactly how. It's time for a council of war."

TWENTY

After a lively discussion in which they threw out ideas ranging from painting the boat to look like a forest—that was Raul's—to hiring their own plane to airlift them to the Aurora Lodge where they could shower—that was Lulu's—they decided to keep moving, sticking to the hidden bays and coves that only a true local would know.

Tristan went on deck to pull up the anchor, while Lulu cleaned up in the galley.

But before they went anywhere, she had to make sure of something. She left Raul drying the plastic plates and tracked Tristan down at the bow of the boat, where a hydraulic lift was hauling up steel cable, spraying water as it coiled around a spool. The noise disturbed the peace of the serene lagoon. She imagined squirrels and birds all in a dither, wondering what was going on.

"Tristan, can you pause that for a second?"

He took his hand off the controls and the lift rattled to a stop. Dark gold scruff covered the lower part of his face, since of course he hadn't shaved this morning. It suited him, made him look like a seafaring lion or a Gaelic warrior. "What's up?"

"I just want to make sure that you know what you're doing."

"Woman, I've been running this boat since I was sixteen. I know what I'm doing." He moved his hand back to the anchor pulley controls.

"No, that's not what I mean. When I saw that plane fly overheard, I thought..." She swallowed hard. "They could have fired at us. We were sitting ducks."

"Very unlikely. That would be an extremely difficult shot."

That didn't entirely reassure her. Or ease her conscience. "The point is, you're putting your boat in the line of fire."

His face tightened and his eyes darkened to thunderstorm gray. "Yeah. I know that. I knew it right about the time I pulled out of the harbor. Actually, even before, when I suggested you stay on the *Desperado* instead of leaving town."

She felt her cheeks heat. A breeze whispered through the rigging, almost like a warning. "But I'm the one who chose your boat, so that's my doing. You didn't have a choice in that."

"What are you getting at?"

She paused to collect her thoughts. " You said you can't make promises. Maybe we're asking too much from you—"

He interrupted in a harsh tone. "It's asking too much to prioritize your lives ahead of my boat? Is that what you think of me?"

Rattled, she scrambled for an answer. "I just...I'd feel terrible if something happened to your boat and it was my fault. Or you," she added quickly. "But also your boat. I know how much you love it."

A shadow came across his face. The morning air nipped at them, causing her to pull her jacket tighter around her. "You don't really know me."

The chilly words drew a gasp from her. "Excuse me?"

"You've known me two days, like you said. I always put my crew first. Even when I fuck it—" He broke off, running a hand through his hair. Droplets of mist spangled across his thick waves.

His suddenly agonized expression surprised her. What had he stopped himself from saying? And why? Apparently she'd stepped on a land mine while intending exactly the opposite. "Maybe you're right. Maybe you chose the wrong boat."

"That's not *at all* what I mean," she cried. "You didn't get to choose, and now here you are, risking everything."

His face went blank, like one of those metal storefront doors that rattled down from above. "I *chose* to be here. Believe that, Lulu. Maybe you think I'm not reliable because I dropped out of the mayor's race."

Her jaw dropped because she hadn't thought that for a moment. "That's absurd. I never thought—"

He went on as if she hadn't spoken. "When it comes to my boat, and the people on my boat...I know exactly what the risks are. I am *choosing* to accept those risks."

"Got it."

She backed away from him, afraid she'd burst into tears if she stayed where she was. Maybe it had only been two days, but they'd been through a lot in that time. She'd opened herself up to him, allowed herself to trust him. Now he was slamming shut a door and it didn't feel good.

"I'm sorry if I offended you. I'll leave you alone."

"Lulu." He snagged her arm and tugged her back to him. "Look, I'm sorry I was rude. You're right, my boat means a lot to me. But nothing's going to happen to it. Not this time."

Not this time. Obviously there was a story there, but just as obviously, this wasn't the moment to ask about it.

"Let's just get out of here, okay?" she said stiffly. "No time to waste."

He nodded, looked like he might say something more, but didn't. As he returned to the anchor mechanism, she hurried down below to stay out of sight. That was part of the plan. The bad guy was looking for a woman and a boy, not a lone fisherman.

But Antonov might know all about Tristan. He'd blown up his truck. Why not his boat? She didn't want more damage on her conscience.

Those questions nagged at her, but she shoved them aside and devoted herself to playing cards with Raul as they chugged through the long inlets and hidden coves of Lost Souls Wilderness.

Occasionally she looked out the porthole and through the scratched plexiglass saw sights so magnificent they took her breath away. Deep ravines with waterfalls that cascaded over hundreds of feet of sheer rock. Groves of spruce so thick and dark it looked like night underneath. Mossy fallen logs the size of boulders. A bald eagle perched on the tip of a tree, gazing down his haughty beak at the lowly mortals below.

It was one way to see Alaska, but she hoped she'd get another chance someday, when she could watch the scenery without looking for signs of a threat.

When Raul got bored with cards, they moved on to charades, which was a game she played with kids on the *Northern Princess*. Charades was a great way to hone one's miming skills. Raul was a natural at it, fortunately.

Even more luckily, the guard Antonov had hired was terrible at pantomime. He mostly stared at his phone during the class, only occasionally looking up to make sure Raul wasn't doing anything suspicious.

Once Lulu had understood what Raul was trying to communicate, she'd recruited Britney, who was a master of flirtation, to distract the boy's guard. That was how she'd finally gotten the full story from Raul.

Watching him now, laughing at his depiction of Wonder Woman, her heart ached for him. Would he ever see his family again? She'd searched online for any mention of Raul's kidnapping in the media. Not a blip. She'd also searched for news about his mother and her family. She'd found plenty there—everything checked out as Raul said—but not a word about a kidnapping or a ransom.

Maybe they'd been ordered to keep it quiet. Or maybe Raul's grandfather was having trouble assembling the ransom money. Or maybe, maybe... Her mind kept spinning with wild theories.

The only thing she knew for sure was that helping Raul escape Antonov was the right thing to do. A risky thing, absolutely. Some might even say an insane thing. She'd inserted herself onto the radar screen of a dangerous man. And she'd even exposed herself to possible charges of kidnapping. After all, she had no more relation to Raul than Antonov did. The FBI would definitely want to interrogate her about her role.

But you only live once. That was what her mother kept telling her, over and over, in her waning days. *"Jump in feet first, Louise. Get into trouble. Fall in love, get your heart broken, stand up for what you believe. Promise me. You've spent enough of your life stuck in this apartment with me. After I'm gone, you'd better live your life. Or I'll come back and lecture you from beyond the grave."*

Lulu shook off the memory, because thinking about her mother was a sure way to get weepy again, and if there was one thing her mother despised, it was too much crying. That was why she'd held back all her tears until after her mother was gone.

Raul flopped onto the bench seat. "Your turn, Lulu. I'm tired. When can we have lunch? I'm hungry too."

"How about some more of those water biscuits?" Tristan kept boxes and boxes of something called Sailor Boy Pilot Crackers onboard. Apparently they took the place of bread, which probably molded quickly in the sea air.

He made a face. "Okay. On my boat, when I'm a fisherman, I will have no crackers. Only tortillas."

"Fair enough." She unfolded herself from the bench and

began to rise to her feet. Raul's eyes went wide, which she didn't understand. Had her shirt come unbuttoned? No, because it didn't have buttons. But something was wrong because he was lunging toward her and flinging himself across the laminate table with the rimmed edge.

"*Abajo!*"

She didn't recognize the Spanish word, but it didn't matter because he'd managed to knock her off balance. She toppled over on her side, tried to brace herself with her hand, but the weight of him made her wrist twist under her. Pain lanced through her arm. But she was more worried about Raul than herself. Somehow he'd ended up under the table. "What's wrong, Raul?"

Another shout came from above. Tristan was yelling something, but pain was singing in her ears and she couldn't quite make it out.

"Raul?"

"I'm okay." He crawled out from under the table and crouched next to her. "Are you hurt?"

"No. Yes." Gingerly, she tried to sit up, but he stopped her.

"Stay down. I saw a man with a long gun through the window."

"*What?*"

So that was why the boat was picking up speed, the engine noise increasing to a full-throated roar. She held tight to the bench with her good hand as she gingerly examined the other one. It throbbed and ached. She needed ice. No, she needed to talk to Tristan. Find out what was going on.

"Hey kid," she managed.

"*Sí.*"

Always a bad sign when Raul reverted to Spanish. It meant he was rattled.

"I need my phone. It's in the pocket of my jacket, but I can't reach it with my good hand. Can you grab it?"

"I'm so sorry, Miss Lulu. I saw the gun and I was afraid—"

"Don't apologize. You did the right thing. I just need to talk to Tristan, okay?"

Nodding, gnawing on his lower lip, Raul reached into her pocket and pulled out her cell phone. He handed it over to her, and she dialed one-handed. No easy feat, since her dominant right hand was still pulsing with pain. But also not the hardest thing she'd done since she'd boarded the *Northern Princess*.

"You okay down there?" Tristan answered, skipping the greeting.

"We're okay. You?"

"I'm getting us the hell out of there. Someone shot at my fucking boat. High-powered rifle. I'm pretty sure it hit us, but the *Desperado* is like an armored truck. It could have hit a window or something. Anything broken down there?"

She went cold. Part of her had hoped that Raul had imagined the gunman. But not only had he seen an actual gun but that gun had been fired. At *them*. If it had gone through a window, it could have hit her or Raul. Raul had possibly, hypothetically, saved her life.

"Not in the galley." She glanced around, confirming that was the case. "Raul saw the gun too. I was starting to stand up but he flattened me. Quick thinking kid."

His eyes huge and dark, Raul managed a smile full of pride.

"Are you okay?" The concern in Tristan's voice made her heart do a funny little flutter.

"Mostly. Might have twisted my wrist."

"Get some ice on it. No, stay where you are. Hand the phone to Raul."

Feeling faint from pain, she did as he said. She could over-hear Tristan's rapid instructions, but they were in Spanish so she didn't understand them.

Raul put the phone on the bench and crawled across the floor to a cooler. He dragged it back under the table and took out an ice pack. "Here, Miss Lulu. *El capitán* says to put it on your wrist."

From her phone, which was still connected, she heard a growl, probably at the word *capitán*. That made her laugh, which gave her enough focus to maneuver her wrist toward Raul. With one hand, he held her hand steady, and with the other he applied the pack.

She winced as the shock of cold hit her skin. But as the numbing effect of the ice filtered into her bones, she relaxed.

"How's it going," Tristan called from the phone. "Lulu, you okay?"

"Good. It feels better. Don't worry about me, just get us out."

"Working on it," he shouted over the roar of the engines. "Pretty much at top speed right now. It's a ride." The hull of the boat slammed into a wave just then, and he let out a whoop.

"Are you enjoying this?" she demanded.

"Not the gunfire part. But the going fast part? Hell yes. Normally I don't like to burn fuel like this."

Exhilaration radiated in his voice. Suddenly, she wanted to be up there with him, sharing the wild adventure, no matter the risks. The pain in her wrist had subsided to a dull ache, so why not?

She ended the call. "Stay here, Raul," she told the boy. "Under the table is safest. I'm going to check on Tristan."

"Is it safe?"

"If that gunman was shooting at us from the shore, we're way out of range by now."

"Can I go in my bunk? It's safe there and I feel a little seasick."

"Yes, good idea."

They both extracted themselves from the galley table. Keeping a low profile, she made her way across the cabin and up the stairs. The lunge and lurch of the fishing boat made every step a leap of faith. Would the floor be where it was a second ago? Total crapshoot.

Somehow, she made it up the stairs without falling on her face. Clinging to the wall, she sidled into the wheelhouse. Tristan stood at the wheel with his legs braced far apart, his hair wild from the sea spray, his dark oilskin jacket flapping like a cape.

He was singing something, too. A sea chanty or a rebel fighting yell, she couldn't tell. When he caught sight of her and turned in surprise, she saw a Tristan she hadn't seen yet—young and free and full of life.

"Lulu! What are you doing here? How's your wrist?"

She held it up, ice in place. "Still attached."

"You should stay below where it's safe."

"I don't want to stay where it's safe." She lifted her chin. "I want to be up here, with you. Raul's in his bunk. Feeling a bit off."

After a moment's hesitation, he lifted one arm from the wheel and beckoned her to his side. She came toward him, helpless to resist that bearded grin, those gleaming wild eyes. He settled her in front of him, her back pressed against his front. She cradled her wrist against her chest and despite the ice pack, felt warm and cozy.

His body heat relaxed her. In the circle of his arms, she felt safe and protected, even though they were on the run from a bad guy who had just upped the ante. She leaned against the hard muscles of his chest and stomach. *This is life*, she thought. A strange life. One she never could have imagined even a year ago, when she was feeding spoonfuls of pureed pears to her mother. But a life beyond her wildest dreams.

Even if it lasted only a day or so more, she was grateful for this time on the *Desperado*. She'd never forget it, or the man with his arms bracketing her, humming softly into her hair.

"Are we safe?" she murmured.

"I wouldn't say that. But no one's shooting at us right now."

She gazed out the spray-flecked window at the gray waters ahead. White lines of foam spread across the ocean as if someone's cappuccino machine had malfunctioned. Birds wheeled overhead, riding invisible currents. "Is a storm coming?"

"Around here? Always."

She laughed, because why not? "If it's not gunfire, it's a storm. I guess it's always something."

He dropped a kiss on her hair. The warmth of his lips reassured her almost as much as his words did. "Don't you worry. We'll be fine."

"Is that a promise, Captain Del Rey?"

His only answer was a low growl that sent tendrils of heat through her body. And she wanted him, hard and fierce and urgent. She wanted to *live*. Not just run. Not just hop on the next cruise ship for the next faraway destination. She wanted to experience those feelings that Tristan brought out in her. She wanted to give back to him. To see another side of Tristan Del Rey—the unleashed sexual side that every fiber of her being knew would be sensational.

"Safety aside, there's something else we have to figure out." She tilted her head back so she was addressing his chin. It was covered in scruff. His Adam's apple moved as he spoke. She smelled sweat and salt and heat.

"What's that?"

"Keeping that promise we made to ourselves." She flexed her lower back against the bulge that had been steadily swelling ever since she nestled into his arms. "Any ideas?"

"Lots. All of them dirty."

"Just the way I like them."

TWENTY-ONE

Tristan had never had to battle arousal while the *Desperado* tackled ten-foot swells. Another first brought to him by Lulu Spencer-Bennington. Face it, nothing was going to be quite the same after this experience with her. For better or worse, he couldn't yet say.

But she sure felt good in his arms. The perfect long-limbed bundle of strawberry-tart sexiness. He would have taken her right then and there, in his wheelhouse, up against his dashboard, if she weren't injured and they weren't caught between a storm and a gunman.

When they were almost to Far Point, Lucas radioed him. "Message from Maya. The FBI is on their way. Come on home."

"Ten-four."

Lulu twisted in his arms to glance up at him. "Should we? Or should we just keep going?"

"If we keep going this way we'll get into Russian waters. Are you ready for another international incident?"

"Sure, pile them on."

Although he laughed, he brought the *Desperado* around.

Now that he was headed toward Lost Harbor, the wind was behind them and they no longer had to battle each wave.

"Toni offered us their place when we get back. She and Bash are heading to Anchorage to pick up their first batch of training camp students. It's better if we don't stay at my place. Antonov might know where I live, and the roof isn't done yet."

"That's very kind of her. But I don't want to bring any trouble to them. He might know she's your sister and..."

"The FBI will scare him off. I don't think he'll take a chance while they're in town. Anyway, Toni's place is as safe as any. And..." He whispered in her ear, her hair tickling his lips. "Very private."

He felt the shiver that ran through her body.

"Raul?" she asked.

"He can have their room upstairs. We can sleep in the guest room downstairs."

"So if anyone's after him, they'll have to get past us first."

"Right. One more reason to stay up all night."

She giggled softly. "What was the first reason?"

He spread one hand across her stomach, then moved slowly up her torso. It took a few moments, because her body was so long. But then, finally, not a minute too soon, he reached her breast. "This."

She squirmed a little when he gently cupped her. He felt her nipple rise. He lingered there, thinking of all the things he wanted to do with her once they had a little privacy. Then he stroked his hand back down her side, curving along her waist, her hip, to her ass. Which he squeezed.

"This is another reason," he murmured in her ear. "This juicy ass of yours. And this." He moved his hand to her front, to the swell of her mound. "Best reason of all, right here. I want to taste you, Lulu. Put my mouth right here and feel you against my tongue."

She hissed in a breath just as a large swell rolled under them, sending the *Desperado* into a sharp lurch.

He whipped his hand away from her and wrestled with the wheel to get them back on track. He couldn't risk his boat foundering, not even to cop a feel from the luscious Lulu.

"You know what? I'll be downstairs." She ducked under his arm, her voice a breathless squeak. "You concentrate on getting us back to Lost Harbor."

"Copy that."

She was right, of course, but he missed her warm, vibrant presence immediately.

"Oh, and Tristan?"

"Yeah?" Now that he'd gotten the *Desperado* safely in line with the direction of the waves, he glanced over his shoulder at her. Just in time to see her lift up her thermal top and flash her boobs. Soft and naked, nipples gloriously erect, the view sent a jolt of heat to his cock. "Damn, Lulu, you want me to wreck the boat?"

"No. Just a little extra motivation to get us to that private downstairs room." With a sassy wink, she danced out of the wheelhouse, then staggered as another wave hit. Of course, being Lulu, she made a comedy routine out of it, making a show of lurching wildly across the deck.

"Careful, babe." But he couldn't help laughing, even though she was going against all his rules for safe onboard behavior. "You fall overboard, you're on your own."

Good thing that was virtually impossible in swells this size. She spread her arms wide, *Titanic* style, and shouted, "I'm the king of the world," before faking a trip and a stumble, windmilling her arms, then righting herself like a toy soldier.

The joy on her face, just before she pretended to pitch down the stairs—"I'm okay!"she called—gave his heart a sharp twist. Lulu was a natural clown. Someone who knew how to make people smile, and loved doing it. That was a real gift. Maybe she was ready to give up her dancing career, but what if there was another way she could express her talent? She ought to be in Hollywood, or on Broadway. Not the damn *Northern Princess*. And definitely not in tiny Lost Harbor, Alaska.

Never mind. He shook it off. This wasn't something meant to last anyway. This was all about getting through an emergency situation. Their chemistry was forged from a crisis. Under normal circumstances, he and Lulu would never have met, let alone connected.

Enjoy it for what it is, he told himself. Which was perfect, actually, because he had no business trying to start something serious.

Another swell sent a shudder through the boat and brought his focus back where it belonged. The *Desperado*. His life. Fishing. Surviving. The simple things. Nothing more.

THEY REACHED the harbor by mid-afternoon. Maya met them at the *Desperado's* slip and informed them that the two FBI agents, Special Agents Clement and Melbourne, had been held up in Grantview, where they had to deal with an unexpected situation that they couldn't talk about. But they'd head to Lost Harbor first thing in the morning.

Lulu was equal parts frustrated and relieved by the delay. Part of her didn't want this part to end, the part where she had Tristan on her side.

"I'm still glad you came back, because it's supposed to blow a gale tonight," said Maya.

"Yeah, it's already picking up." Tristan shook sea spray out of his hair. "Maya, we have another problem. Lulu left a little something out of her story. Or a little someone."

He motioned for Raul to come forward from his hiding place behind Lulu. The boy gave Maya an almost formal-looking bow. "I am Raul Gastón Perino."

Maya looked bemused. "Police Chief Badger. Nice to meet you."

Lulu explained the entire situation to Maya, whose expression got more and more stern as the story progressed. "It's a good thing the FBI is coming because this is out of my jurisdiction," she finally said. "This is international. I should let the agents know what to expect."

"You should also tell them that someone shot at us in Lost Souls Wilderness. We don't know if it was him, or someone working for him, or completely unrelated."

Maya glanced at Tristan with her eyebrows raised. He confirmed with a quick nod. "High-powered rifle. I'm not even running for mayor anymore, so it wasn't aimed at me."

His attempt at a joke fell a little bit flat, though Lulu snuck her hand into his and gave it a squeeze. When she tried to draw her hand away, he held onto it for an extra length of time. Warmth radiated through her.

Tristan at her side. She could get used to that.

"This complicates things a lot," Maya was saying. "We need to keep you under guard until the FBI gets here. Unfortunately two of my sergeants are sick right now. But we'll figure it out, don't worry."

"You think it's necessary?" Tristan frowned.

"Yes. I'm putting my foot down this time." Her handheld radio beeped, and she pulled it out to listen. "Damn. Got an incident out on MacKenzie Ridge. A bear broke into a truck and ate an entire five-pound bag of chocolate chips."

"Is that a crime?" Tristan asked. "Are you going to arrest the bear?"

"No, but old Lenny Dimov is going after it with a golf club. Probably drunk."

"No, he quit drinking. That's why he's been chowing down the chocolate chips. Go easy on him, Maya. He has mental issues."

"I know that." Maya shot him an irritated frown, her smooth brown forehead wrinkling. "But I didn't know he'd quit drinking, so thanks."

She quickly fired off a text, then blew out a breath.

"Okay, here's the plan. See that police cruiser up there?" She pointed up to the road at her rig. "Consider that your chauffeured limousine. I just called in Sergeant Hollister on his day off. He's about two minutes away. I'll borrow his car, and he'll drive you in the cruiser. Are you guys staying at Toni's tonight?"

Tristan and Lulu nodded.

"Good. I'll meet you there. Don't worry, I'll be outside in the cruiser. Go straight from here to Toni's. No extra stops. Except..." She glanced down at Raul. "Trixie's giving away free ice cream cones—locals only. She's trying to drum up votes. But she might make an exception for you, Raul."

The kid brightened at the mention of ice cream. The poor boy had a smudge of dirt on his forehead and what might be fish guts in his hair, but he still held himself like a prince. "Can we go, *Capitán?*"

Lulu rolled her eyes at the way Raul looked to Tristan as his authority figure, even though she was the one who'd helped him escape the cruise ship. Either sexism was alive and well in Colombia—a good bet—or Tristan just had that leadership quality—also a good bet.

All credit to him, Tristan gestured to Lulu to make that call.

"Sure, ice cream sounds wonderful. Assuming Trixie isn't still furious with you, Tristan."

"Oh, she's furious, all right." Maya laughed. "One stop only.

Ice cream. Sergeant Hollister will meet you in Trixie's shop. Then get in the cruiser and go directly to Toni's. I'll meet you there. Understood?"

After everyone nodded their understanding, she hurried up the ramp to the boardwalk. Following more slowly, Lulu steered Raul up the ramp, with Tristan close behind. She could sense his watchfulness as they reached the boardwalk, which was crowded with quaint shops and jumbled walkways.

Some of the buildings were little more than shingled shacks with bright hand-painted signs advertising native artwork or slices of pizza. Seagulls hunted overhead, and limp, frostbitten flowers drooped from barrel planters. The boardwalk had a ramshackle quality, as if every winter a roof blew off or a planter got rolled over.

Wedged between Wild North Kayaks and a rack of bicycles for rent, they found Trixie's ice cream shop—Soul Satisfaction. Painted in dreamy swirls of ivory and palest orange, even the exterior made Lulu's mouth water. The hand-carved sign depicted a sea otter floating on the ocean, with a backdrop of glaciers and mountains, with a double-scoop cone resting on its belly.

Adorable. She wanted to move into that sign and live there.

"You'd better go first," Tristan murmured. "If she sees me she might haul out her Reddi-whip."

"Reddi-whip?" Was Trixie some kind of lion tamer, or maybe a dominatrix?

"Whipped cream. It's her go-to weapon of choice, though she's also been known to fling a cherry or two if she's really mad."

"Oh, you mean squirty cream. The stuff in a can?"

"*Squirty cream?*"

On that astonished note, Tristan pushed open the door. Trixie sat on a stool behind the ice cream display, a pink neon ice cream cone lighting up the wall behind her.

"Hello, worst campaign manager ever," she said when she caught sight of Lulu.

"That's fair," agreed Lulu. "How's the campaign going?"

"Shitty. All the fishermen are going for the rooster just to piss everyone off. Did someone say 'squirty cream?' That sounds like something I should know about."

"It's British for Reddi-wip," Lulu explained.

"Are you sure? Because to me it sounds—" She changed gears as she caught sight of Raul. "Who's this now?" She smiled at the boy.

"This is someone who could really use an ice cream." Lulu didn't want to share his name, just in case.

"Coming up. What looks good to you, kiddo?" Raul peered into the glass display case of flavors with their handwritten descriptions. "I just came up with a new flavor. Tristan the Traitor. It has black licorice for betrayal."

Tristan closed the door, taking a moment to make sure no one suspicious was right behind them. "Jesus, Trixie. Feels like you weren't this mad when I was running against you."

"That's true."

Trixie hopped off the stool and came around the counter. She wore red platform boots that gave her an extra five inches of height. Her hair was twisted on top of her head, with a jaunty feather stuck in the pile. And she held a can of Reddi-wip. Lulu edged closer to Tristan in case he needed protection from his furious former competitor.

"But you have no idea why I'm mad, do you?"

"Because I endorsed Malcolm? It wasn't personal, Trix. I just think it's time for the native community to take a leadership role."

"Well, as a matter of fact, Malcolm and I are looking into some kind of coalition. We agree on most things, and maybe together we can beat Cockles the Rooster."

Lulu folded her lips to hold back the laughter that threatened every time someone mentioned that rooster.

"That's not why I'm mad," Trixie said steadily. "I'm mad because you're selling yourself short. Tell him, Lulu. Maybe he'll listen to you."

"To me?" Lulu's eyes rounded. "Why would he listen to me?"

"That British accent of yours. It's so sexy and authoritative."

Lulu laughed, deciding that she liked Trixie—a lot.

Just then, Raul announced that he'd chosen his flavors—a scoop of Frosty Fudge and one of Midnight Delight. Trixie scooped his cone for him, and waved off Tristan's attempt at payment.

Sergeant Hollister arrived a moment later. He looked a little like Santa, with a fringe of white beard. He shepherded them all out of the shop, toward the police cruiser, paying extra attention to Raul.

Lulu lagged a bit behind with Tristan.

"I like Trixie," she told him. "Is she your ex-girlfriend?"

"Definitely not." Tristan's fine mouth curved in a piratical smile. "We're friends, and a little more than that a couple times. But only in times of extreme crisis. After my divorce, for instance. We decided anything more would be a disaster. Trixie's a handful."

"What was she on about?"

"I don't know. You'd have to ask her," he said vaguely.

"She gave you quite a bollocking. I'm surprised she didn't unleash the squirty cream on you."

Tristan nearly choked on a snort of laughter. "Please stop saying that. A guy can only take so much."

TWENTY-TWO

The nice police sergeant drove them to Toni and Bash's house, where he and Tristan did a thorough search while Raul and Lulu stayed in the vehicle. Lulu gazed at the house in wonder. It was a fairytale cottage with a steep shingled roof, surrounded by wild roses and towering delphiniums at the end of their season. The place felt so secure, as if a fairy godmother had cast an enchantment over it.

When the sergeant was satisfied, Tristan beckoned for Lulu and Raul to come in. The interior was much more utilitarian. A sturdy couch unholstered in sage-green, straight-backed dining room chairs that could handle a giant's weight. She remembered that Toni's partner was a former pro fighter. He probably demanded unbreakability from his furnishings.

"I'm going to bring the cruiser to Maya," said the sergeant. "She'll be here overnight, but I don't think you'll have any trouble."

"Thank you so much for coming in on your day off," Lulu told him.

"Been doing that a lot. Two of us are out sick and that's

almost half the department. You take care. Maya will take you to the police station in the morning, soon as the Feds are there."

They played cards and took turn taking showers until it was time for dinner. Raul kept yawning, the poor boy. Shortly after dark, Maya arrived. She told them she had work to do in her cruiser and plenty of provisions.

"I'll see you at breakfast," she told them. "Get some rest. Did you check the fridge? Alastair said he left you some dinner."

Dinner was almost an understatement. This Alastair person, who was apparently an incredible chef, had made them a fabulous paella type of dish. They all ate ravenously, and by the end, Raul was dozing off in his seat.

Lulu got Raul tucked into the bed upstairs and watched him fall asleep almost instantly. Her heart twisted as she thought about what might happen tomorrow. Would the FBI agents take him away? Would they allow her to come along with them? Or would they arrest *her* for getting involved? Would they be able to contact Raul's family?

Whatever happened, things would be different. She would no longer have responsibility for this child she'd come to care about. Even more terrifying, she'd have to figure out her next move. Best case scenario, she was an unemployed dancer stranded in a small Alaska town with winter coming on and about a thousand pounds to her name.

But all that could wait, she decided as she skipped down the stairs to the ground floor. There was a rugged fisherman making up the bed in the downstairs guest room, and that was all that mattered right now. She had tonight with Tristan Del Rey, one night only, and she was going to make the most of it.

He obviously had the same idea, because she found him striking a match to light the candles clustered on a nightstand in the guest room. As the first candle flamed to life, candlelight flickered across his bearded face and gave a soft gleam to his sea-gray eyes. His hair, still damp from his shower, was slicked back from his face, drying in rough waves.

He wore cotton sleep pants that hung low on his hips. The candlelight shimmered over the hard ridges along his sides, and the smooth swell of his abdominal muscles. There was something bear-like about him, she thought. Maybe it was the golden hair that covered his chest and lower belly. Or the husky width of his shoulders. Or maybe it was just the protectiveness that she'd seen from him. Who wouldn't want a fierce golden bear watching over them?

She leaned against the doorjamb and folded her arms across her chest. "Planning to burn down your sister's house, are you?"

"Hell, yes." He straightened, light sliding across his skin and held out his hand. "Can't do it alone, though."

Her stomach in knots, she stepped forward. She wanted this —God, how she wanted it—but at the same time it terrified her. Getting sexually involved with someone seemed like the worst possible thing to do, given everything that was going on. She should stop this before it started. Before she did something she couldn't take back.

Live your life. Take chances. Get your heart broken. Her mother's words were so clear they might have been whispered in her ear.

Okay, Mama. Leave me alone. Inappropriate.

With his hand still extended, Tristan cocked his head at her. Quiet and steady, he locked eyes with her. "Second thoughts?"

"No. Maybe. I don't know."

"Hmm." He glanced around the room. "Is it the candles? Am I coming on too strong? After all the cold and discomfort on my boat, I thought it might be nice."

He felt just as nervous as she did, she realized. That knowledge eased her mind. If they were both stepping into the unknown together, that was different.

"I'll blow them out." He puckered his lips to blow out the nearest candle, but she grabbed his hand to stop him.

"No, leave them. They're pretty. I'm just nervous because, well, it's been a while."

His expression showed nothing but understanding. "For me, too." He tugged her a step closer.

"No, I mean a long while. At least five years. When my mother got really sick, I just..." She shook her head, "I couldn't handle anything else."

Saying nothing, he drew her against him and cupped both hands around her face. Slowly, deliberately, he lowered his mouth to hers. A kiss. But more than a kiss. An appreciation in physical form. As if he was communicating all sorts of complimentary things with each movement of his lips. *You're beautiful. You deserve joy. You deserve to be lavished with pleasure. I want you.*

She leaned against him, her body fully pressed against his, hip to shoulders, and ran her hands along his back. The hard muscles flexed under her touch.

"Not sure if I can handle this," she said more lightly. "All these muscles and so forth. It's a lot, Captain Del Rey."

"And here I am wondering if I can handle the smoking-hot dancer with the legs that don't stop. You might high-kick me into oblivion."

Laughter filled her chest. "That I might. Care to risk it?"

"I'm ready to take a chance if you are."

"Your wrist?" He touched her right hand gingerly.

"Good as new."

He slid his hands under her rear and lifted her off the ground. She wrapped her legs around him, bringing a groan of arousal from him. "Those legs...damn. You're killing me. Doesn't even take a high-kick."

He spun around to carry her to the bed, while she peppered

kisses into his bare neck. The taste of his skin went right to her head, that mixture of fresh shower dampness and underlying man flesh. So warm and alive. *Alive.* She was alive, she really was, and her heart was beating and her nerves jumping and her skin prickling.

All her hesitation evaporated in the strong hold of Tristan's arms. This was exactly what she needed. All of her body parts were telling her the same thing. Her nipples pulsed, already sensitized from being pressed against Tristan's chest. Moisture sprang between her legs, hot and juicy. As a dancer, she was used to listening to her body. The message it was sending was clear as well-water. *I want Tristan.*

They tumbled together onto the bed, and whatever slow pace they'd started off with shifted into a frantic pile-on. All their clothing got flung to all corners of the room until they were both completely naked and breathless. She had no idea where it had all gone and didn't care. All she saw was the magnificent muscled man tangled up with her.

Some piece of clothing must have come close to a candle, because the light flickered.

"No burning down the house." Tristan stretched over her, arms braced on either side of her. "At least not until I've been inside you."

"Yes, Captain." Demurely, she blinked at him. "Whatever you say, Captain."

"I say stay where you are. There's something I have to check on."

"What?"

But he was already gone, disappearing down her body. She lifted herself onto her elbows and watched that blond shaggy head nudge apart her thighs. His tongue against her clit made her muffle a shriek.

"Wanted to see if you tasted like strawberries." He lifted his head, his eyes a dark gleam of light. "But you don't. You taste better than strawberries."

She let her head fall back as he dipped his head to her sex again. Closing her eyes, she lost herself in the world of pleasure he generated with each stroke of that warm tongue. It was the most luxurious feeling. She didn't have to do anything except receive his attention. She didn't have to run or plan or worry or prepare. All she had to do was *enjoy*.

He parted her legs farther and ran his hands up and down her inner thighs. She shook with pleasure, since that was one of the most sensitive parts of her body. Her hips arched upwards, seeking more friction from his mouth. He gave her what she wanted, circling her clit, pressing just enough to make her cry out...but not come.

God, she was ready, but she didn't want to, not yet. She wanted to draw this out as long as possible, she needed this escape, this oblivion. He must have felt the same, because he kept bringing her right to the edge, then pausing as she trembled and moaned.

"I need to be inside you," he finally said through gritted teeth. "It's an urgent situation."

"Yes," she gasped. "I'm in favor."

He reached past her to the nightstand next to the bed. Craning her neck, she saw that a small pile of condoms sat behind the candles.

"Did you put those there?"

"I did. I'm an optimistic guy."

"I'd say realistic." She laughed at him as he ripped one open. "You knew I wanted you."

"And you knew I wanted you. From pretty much the moment you helped me with Fidget."

"Really?" She was touched by that confession. "I thought you were quite annoying at that point."

"Annoying, eh?" He flipped her over onto her stomach and slid a hand between her legs. She moaned as he touched her already hyper-aroused clit. "Take that back."

"Or what?"

"Or I'll make you scream for mercy." The hot rough edge in his voice made her inside pool with heat. His other hand, the one that wasn't planted between her legs, took her breast—no, both of her breasts, that was how big his hand was. Her nipples pulsed as he fondled her, both gentle and rough, hard and tender, keeping her off balance and yet arrowed toward that sweet, sweet destination shimmering ahead.

She came, bucking against him, glorious pleasure sweeping through her and washing everything else away. He rode out her climax with those magic hands of his. When the waves of sensation had diminished to a low throb, he flipped her over again. She landed on her back, panting up at him, buzzing with full-body satisfaction.

"I want to watch this time," he told her roughly. "I want to see your face when you shatter."

This time? Goodness.

Almost dizzy from her release, she reached for his erection. Thick and hard inside its casing of latex, it throbbed against her hand. "I never got to taste it," she said, almost mournfully. "Now it's all wrapped up like a sausage."

He gave a spurt of laughter that had a strained quality to it. Probably because she was enclosing his penis in her fist. Under her caresses, his body tensed as he braced himself over her, his big shoulders rigid. His breaths came rough and hard, and so did hers. Watching him got her heated all over again, or maybe she hadn't come down from her arousal.

She guided him toward her opening. "Ready if you are, desperado."

"Yeah?"

"Oh yes." She was pretty sure a woman couldn't be readier than she was. The orgasm he'd given her still rippled through her, but it wasn't the end of this story. Something enormous was waiting for her, coming closer and closer with everything Tristan did to her.

Oh yes, she was ready for that.

At least she thought she was, but when Tristan eased himself inside her, taking her inch by inch, filling her up, he tipped her into another realm of connection she hadn't foreseen. This wasn't just sex; he was part of her, she was surrounding him, embracing him with the most secret parts of her body.

When he moved inside her, they quickly fell into a shared rhythm that sent vivid pulses of pleasure all the way to her fingertips. They panted and strained together. She wanted everything for him. Joy, pleasure, release. For her too, of course, but this time, she wanted to see *him* lose control. She wanted him to experience the soaring bliss that saturated her being.

And when he came, rocking his hips into her, his body rigid and trembling, her heart nearly exploded along with the orgasm that shook her all the way to her core.

TWENTY-THREE

Tristan eased his still-pulsing cock from Lulu's body. She lay with her arms spread out, utterly relaxed, the picture of boneless bliss. He needed a moment to collect himself, so he pressed a lingering kiss to her lips and murmured, "Be right back."

She blinked at him with hazy blue eyes. "Washroom?"

And even that was adorable, the Britishism of washroom instead of bathroom.

He grabbed one of the towels Toni had piled on the dresser and wrapped it around his hips. In the downstairs bathroom, which was still unfinished and awaiting tiles, he disposed of the condom, cleaned himself off, and braced his hands on the sink. He looked at himself in the mirror and said one word.

"Fuck."

He knew what it meant. He didn't have to explain himself to his reflection. It meant that things with Lulu were getting...out of hand. Out of his don't-get-too-deep comfort zone. Out of his never-doing-that-again rut.

He splashed water on his face and reminded himself that she

wasn't going to be here for long. In a matter of hours, she'd probably be gone.

That didn't make him feel any better. In fact, he didn't like that idea one bit. He and Lulu had formed a connection—he didn't want to say relationship because that would be overstating it—that meant something to him. She'd brought out a part of him that he'd lost sight of.

Lulu, along with Raul, once he'd appeared, had inspired him to put himself on the line.

He didn't want to back away from that. So maybe the only thing to do was to take it even further.

Hell, she was leaving anyway, right? And he could talk to her the way he couldn't talk to people he'd known all his life. He'd already noticed that. With Lulu, he could admit things that he didn't necessarily want Lost Harbor knowing about.

Filled with determination, he strode back into the guest bedroom. Lulu was still awake, judging by the slit of blue peeking through her mostly closed eyelids. She'd drawn the comforter over some of her body, but not all. He caught a glimpse of one bare leg, bent at the knee, and her beautifully molded collarbones and shoulders.

Ignore, ignore.

"Few things you should know about me," he said from the doorway, arms folded.

Her eyes opened wider, though they still held the same sleepy satisfaction. "Is this the part where you explain how you don't get involved in relationships and you always keep it light and you never spend the whole night with a woman, blah blah blah? I think we can skip that speech, since I'm probably leaving tomorrow."

"What? No." He shoved a hand through his hair. Why wouldn't he want to spend a whole night with a woman? That made no sense, especially in Alaska. Body heat was important. "That's not what I'm talking about."

She sat up, the comforter falling to her waist, exposing her breasts, with those pink rosebud nipples. If she didn't cover up right away, he might forget what he wanted to say.

Luckily, she drew the comforter all the way up. "All right, then, let's have it. Is this deep dark secret time?"

"If you want to just get back to the sex part—"

"No." She made a little face. "Sorry, it's just a habit of mine. I'm interested. Go ahead."

"I'm divorced," he began.

"You mentioned that already."

He continued on, because she didn't know it all. "I failed. I had the idea that since I was the breadwinner, I didn't have to do anything besides work and bring home the dough. I did that part just fine."

Lulu rested her head against the headboard, her hair tumbling over her bare shoulders. "It sounds like you were young and trying to take care of business."

"No. I was just young and stupid. My father tried to warn me but I was a cocky little shit. Then I found out that Julie had slept with someone else, and I couldn't forgive her. She cried and tried to explain how lonely she was, but I was so full of myself I couldn't listen. She left after that. I felt like such a fucking failure. It opened my eyes."

Lulu was listening closely but for once, he couldn't read her expression. "To what?"

"That things weren't as easy as I thought. I failed at marriage. But I always told myself it's okay, at least I'm a great fisherman. Captain of my own boat by the age of twenty-four, I got it paid off in full three years later, kind of a superstar, honestly. Crew respects me, they make good money with me. Excellent safety record. I figured that was my life. My zone. My thing. And then..." He touched the side of his head, the scar hidden behind his hair, which was still growing out now.

Lulu sat up and beckoned for him to come next to her. "I noticed that patch there. I was too polite to ask, and also we were being chased by a kidnapper. What is it?"

He stepped to the side of the bed and sat down with his wounded side facing her. With her fingers, she lightly explored the puckered scar on his skull. "Surgery for a brain bleed sustained during an accident at sea. It was my fault. Huge storm off the coast of Kodiak Island, and I knew it was coming. But our onboard freezer was failing and I had a huge catch to bring in. I took a chance that we could skirt the storm and get home."

"What happened?"

"We struck a sandbar and nearly got swamped. Bo, the new deckhand, awesome kid, nearly got swept off the boat. I went after him and managed to grab him, but a piece of the crane came loose and slammed me in the head. He had a concussion too. Nineteen, first time at sea. Another of my crew, Ralphie Reed, got impaled right through the shoulder."

He felt her hand move from his scar to the back of his neck. She stroked him lightly there, kneading out the tension in his tendons. "I've heard that commercial fishing is dangerous."

"Very. It's always up there on the list of most dangerous professions. My insurance is ridiculous. I think that's one of the things that draws us to it. Life on the edge, you know." He gave a wry laugh. "Until something happens. It hits a little different after that."

"So you had brain surgery...is it all better?"

"I don't know. I think so. Dr. Finnegan says I'm in good shape. But brain trauma is tricky. I wish I'd gotten some other injury. Broken bone, severed artery, amputated foot. I know that sounds morbid, but knowing that someone had to go inside my brain and take out a blood clot—fuck, it messed with my head. I got depressed afterwards. I couldn't stop thinking about how I'd failed my crew, and even my boat. The *Desperado* needed repairs after that. Nothing new there, she needs repairs every winter, but this time it was my fault. And Bo, poor kid... " He scrubbed a hand through his hair, shaking her away. "I just want you to know I'm a fuckup, that's all. Seems like you should know."

A short silence followed that embarrassing confession. The moments ticked past, painfully.

"You might have mentioned that earlier, before you heroically saved me and Raul from kidnappers," she said eventually.

"Not heroic—"

"Wait, didn't you save Bo's life? Or did I get the story wrong?"

"I saved him after I put him in danger," he corrected. "Big difference." Surely anyone could see that.

She clapped her hands together. "Your dream! Was this what you were talking about the other night? The dream that wasn't a dream?"

"Yes. Happens now and then, like a dream but it's exactly what happened. I'm reliving it all over again."

Nodding, she drew up her knees and wrapped her arms around them. "I do that sometimes. It sounds like a scary experience. Did anyone on your crew die?"

"What? No." The thought made him scowl and mutter a quick and silent prayer. *Please don't let me ever lose a crew member.*

"And your boat is still functional. *You're* still functional. I'm no expert but it sounds like a successful disaster."

"A successful disaster?"

"My mother's terminology. She always said that disasters happen. It's a general rule of life. The question is how you handle them." Her voice caught, and he glanced over at her.

"Sorry," she said, clearing her throat. "Her disaster was

getting sick. Well, I suppose she had other disasters too. Leaving home, getting dumped by my father, being stuck with me."

"I'm sure she didn't see it that way—" he began, but she cut him off.

"Oh, she did when I was a baby. My mother didn't dance around things. My mother was very...blunt. She didn't believe in being mopey or maudlin. She was the most unsentimental person I've ever known. You know what she would have told you?"

He pulled a face. "Something about a successful disaster?"

"Probably. She would have told you to buck up and get on with it. But I'm not her and I would never say something like that. It's too simple, you know? Easy for her to say. We used to argue about it. She'd say," here she launched into a more-proper British accent, 'I'm the one dying, and I say buck up, Louise.' And I'd say, 'I'm the one who's going to get stuck grieving for you, so don't tell me what to do.'"

She laughed, the sound riding on a sob. This time he was the one who rubbed her neck, comforting her the way she had him.

"She sounds like a real firecracker."

"Yes. We were quite close. Only child, single mother. But all of that's beside the point. You wanted to tell me a few things about yourself. Is that it? The divorce and the accident?"

"And the surgery."

"Brain surgery. Got it. What else?"

He thought about it. "Dropping out of the mayoral race was kind of a dick move."

"Okay. Go on. What else? And why do you want me to know all this?"

He looked at her helplessly. "I'm not sure. It just seemed right. You're counting on me in this crazy situation and it seems like you ought to know who I really am."

Her forehead crinkled, then she tossed her head back in a laugh. "You really should have told me all this before you whisked me off in the *Desperado* while I was asleep. Or maybe when you were sleeping on deck to make sure no one surprised us. Or possibly when you got us away from the man with the rifle. You know, when you were *proving* you were someone I could count on."

She was making good points, he supposed, but totally missing the overall picture. "That's the thing. Just because I've been protecting you and Raul doesn't mean shit."

"Are you planning to walk away?"

"Of course not. I'm planning to do whatever you need until that kid is safe. Jesus, Lulu, you're not getting it."

"Then spell it out for me. Like I'm a child with the absurd name of Lulu."

"I like the name Lulu." He stretched back on the bed, propping himself on his elbows. He caught her gaze sliding down his chest. His cock stirred under the towel. Not his intention going into the conversation, but not much he could do about it. Besides, he'd done his part. He'd warned her about himself. If she didn't mind going another round with a divorced fuckup, he wouldn't say no. "I'm a fuckup, not a hero," he said. "I just want that crystal clear."

"Couldn't you be some of both? And many other things? Isn't everyone? Why does it have to be black and white? Is that a man thing? Can't admit weakness or flaws?"

He didn't answer, since maybe she had a point, a good one, but maybe he didn't want to talk about being a man right now. He *was* a man, a man with an erection that was rearing its eager head again.

"I've said my piece. I'm ready to get back to boning if you're still up for it."

He tugged the comforter down her body to reveal her breasts. She didn't resist, nor did she protest when he skimmed a thumb along the tender undercurve of one breast.

She burst into laughter. "You're even more blunt than my mother."

"I'll take that as a compliment." Grinning, he pulled her closer so he could close his mouth around her nipple. She shut her eyes and hummed in contentment as he probed the swelling flesh. "You're really good with nipples."

He had to pull his mouth away so he wouldn't hurt her when he howled in laughter. "Gee, thanks."

"I mean, other things too," she said quickly.

"Yeah? Like what?" He decided to get busy with his hands and fingers instead of relying on his mouth. Just in case he had to laugh again. Lulu had a knack for that.

"Oh, you know. All the rest."

Chuckling, he pulled her on top of him and let her feel the hard thrust of his cock. "Whatever it takes, princess. Whatever it takes."

And they moved back into a world of sensation and touch and murmurs and moans.

They made love twice more that night, and each time he wondered if it would be the last. Each time felt different, sort of... further. More. Sometimes slower, sometimes more frenzied. Each time took them deeper into a magical journey, destination unknown.

From now on, he wasn't going to fight it, he decided at some point in the dark of night. No more warnings or caution or doubts. This thing with Lulu had a life of its own and wherever it led him, that was where he wanted to be. With her.

TWENTY-FOUR

By the next morning, Lulu was in a state of physical contentment she'd never experienced before. Every inch of her body was sated and humming with happiness. Her mind and heart too, she realized. Tristan's "confession," for lack of a better word, had opened her heart to him even further. The man was so hard on himself, which to her meant one thing only—that he had a strong conscience and sense of duty.

Also, he was straightforward. He didn't want to deceive her or manipulate her. He wanted her to know the truth, or at least the truth as he saw it.

Her interpretation was different from his. Maybe he'd fucked up, but he wasn't a fuckup. Maybe he didn't see himself as a hero, but he'd acted heroically on her and Raul's behalf. In her eyes, he was a hero, no matter what he said.

Her body certainly thought so, and who was she to doubt her body?

Maya joined them for breakfast and told them the night had been completely peaceful except for a curious moose. Rune, her boyfriend, had kept her company for part of the night, which had allowed her to get a few hours of sleep.

The four of them ate a quick breakfast of shredded wheat and some blueberries from Toni's refrigerator. Raul seemed oblivious to the way Lulu and Tristan kept sharing hidden touches and the occasional secret kiss. But it would be hard to hide much from Maya.

Amazingly, things between her and Tristan didn't feel strange or awkward. They felt right. No, not just right. Beyond that. More like life-changing. Whatever she and Tristan had forged together had wound a spell around her heart. And every time she looked at him, she saw the same wonder in his eyes.

Was this real? Could it have a future?

They gathered their things and Maya drove them to the police station in the cruiser. Lulu tried not to think about the reality that their time together might be almost at an end. Even if she left with Raul, they could stay connected in so many ways. Phone, text, social media, Zoom. Maybe she could come back to Lost Harbor after Raul had been reunited with his family. Or maybe the FBI would allow Tristan to come with them.

This wasn't going to be the end. She knew it. Or at least *hoped* it.

When they reached the police station, they found the two FBI agents already waiting for them. They both proffered their badges, although since Maya already knew them, it hardly seemed necessary. Special Agent Melbourne was a fit man in his thirties with a sharp-angled face, like a knife in human form. Agent Clement seemed less intimidating, although that might have been because he kept pulling out an oversize handkerchief to blow his nose.

"I want to assure you that you're not in any trouble," Melbourne told Lulu right away. "We've been in contact with Raul's grandparents, the Perinos, and they're very grateful to you.

They were one day away from transferring the ransom payment. You saved them a lot of money."

"You talked to them?" Raul cried.

"We did. Your grandfather will meet us at the airport in Anchorage."

Tristan frowned. "He got here from Colombia that quickly?"

"The FBI is very efficient," the agent said, with an edge of pride. "We located them within ten minutes of getting the call from Chief Badger. He boarded the next available flight. He should be landing within the hour."

"Why did you drive down instead of taking a plane?" Tristan asked.

Lulu glanced at Tristan, wondering why he was asking so many questions. Did he think something was off about the two agents? Maybe he was having a hard time letting go of his protector role. So was she.

Melbourne lifted an eyebrow but answered the question calmly enough. "We had a meeting in Grantview, so we needed a vehicle. It made more sense to drive than fly and rent a car."

That matched what Maya had said yesterday.

"What about Seb Antonov?" Lulu asked anxiously. "Have you located him yet?"

"He and an accomplice have been spotted on their way to Canada. They won't get past the border." Agent Clement blew his nose again.

Maya spoke up at that point. "Lulu and Tristan, you two have done an incredible job keeping Raul safe. All credit to you both. Until they've arrested Antonov and his minion, you need to be on guard. The man's unpredictable. If I had my way, you'd lie low and stick close to Lost Harbor."

Lulu and Tristan shared a secret amused glance. That didn't sound bad to her.

"What happens next?" she asked.

Melbourne answered. "Now we take some statements—from you and Raul here—then I take this boy to his family. Sound good?"

Raul cheered, but a pang struck Lulu right in the heart. This was it. Goodbye to Raul. Ever since that fateful miming session on the *Northern Princess*, her mission in life had been to protect him and get him back to his family. In the process, she'd grown very attached to the kid. He was so polite and courageous. Like a mini-Prince Valiant. He also made her laugh with his obsessions with all things American. When she'd snagged a hamburger for him that first night in Lost Harbor, before they hid behind the dumpster, he'd gobbled it down with so much carefree joy that she'd almost forgotten they'd just fled the *Northern Princess*.

She crouched down next to him and gave him a hug. He wrapped his arms around her and clung to her. "*Gracias por todo,* Lulu. Maybe I will see you again soon."

God, she loved the formal way he talked. "I'm going to miss you, *profesor.*"

His giggle sounded more boy than professor. Maybe now that he was going home, he could let his guard down.

"Oh, and thank you for saving my life," she added, shaking out her wrist. "We had some fun times, didn't we? Maybe best not to tell your grandparents about *all* of them."

"I will tell them everything," Raul said fervently. "I'm going to write a book. You will be the heroine."

"Oh. Well, in that case..." Laughing, she gave him one more squeeze and stood up. She banished her tears to the back of her mind, determined not to rain on the boy's happiness.

After their goodbye, Tristan took his turn. He bent down to shake Raul's hand. "Nice work out there. You can be my crew member any time."

"*Gracias, Capitán!*"

Tristan didn't even scowl at his use of the hated *capitán,* which just proved that Raul had won him over too. As Lulu blinked away a tear, she noticed that Tristan was slipping something into Raul's jacket pocket. Chocolate bar? Jerky? Whatever it was, she couldn't identify it, but Raul smiled happily at Tristan.

After Lulu and Raul had finished their statements, she walked outside with the boy to wave goodbye to him and the agents. A brisk wind cut through her thrift store jacket and made her cheeks go numb. A grove of spruce trees swayed back and forth like priestesses in prayer. Gray-bellied clouds roamed overhead with their threatening loads of what...rain? Sleet? Snow?

She got the message. *This* was the real Alaska—when the forces of nature take over and the humans turn their focus to survival. Something deep inside her thrilled to the challenge, to the dare flung down by the autumn wind. Can you survive? Can you do more than survive? Can you *live*?

The FBI agents' car pulled out of the parking lot, with Raul turning to wave at her through the back window. Then it turned the corner onto Main Street and disappeared behind a stand of birch trees that had lost nearly all their leaves. Their branches twisted white and naked against the sky.

She stared after the vehicle, feeling blank and empty, until other things filled her field of vision. The art store on the other side of Main, the physical therapy office, the teenager skateboarding down the sidewalk, a banner for the community college.

Footsteps sounded behind her and a warm hand settled on her shoulder. Without turning around, she knew who it was. Her body recognized his touch and initiated a slow melting process from her belly to her heart.

Tristan.

She was going to stay in Lost Harbor, she decided. She couldn't walk away from someone who made her feel like this with one touch on her shoulder. Random chance had deposited her in Lost Harbor, but that didn't mean she couldn't make the most of it.

She would stay for the fall. Or even the winter, maybe. She'd find her own place and her own work and she and Tristan could... date. They could see where this thing between them led—without the pressure of a kidnapper chasing them.

Filled with the joy of making that decision, she spun around to share it with Tristan. Then froze at the look on his face.

He held his phone in one hand, while the other fell away from her shoulder. "I just got a call. My father's in the hospital."

"Oh Tristan." Her stomach clenched, her body reacting viscerally to the worst kind of news. "What happened?"

"I'm not sure. My mother was nearly hysterical, it was hard to understand her. I'm going on the next flight."

The next flight. Tristan was leaving?

"To...*Chile*?"

"Yes. I don't know how long I'll be gone. Will you...do you know...?"

She filled in the blanks. "What I'm doing? No."

A second ago, she had known. But now? Did she really want to stay here if Tristan wasn't around?

She'd decide that later. This was an emergency. All hands on deck.

"But don't worry about me, Tristan. How can I help? I can help you pack. Drive you to the airport. You just tell me what you need."

The lines of tension in his face eased and he ran his fingers through his thick hair. "Fuck, I don't even know. My boat, the roof on my house, winter preps, my sister...shit, I need to call Toni."

"Come on." She spread a hand across his back and steered him toward Toni's truck. "You make phone calls while I drive.

I've always wanted to try driving on the wrong side of the street. How hard could it be?"

Her tiny little joke brought a twitch of a smile to his face.

Following her suggestion, he called Toni while she drove them back to the fairytale house. Tristan and Toni decided that he should travel to Chile first, because she was in the midst of helping Bash with the first session of their fight training camp. If things looked dire, he'd tell her right away and she'd fly down.

"Papa will want you there," she heard Toni say. "It'll reassure him to see your hairy face."

She could relate to that. A kind of panic was brewing inside her at the thought of Tristan leaving. Why should that be, when she'd only just met the man?

Shoving aside all such thoughts, she helped him pack and tidy up Toni's kitchen.

"You're welcome to stay here," Tristan told her as he zipped up his duffel bag. "I checked with Toni. They'll be back either tomorrow or the next day, but there's plenty of space."

"That's very kind, but no." She didn't want to intrude on Toni and Bash, who she barely knew. Nor did she want to sleep in the guest room where she and Tristan had spent such an intense and glorious night.

"Are you leaving then?" Tristan asked her, almost casually, as if he was no more than mildly curious. She couldn't blame him, of course. He had bigger things on his mind—life-and-death things. Family things.

"As I said before, don't worry about me." She checked her phone. "We have thirty minutes to get to the airport."

"Shit. I haven't even been down to my boat." He shouldered his duffel. "And I still have to get to my house and grab my passport."

"Let's go, then. Tell you what, make a list while we drive. What needs to be done, and who I should contact about getting it done. I won't leave Lost Harbor until everything's under control. If I know one thing about this town, it's that the people will be there for you. They were there for me and they didn't even know me."

"Yeah. Good plan."

They hurried out to Toni's truck, where she slid behind the wheel again. Definitely a strange feeling, driving on the left side of everything, but she was already getting used to it. The biggest problem was getting distracted by the incredible scenery—russet hills covered in dying fireweed, a burst of yellow from a lone birch tree, the silver surface of the bay, the parting of clouds to reveal a snowy mountaintop.

"Termination dust." Tristan took a break from dictating a list into his phone to wave at the mountain on the other side of the bay.

"What's that?"

"First snowfall in the higher elevations. Signifies the end of summer. Hence the termination."

"That's rather grim."

"Only if you don't like winter. Some do."

"Do you?"

"I love winter. That's when I get to take a vacation." He returned to his list. "Boat. Lucas Holt can handle everything. Tell him to check for bullet holes. Ask him to call Morty at Northern Welding to postpone. I'll haul my boat out later on."

By the time they reached the tiny Lost Harbor airport—more like an airstrip with a small terminal building—the list took up a lot of space on his Notes app.

He sent it to her with a *ding* on her phone. "I owe you, Lulu. I don't like dumping all this on you, but it's mostly just connecting with the people who will actually do everything."

"You don't owe me anything. I owe you." She stopped the

truck with a jerk. "I'll never forget what you did for me and Raul."

He turned toward her, his sea-gray gaze sweeping across her face. He still hadn't shaved. Her hands itched to feel the thick golden scruff, but she could tell that his entire focus was on getting on that plane.

"I'll see you again," he said, as if it was absolutely certain.

She smiled, neither agreeing or disagreeing. Who knew what the future held? Not her, since a week ago she didn't know Lust—ahem—Lost Harbor existed. It sure was living up to its name—both of them.

"Take care of your father," she said softly. "Don't let the medical stuff distract you."

His gaze zeroed in on her, and she knew he was really listening. "Go on."

"Just be with him. Give him your best. This time will never come again." Such bittersweet advice. She twisted her mouth to one side, refusing to add tears to this moment.

He leaned forward and tipped up her chin with one hand. "This isn't over, Lulu. I promise."

"Oh? How do you know I'm not going to hop on the next plane after yours and take off for Fiji?"

"I don't. But if you do, expect me to show up in a thong when you least expect me."

A smile trembled on her lips, only to be captured by his mouth, along with her sigh. This kiss held so many questions, so many reassurances, so much possibility. She surrendered to it completely, immersing herself in the powerful, drugging sensations. *Tristan. I think I might love you.*

Finally, after what felt like an entire story packed into one kiss, he drew away. Shaken by her last thought—*I think I might love you*—she touched her fingers to her mouth.

"Get on with you, then," she said in her best Cockney accent. "Time for kidney pie, don't you know."

"Excuse me?"

"Goodbye. Kidney pie. It rhymes."

"Okay." With a perplexed laugh, he swung his long legs out of the truck. "No need to come inside. The truck is yours as long as you want it. Toni's idea. They have Bash's rig."

"Now that, I'll take, since I'm not keen on hitchhiking from the airport. You'll let me know how your dad's doing?"

"Of course." Turning away from the truck, he pulled his phone from his pocket and texted something. Her phone dinged. And then he was gone, disappearing inside the terminal, giving her one last glimpse of his tall form before the glass doors closed behind him.

And then, she really was alone.

Not wanting to draw things out too long, she drove slowly out of the airport parking lot. It wasn't until she reached the next stoplight that she glanced at her phone to see what Tristan had texted.

This isn't over. I promise.

TWENTY-FIVE

At least once a year, Tristan traveled to Chile to visit his parents, and every time he had to adjust to speaking Spanish all over again. And every year, it seemed his accent got worse. This time, he had to get used to a lot of medical terminology that he barely knew in English.

From the Santiago airport, he took a taxi to the Centro Medico Nuestra Señora de la Paz, where he met his mother outside his father's room. She clung to him, shaking so hard he worried she was having a medical crisis of her own.

"It's okay, Mama. I just saw the doctor and he said Papa needs heart surgery but that he should come through it fine. He's in good health otherwise. I guess all those years fishing paid off."

But his mother just sobbed on his shoulder. His jacket grew wet from her tears. "I'm glad you're here," she said when she'd finally gotten through her tears. "I didn't want Victor to see me crying. I feel better now. Go on, say hello to your father. He's been asking for you."

"Are you sure you're okay?" He held onto her, hands on her upper arms. Her dark eyes, so much like Toni's, cleared.

"*Si, Tristán.* I'm fine. I'll find some tissues and clean my face off. I don't want your father to get upset. Go ahead."

Drawing in a long breath, he pushed open the door and found his father stretched out on the hospital bed, electrodes on his shaved chest, monitors blinking green. His eyes opened when Tristan walked in, and he managed a wide smile. "Good to see you, Tristan."

Tristan got his build from his father, along with his gray-green eyes and his deep love for the ocean.

"*Far,*" he said, using the Danish word for Dad, which he and Toni liked to do sometimes. He bent over to hug him gingerly. "You look pretty good, considering."

"*Ja.*" As a Dane, Victor Gammelgaard had learned English early in life, and had very little trace of an accent. But occasionally a Danish word would slip through. "No flattery. I'm glad you're here, Tristan. Your mother needs you."

Tristan tucked away a smile at the fact that both his parents were more worried about each other than themselves. No surprise there. They were the most passionately-in-love parents an embarrassed kid could have. He and Toni used to roll their eyes at their constant displays of affection.

"I came right away. Soon as I heard. The doctor says they're going to operate tomorrow."

"*Ja. Mit hjerte.*" He spread a hand across his chest. "No more fishing for me, they said. I'll have to be careful from now on."

"Well, it's a good thing you're retired."

"A fisherman never retires." His eyelids lowered, as if he was having trouble staying awake. "He just catches fewer fish."

Tristan found a chair and drew it close to the edge of the hospital bed. He kept quiet while his father drifted off to sleep. The hypnotic beeping of the monitor made him drowsy too. He'd barely slept on the long flight. He kept thinking about Lulu and what he'd texted her.

I promise.

He didn't make promises. Not to anyone. Not anymore. He knew better. And yet he'd not only spoken one out loud—"This isn't over. I promise"—but he'd written it into a text.

Where had that come from? It was probably just the heat of the moment, after all the drama they'd both been through. They'd connected in such an intense way, but maybe that was just the "crisis effect." It would wear off, and he and Lulu would go back to being strangers to each other's worlds.

After all, he knew exactly what happened when someone from another place tried to settle in Lost Harbor. He'd *lived* it. He couldn't go through that again, and anyway, Lulu hadn't given any hint of wanting to stick around town. She hadn't even wanted to stay at Toni and Bash's house. He had no idea what she was going to do.

His phone dinged. Oh good, international texts were going through.

It was Toni, checking on things. He answered her, taking care to remember each detail the doctor had told him. *Blocked artery, surgery tomorrow, prognosis good. Mama wants me to stay for a while.*

Can you do that?

For a while. Sure.

What about Lulu? She texted me that the truck is parked at my house. What are her plans?

Don't know yet.

A short time after that, he sent Lulu the same information. Surgery, the need to stay longer.

When she texted him back, his heart leaped into his throat, almost as if she was right there in front of him, long legs and laughing eyes and all. *You should absolutely stay. This time won't come again.*

HE THOUGHT about that phrase often over the next few weeks, as things grew more and more difficult. The first heart surgery didn't go as expected. They had to perform another surgery, this one even trickier. The doctors moved his father into the critical care unit. His mother cried herself to sleep at night; he could hear her from the sofa bed in the living room of their little high-rise condo.

He immersed himself in taking care of both of his parents. He cooked for his mother. He grilled the doctors. He sought out second opinions. He spent hours with his father at the hospital as he came in and out of consciousness.

Everything else faded away.

For a while he followed the news about Seb Antonov. With the help of Lulu and Raul's statements, as well as information from the *Northern Princess*, the FBI arrested him and his accomplice as they tried to cross the border into Canada. They were extradited to Colombia, where charges of kidnapping and child trafficking were filed against him, and accessory charges against his helper.

After that, Tristan lost track of the news and sometimes forgot there was a world outside of the hospital and his parents' condo.

Except for Lulu.

He didn't forget her because she texted him often, and always just when he most needed her bright spirit. She sent him encouraging words, silly jokes, or a link to a song. Once she sent him a news article about Raul and his escape from the *Northern Princess*.

They spelled my name wrong, she complained. *But I kind of like it, so you must now call me Fufu from now on.*

Her texts were like beams of light in the forest. Whenever he had a spare moment, he sent her an update or a joke or a random snapshot of Chilean hospital food. He kept expecting her to leave Lost Harbor, especially after Antonov was arrested, but week after week, she didn't. A sneaky sense of hope sparked in his heart that maybe she would still be there when he got home.

Toni called every day. "Should I come? I can get on a plane tomorrow. Bash can handle these kids. He could handle twice as many. Tell me the truth, Tris."

"The valve replacement went well. The doctors don't have that grim look about them anymore. They say Papa's going to be fine, it's just going to take a while."

She sighed in relief. "Thank God. So should I come? You didn't answer the question."

"It's up to you, but I don't think we both need to be here. They're hoping you'll come next year for their fortieth anniversary."

"I can't believe they've been married that long. How do they do it?"

"I asked Papa that. He said it's all about one word."

"Love?"

"No. Paying attention."

"That's two words."

"He's in a hospital bed, what do you want me to do, correct him?"

She laughed. "You know, I'm kind of surprised you even got two words out of him. He doesn't usually talk about stuff like that."

"I know. He's been pretty chatty. Maybe it's the drugs."

"Well, make the most of it. Maybe I can send you a list of questions for him. Like why didn't he stand up for me when Mom made me wear all those girlie dresses I hated?"

At the other end of the hospital corridor, he spotted the nurse on duty heading into his dad's room.

"I can answer that one myself. Because you stood up for yourself just fine. I gotta go, Toni. The nurse is here and I want to talk to him."

"Keep me posted and let me know if *anything* changes."

"You know I will. Wait. Before you go. How's Lulu? She sounds good in her texts."

"She's really good. Lulu's a busy girl. I barely see her. Seems like she's having fun."

He wanted to drill down on what kind of "fun" Lulu was having, but didn't want to miss his opportunity to talk to the nurse. So he ended the call and hurried down the corridor. Was she having fun causing random disasters? Having fun meeting new people? Dating?

He and Lulu didn't have any kind of official relationship. They'd never discussed such a thing, or even their feelings toward each other. They'd met, bonded, slept together, and gone their separate ways.

She probably *was* dating other people. A beautiful, fun, fascinating woman like her, dropped into the middle of a remote Alaska town filled with hard-working single men—shit, they could make a reality show out of that. *Alaskan fishermen vie for the heart of a British royal-adjacent dancer. Streaming now on Netflix.*

He should have spoken his piece before he left. He should have asked her to wait. Told her that he believed they really had something together. That he hadn't experienced feelings this strong since Julie, and that it was a completely different kind of emotion. More mature, more real. Less fantasy.

But maybe it was a fantasy that two such wildly different people could find love with each other. She was practically a princess, for God's sake. And he was...just a fisherman.

TWENTY-SIX

Lulu waltzed into the office of Lost Harbor Physical Therapy and waved hello to Bridget, the receptionist who was almost as new as she was.

"How was your date last night?" she asked.

"I know more about marine welding than I ever imagined. I could teach a class now."

Lulu laughed. "That's one way to get an education. Date different professionals and take notes."

"Next time, I'm making you come with. Double date. That's the way to go. It spreads out the risk, you know?"

Lulu offered her a sympathetic smile, but didn't commit to anything. She didn't want to go on a date, not even a double date. But as the days ticked onwards and Tristan stayed in Chile, she was starting to wonder if she was being ridiculous.

Other parts of her life were coming along nicely. After she'd taken Tristan to the airport, she'd remembered the sign she'd noticed across from the police station. Although she wasn't a licensed physical therapist, she had lots of experience from working with her mother. She'd taken a few classes on anatomy and musculoskeletal treatments. On the cruise ship, she'd assisted the overworked and understaffed medical unit.

All of that added up to a job as an assistant to the physical therapy team. She didn't prescribe the exercises, but she worked through the recommended sets with patients and reported back to the therapists. She liked to keep it as entertaining as possible, which they seemed to appreciate.

Once she'd been offered the job, she'd looked around for a short-term apartment of some kind. Her funds would only last so long while paying for a room at the Sweet Harbor Bakery and Bed and Breakfast—especially when she couldn't resist the daily special every morning.

Megan Holt had told her about the log cabin she'd lived in when she first came to Lost Harbor. Although tiny and cave-like inside, it had a wonderful open deck with a view of Misty Bay and the drifts of clouds that wandered past.

She'd signed a month-by-month lease, and every month she thought about whether she should leave or not. So far, two months in, the answer had been no.

It was early December now, and a thin layer of snow covered the ground. Christmas was approaching. It would be her first Christmas without her mother and she could barely think about what that would be like.

Would it be better to go back to England and open up her mother's apartment? Or go back and stay with a friend in London who kept inviting her? Or would the memories simply be too painful? At least here in Lost Harbor, she had no ghosts haunting her. Americans celebrated Christmas differently, as far as she could tell. No Boxing Day, no rum cakes. Instead, people put up a lot of decorations and made long shopping lists and baked many cookies.

If she stayed, she could look at it as an anthropological exercise. English Christmas compared and contrasted with Christmas in Alaska. Maybe that would remove some of the sadness.

Her first patient of the morning was Janet Holt, the harbormaster's mother. She wore a handwoven poncho over her joggers. Her long gray braid was fastened in a coronet atop her head. Lulu happened to know that she'd knitted her own socks. She knew this because she was now a regularly attending member of stitch-and-bitch, a crafting slash gossiping group.

"Good morning, Janet, how's the knee feeling?" she asked her patient.

"Like it got kicked by my yak," the older woman grumbled.

Lulu squirted some sanitizer on her hands. "That wasn't very nice of it. Wait, did you say *yak*?"

"Yak. Yes. Normally he's well-behaved, but he was in a mood yesterday. It was our anniversary," she explained.

"You and your yak have an anniversary?" She checked the computer terminal where Mrs. Holt's exercises were listed.

"He's my husband, come back as a yak. Took a while to see it, but there was something about his chin that gave it away."

"Ah." If there was one thing she'd learned about Lost Harbor, it was that the town had no shortage of eccentrics. Maybe such unique characters were drawn here, or maybe living here turned you peculiar. She didn't know which. But she loved it.

Actually, there were two things she'd learned about Lost Harbor. People here really did help each other out. It made sense because there was always something trying to kill you here. The cold. A storm. An avalanche. A bear. Even though the residents tended to be self-sufficient and independent, when someone needed help, no one hesitated to offer it. That was how this tiny outpost on the edge of the wilderness had survived so long.

She told Janet to lie on her back for the first set of exercises. "Show me how you've been doing the clamshells. I have a note here that says to make sure you're not overdoing it. Are you an overachiever, my friend?"

The older woman chuckled. "You should ask stitch-and-bitch about that. You'd get some bitching for sure."

"From what I can tell, it's already about sixty percent bitching and forty percent stitching."

She'd been to three meetings of Stitch and Bitch already, and loved every second. Not so much because of the knitting, although she'd always enjoyed that, but because of the gossip.

For instance, she'd heard all about Tristan's ex-wife. No one had liked her much because she threw a tantrum every time he had to leave for a long trip.

"Of course there are two sides to every story," Mrs. Bellini had allowed. "But Tristan was just trying to pay for his boat. How else was he going to make a living? He's a fisherman and you have to go where the fish are."

"Good thing there's other fish in the sea." Zoe Bellini's crack had made them all laugh. "Especially for Tristan."

"No one serious, though. Not since Julie."

Zoe and the others had eyed Lulu curiously, since everyone knew she and Tristan were...something. But no one knew what, exactly. Including her. She'd simply folded her lips together and glanced at the ceiling, the picture of innocence.

Which had gotten a general chuckle from the group.

"If you don't have other plans, we'd love to have you come out to the homestead for Christmas," Janet Holt was saying as she pushed her legs against the resistance band.

"That's so kind. Now when you say we, are you referring to yourself and the yak, or you and..."

"Me and Lucas and Megan and Ruby, and probably a few others. Jack never liked Christmas much, other than the rum punch I always made. I'll probably give the yak a sip or two just for old times' sake."

It might be worth accepting her invitation just to meet this yak. Also, sometimes Mrs. Holt reminded Lulu of her own mother, even though their exteriors were entirely different. Her mother had refused to show the world a single gray hair. Lulu used to bring in a hair colorist to touch up her roots. But both of them had a certain bluntness to them. As a matter of fact, Lulu drew a great deal of comfort from Janet Holt's presence.

"Thank you, Janet. I'm not yet sure what I'm doing this Christmas. I have friends in England who are worried I won't be able to find my way back from Alaska."

"It's easy to get lost here." Mrs. Holt lowered her hips back down on the table. "Or found, depending on how you look at it."

Lulu didn't look at it either way. She wasn't lost or found. She was like a piece of kelp that had been deposited on the high-water mark at the beach. In time, another higher than normal tide would pick her up and sweep her away again. This was purely temporary, this time in Lost Harbor. One day at a time, as they said.

And one day at a time, she grew more attached to the place. She loved exploring the hiking trails in the hills above the town. When Toni found out she was going off on her own, she gave her a strict lecture about bears. After that, she regularly received invitations to hike—from Ruthie Malone, Chrissie Yates, Megan Holt, or Zoe Bellini.

With Zoe, she went on beach walks and helped her collect random bits of debris for her artwork. Ruthie was trying to get into shape for her upcoming wedding, so she was always up for a jog or a hike. Chrissie asked Lulu a zillion questions about herself, which made sense once Lulu remembered that she and Tristan had been high school sweethearts. She was still looking out for her former boyfriend. And Megan...she adored Megan, who was also a newcomer to Lost Harbor and made a special effort to reach out to her.

She got to know the Morrison sisters—Dr. Bethany Morrison and her younger sister, Gretel—because Gretel's Café became her favorite place for her morning cappuccino. One day in late October, Gretel invited her to a rehearsal for the local amateur production of *The Nutcracker*.

When the director, who was the high school music teacher, discovered that Lulu could dance, she got roped into joining the production herself. Now she was busy choreographing her own solo, which she would perform for the Rat King and his court.

When the other cast members saw her dance, all of a sudden she was deluged with other invitations. The teen rec center begged her to put on a dance workshop. The local community college campus asked her to propose a class for the next semester. A fun women's burlesque group, the Harbor Hotties, invited her to join them for a show.

It was almost overwhelming. In the last months with her mother, her world had closed in and become very small—just her and her mother and the stream of hospice nurses from the NHS. After her mother had died, all of that had stopped. She'd felt completely at sea.

And then she'd literally *gone* to sea. On the cruise ship, she'd been surrounded by people, but had formed mostly superficial friendships with her fellow dancers. When you knew it was just a temporary gig, you didn't become attached.

But Lost Harbor was working some kind of spell on her. With each shift in the weather, she wondered if it would finally become too cold or too icy or too dark for her. But it never happened.

Halloween brought a slew of parties. She dressed up as Ringo Starr and handed out caramels to Ruby and her cohorts. Then she danced until dawn at the Olde Salt with Pedro Davila and other crusty but endearing fishermen.

In November, Malcolm Crow was elected mayor of Lost

Harbor, and he immediately appointed Trixie Tran to run a new business outreach department. Cockles came in third, but seemed to hold no grudges and demanded no recounts.

The first snowfall meant invitations for sledding from Gretel and the Ross boys. And best of all, a dog sled ride. She went skating on a frozen lake with Kate Robinson, who was trying to improve her skating to keep up with her fiancé, the fire chief Darius Boone.

"Did you know Lost Harbor has a women's hockey team?" Kate told her. "You should join up."

"Kate, I would, but I'm so overbooked with rehearsals and workshops. I've never been this busy in my life!"

Kate laughed, windmilling her arms to keep from tripping on an air bubble frozen into the lake. Someone had hot-mopped the surface to make it smooth, but it wasn't perfect. The setting made up for it, though. Shoreside alders bowing under the weight of the snow, the sky a blue so pure it made Lulu's heart sing.

Winter brought an unexpectedly delicate beauty. For instance, the alpenglow, the pink aura of light clinging to the mountainous horizon. Lulu had never seen anything like it. The sunsets seemed to stretch for hours, from afternoon to evening, pastel clouds shifting from rose to pale apricot to lavender. At night the stars were so brilliant she had to shade her eyes to gaze up at them. After windy nights, she'd wake up to snowdrifts carved into wild and whimsical shapes.

Winter here had a playfulness that was new to her. In London it was mostly gray skies and bitter wind. When snow came, it didn't generally linger. If it did, it quickly became dirty and inconvenient.

But in Lost Harbor, she looked forward to fresh snowfall, even if it meant she'd have to bring out the cabin's big push shovel. The new snow felt like a clean slate, like a chance to start fresh. She loved waking up in the morning and finding tiny bird imprints on the surface of the new snow. Or surprising a bunny rabbit, its creamy fur barely visible against the white snow.

Snowshoe hares, they were called. In the winter they grew a special coat of white fur, which they shed in the spring in favor of brown—the better to hide from predators.

As for her own predator, the one who had been hunting her and Raul, he was safely under lock and key, last she'd heard. The authorities in Colombia had taken custody of Seb Antonov. Agent Melbourne sent her updates on a regular basis; the last one had come about a month ago. Antonov and his accomplice were in jail awaiting trial.

She hadn't heard anything from Raul, but she wasn't surprised by that. He was safely back home and should be focusing on having a childhood and putting his traumatic experience behind him. His mother and his grandparents had both sent her 'thank you' cards, which had miraculously made their way to her despite being addressed to Lulu from the Northern Princess/Lost Harbor, Alaska.

She'd propped those cards on the mantel of the hearth in her little log cabin, along with some interesting stones and shells she'd found on her beach walks with Zoe. In a place of honor, she displayed her favorite photo of her mother. And then there was Tristan's bandana from the *Desperado* that had somehow ended up in her backpack.

If Tristan ever came back to Lost Harbor, she'd return it to him. That was why she kept it on the mantel, she told herself. To remind her to give it back to him. Not because it was a tangible reminder of her time on the *Desperado*. Not because it brought back the memory of Tristan's wide grin flashing through his beard, and his sea-green gaze. Not because he texted or called almost every day. Not because with each one, she felt closer to him and so very far away.

TWENTY-SEVEN

Tristan listened closely to the latest update from the nurse, who relayed it in rapid Spanish that Tristan understood more easily now. They were going to try taking him off the intravenous blood pressure medication and see how he did.

"You're unhooking it now? What's the worst that could happen?"

"If his blood pressure goes up too much, we'll either put him back on this medication or try another." He rattled off the name of the medication. Tristan made him slow down and say it again so he could look it up later.

From the bed, Victor spoke in English. "Stand down, Tristan. They're doing a good job for me."

"I know that." But were they doing such a good job because Tristan was there, hounding them? That was the question that kept him here. That, and feeling close to his father in a new way. Never before had he felt that his Viking-like father *needed* him. He'd always been so mighty and self-contained.

"*Gracias por todos,*" his father said to the nurse. "*Mi hijo es protector.*"

The nurse finished his work with the IV and left, muttering something about other, probably much easier, patients.

Victor adjusted his position on the bed. "Help me get up. I want to take a walk."

"Did you ask the nurse?"

"I can walk whenever I want. They say it's good for me."

"But they just took you off that blood pressure medication."

"Son. Either help me or go back to Alaska." His irritation made Tristan jump. His father usually kept his frustrations to himself. "I'm not a child. Still got life in me."

After he swung his legs over the side of the bed, he grabbed onto Tristan's arm to come to his feet. Tristan hooked the IV onto a wheeled stand that allowed his dad to go mobile.

"A lot of life." He helped his father pad away from the bed in the felted slippers Mama had made for him. He was even taller than Tristan, a barrel-chested burly man who'd always seemed like a giant to his children. His formerly blond hair was mostly a silvery white now, and he'd lost some weight. But his presence still had the same imposing effect. "You're not even seventy. You could come back and crew on the *Desperado* with me."

He chuckled. "I never was a very good crew member."

"That's because you were the best captain in Lost Harbor. You were the leader of the fleet. They all looked to you when big issues came up. Remember the time the cruise ship companies wanted to expand their dock and take out half the harbor?"

"I do."

"You organized everyone to stand up against it. You got a TV reporter to come down and do a story on it. You saved the harbor." The pride of that event still hadn't left Tristan. *His father* had done that. Victor Gammelgaard.

"It was all of us, standing together. They didn't expect that."

"But you were the leader."

Tristan nodded to a doctor hurrying past them. She was

attractive, around his age and single, she'd let him know. But he hadn't made even a hint of a move. He told himself it was because of the situation, that he was here for his dad, not flirtation, but it wasn't that. It was Lulu. Or should he say, Fufu.

"Someone has to be the leader," his father was saying. "You know how it is."

"Me? No. I dropped out of the mayor's race. I endorsed Malcolm Crow." Hadn't he told Papa about that? So much had happened right around that time, it was hard to remember.

"He's a good choice. He'll be good for Lost Harbor." They turned the corner and passed a pretty glassed-in room filled with greenery in pots. It was billed as a respite room, and Tristan had spent a fair amount of time in there. "You'll do something else."

"Yes, I'll do my own thing and not worry about everyone else." Tristan tossed off the comment lightly, in a half-joking way meant to mask the fact that he meant it. Maybe once he'd seen himself as a leader. But no more.

"No, you won't."

Tristan jerked his head around to catch his father's frown as he shuffled down the hall. "Why won't I?"

"Because you won't be happy that way. You'll be lying to yourself." He stopped to take a short rest. "Remember when you first bought the *Desperado*? You were twenty. Asking men ten, twenty years older than you to follow your command. And they did."

"Because it was their job." Tristan remembered the stress of that first trip very clearly. Managing a crew in which every single person was older than him had kept him up nights.

"They could have gotten jobs on other boats. No, son, they saw something in you."

"Money. I was a crazy kid hell-bent on making my mark."

"You had a record-making catch that year." The pride in his father's voice echoed the pride he'd felt, reminiscing about the cruise ship battle. "And those fishermen on your boat, with maybe sixty years' experience combined, they knew you were going to be something special. You're a leader, Tristan. Where you lead, people will follow. You can't pretend you aren't who you are."

Tristan blinked at him. Since when did Victor Gammelgaard talk about this kind of stuff? Besides, he had it all wrong.

"I led my crew into a bad situation on that sandbar. People are better off not following me. I learned that the hard way."

His father waved his hand, nearly dislodging the IV bag from the stand. "Accidents are part of the job. You kept it from getting worse. In a crisis, you did what a captain does. You led."

Tristan wanted to protest, to argue. To say that he'd fucked up and other people had paid with their blood. That it didn't matter what happened *after* they hit the sandbar. Because everything after that moment was on him.

But he didn't want to upset his father, so he held his tongue.

His father took another step forward, leaning on his walker, his large body tilting forward. Even while recovering from surgery, Victor Gammelgaard was a man you listened to. Even if —or maybe especially if—you were his son. "You led in the mayor's race too."

"I have no idea if I was leading before I dropped out."

"No, I mean that you led. You gave your support to Malcolm. And he won."

Tristan laughed. "He almost got beat by that rooster."

"That damn Cockles," muttered Victor. "He belongs in a stew pot. And you belong wherever you decide. But you won't be happy unless you accept who you are. That's true for anyone."

"Fair enough."

They walked a few feet more, but Tristan could tell that his father was tiring. Not that he'd ever say so.

"Ready to turn back?"

Victor nodded wearily, and they turned back to retrace their steps, more slowly this time, with more frequent breaks. Love for this normally taciturn man, the giant of his childhood, his inspiration in so many ways, swept through him.

"I'm sorry I let you down," he said abruptly. And as soon as he said it, he knew he'd been feeling that way for a long time. His father was his role model. Victor had never gotten divorced. He'd never led his boat onto a sandbar. "The accident. My surgery." He ran a hand across his scar. "The divorce."

"*Ja?*" His father swung his head to glare at him. "Did I say that? Did I say you let me down?"

"No. You didn't have to. Divorce..." He shrugged. His mother had been raised in the Catholic church, so she'd struggled with that news. Dad had never said much about it. "It didn't win me any points."

"What points? There are no points. How's Julie now?"

"She's remarried with a kid," he said. "I check in with her now and then. Her husband's a good guy. They live outside Chicago."

"Son, my feet are starting to hurt so my patience is low. I cannot stop you from blaming yourself about Julie. But don't accuse me of doing so. I never had an opinion about it. Other people's marriages, even your son's..." He shrugged. "Best to stay out."

They reached his room—Cuarto 212—and Tristan helped him through the doorway. He wished he'd brought this up with his father long ago. Maybe he would have stopped beating himself up. Because that was exactly what he'd been doing—and assuming that his father felt the same way.

"That's very interesting, *far*, because you just expressed a whole lot of opinions about my life and who I am and so on and so forth."

His father eased himself onto the edge of the bed and shoved aside the IV stand. "Don't argue with an old man in his hospital bed."

Tristan helped him lift his legs onto the bed, then covered them with the lacy blanket Mama had brought from home. "What old man? I just see my next deckhand," he teased.

Victor lay back with a long sigh. Tristan adjusted the pillows under his head and stood up to go.

"Wait." He closed his hand around Tristan's wrist. "I know what it is to disappoint a father. I did that when I left the dairy farm to go to sea. I never returned."

Tristan stilled. He'd never heard the details of this story, just the general outlines.

"My father was harsh. He didn't talk. When I met your mother, there were so many words, so many feelings. I thought, this is life. I can't go back. My father never asked me to come back. He had five other sons and the farm was fine. But I knew I'd disappointed him. I felt it. It's a terrible feeling. So I repeat, Tristan. You have not disappointed me. Maybe I've disappointed *you* because I didn't say this earlier. We men, we can't be afraid to speak."

"Disappointed *me?* Of course you haven't—I've never thought—" The idea that the mighty Viking could let anyone down, especially Tristan, blew his mind.

His father threw up a hand, eyes gleaming. "Don't argue with the old man in the hospital bed. I need to sleep now. You go check on your mother."

Practically reeling, Tristan stepped back from his bedside. That was more words than his father had spoken, all at one time, than he could remember. He probably should have recorded it; Toni would never believe him.

Instead, he went right to his go-to these days. He texted Lulu.

TWENTY-EIGHT

Whenever a text from Tristan dinged on Lulu's phone, her heart jumped. Sometimes his texts were light and flirty, and sometimes they were more serious.

Had a convo with my dad today. Pretty intense. He brought a few things to my attention and made me think. He says I beat myself up too much and I'm not letting myself be everything I should be—or something like that.

She'd thought a long time before replying. *Maybe you beat yourself up because you're a good person. But you don't need to. Because you're a good person.*

He sent back an exploding head emoji. She rejoined with an emoji of someone meditating.

Been doing plenty of that here in the hospital. There's a court-yard. He attached a photo of the courtyard that also showed part of one of his arms. It looked so good, that arm. White sleeves rolled up, light golden hairs, corded muscles under tanned skin. Her mouth watered and she missed him in a starkly *physical* way. Wanting to smell his scent, touch his solid body.

She sent back a similar photo of her own arm and the snowy

backdrop of her front deck. *Lots of time for reflection here too. When I'm not shoveling.*

Reflecting on what?

What wasn't she reflecting on? The last five years. Her mother. The escape from the cruise ship. Her future. She was thirty now. That was generally regarded to be an important milestone in life. But for her, it was even more than that. She was thirty and alone in the world.

Which sounded absurdly dramatic, honestly. Of course she wasn't alone. She even had a cat now. Or rather, the cat seemed to regard her as relevant somehow to its life. *His* life, according to the vet. The cat allowed her to feed him and give him shelter occasionally, but most of his life took place in the woods where he wreaked who knew what havoc.

How I just became a 30yo cat lady, she answered Tristan.

Meow. That's hot. He included some kitten ears with that text.

Come and get it, she wanted to say. Get your ass back to Lost Harbor before a change in the weather sends me on my way.

But she would never say that, because she, more than anyone, knew how important it was to be where he was, doing what he was doing.

They talked about some pretty serious stuff in their texts.

When I get back to LH, I'm going to try the brain support group again, he told her one night.

You tried before?

Sort of. I was afraid of people thinking I was weak or something. Seeing my father like this, it feels different now. I respect him even more, you know? He's working so hard to get better.

Good for him. And you. (Thumbs up emojis and cheering emojis.)

Sometimes, when he had time at the hospital, they spoke on the phone, long, rambling conversations that covered everything from why Lulu loved dancing so much—it transported her into a world of joy—to why they both loved old-school Queen music. They shared childhood stories, laughed, flirted.

One snowy night in early December, he texted her, *I want to take you to dinner. Will you go to dinner with me?*

Curled in the armchair next to the woodstove, she laughed out loud. *Long-distance virtual dinner?*

Sort of. Tomorrow at the Lighthouse Brewery at 8. Ask for Alastair when you get there. Tell him I sent you. Gotta go. Tomorrow! Don't forget.

Ooh, that sounded intriguing. A long-distance date. How exactly would that work? It wasn't exactly the same as being with Tristan, kissing him, touching him. But she was touched that he was thinking of ways to stay connected despite nearly thirteen-thousand kilometers of distance.

The next night, she drove the Toyota truck she'd bought from Pedro Davila to the Lighthouse Brewery, which she'd never been to before. It was located in a homestead farmhouse near a lighthouse perched on a bluff overlooking the bay. Remote, romantic, buffeted by the wind, it suited her mood to a tee.

Inside, hurricane oil lamps gave the brewery a cozy atmosphere. In the summer, outdoor picnic tables and a large yurt provided extra space, but in the off-season, all the guests were served in the farmhouse itself.

But there were no other guests. She was the only one.

"Hullo?" she called into the inviting space.

A moment later, a tall man in a heather-gray sweater and an apron strolled out from the kitchen, wiping his hands on a towel.

"You're Lulu?" he said with a kind smile. "Alastair Dougal."

She recognized that accent with a thrill of familiarity. "Lovely to meet a fellow UK exile. You're Scottish?"

"I am. I'm the chef here. I've been whipping up a feast for you, on orders from Tristan Del Rey. He also hinted that you might be interested in how I wound up in this little dot on the shoreline."

"I'm so interested!"

"Then have yourself a seat and I'll tell you the tale over a bit of home-brewed ginger ale. Tristan mentioned you prefer that to alcohol."

Tristan's thoughtfulness seemed to have no limits.

Alastair showed her to a table that held a vase of fresh daisies. She noticed a note tucked between two stems. *Thanks for being the daisy next to the seaweed*, it read. With a laugh, she sat down, and Alastair poured them both a glass of sparkling brew.

They had a long, heartfelt chat about his story, and how it felt to be so far from your native land, and how he'd come to realize that he belonged here, with his fiancée Ruthie Malone.

"It had been many years since I felt I had a home. Then along came Ruthie and there I was. Home."

"That's lovely." It must be wonderful to feel so certain that someone loved you, and that you loved that someone. But it didn't seem very relevant to her own life. She and Tristan were in a very different situation. This was their first real "date"—and they weren't even on the same continent.

"Are you hungry? Tristan ordered up a parade of dishes for you. There's a theme. He said you'd recognize it."

"Is he...coming? Or am I eating alone?"

Just then her phone rang with a FaceTime call. Tristan's beaming face appeared. Even over a sketchy video connection, he made her weak in the knees.

"God, you're a sight for sore eyes," he said. "My internet won't hold up for long, but I just wanted to put my eyes on you."

"Likewise, desperado. Nice touch, with the daisies and the fellow Brit."

He laughed. "Just wait for the food."

"You've put a lot of thought into this."

"Well, I think about you a lot." The intimate tone made her heart jump.

At that point, Alastair began bringing out one dish after another. Smoked salmon dip with crackers. Salmon chowder. A salmon filet crusted in macadamia nuts.

When the video connection failed, she and Tristan switched to texting. It felt almost as intimate as being together in person, or maybe intimate in a different way. *I think I've guessed the theme,* she told him.

I had that salmon delivered to Alastair from my own catch.

Is that why it tastes so good?

That might be thanks to Alastair.

She laughed and devoured every bit of the delicious bespoke meal. *I draw the line at salmon for dessert.*

Good, because I have something else in mind for dessert.

Oh really? Her pulse picked up, and her breathing quickened. What did Tristan have up his sleeve next?

When Alastair brought her chocolate fondue, at first she was almost disappointed, although of course she loved chocolate. But midway through a bit of strawberry dipped in fondue, Tristan texted again.

That's just a preview of dessert. The real one's back at home. But there's a catch.

What catch?

We have to be naked.

TWENTY-NINE

If only they could keep up the FaceTiming for this part of the date. But Tristan didn't ever have enough privacy for anything like that. At his parents' high-rise, he slept on the couch in the living room. The condo was tiny and his mother had very good hearing. Anything X-rated and out loud was out of the question.

But texting worked just fine.

Are you naked yet? He texted when he'd given her enough time to drive home. He'd pictured her every step of the way—rounding the steep bluff where the wild strawberries grew, passing between the snow-loaded spruce groves near the hospital. Then parking next to her little cabin, running inside, and hopefully ripping her clothes off.

After a few moments she answered. *Yes. I'm under the covers and they're kind of scratchy on my nipples.*

Trust Lulu to make him laugh in the middle of sexting. *Better touch them. Imagine me licking them. Put your fingers in your mouth and get them wet. Then squeeze your nipples.*

Mmmmm. Feels good. Getting kind of aroused.

Kind of? We can do better than that. Imagine my fingers inside you. Stroking you. Making that sweet pussy purr.

Oh, did I tell you I got a cat?

Okay, that went in a direction he hadn't expected. *You mentioned being a cat lady. Are you fondling yourself? Are you wet?*

Very juicy. Slippery. Mmm.

Tell me about this cat.

Don't want to talk about my cat. Are you touching yourself too? How's that beautiful cock of yours?

Talking about the mayor?

Haha. Didn't you hear? Malcolm Crow got elected. Trixie and the rooster split the pro-cruise ship vote.

He kind of liked this mixture of sexting and casual conversation. It felt so natural, as if they were lounging in bed together catching up on the day's news while getting in the mood.

Good news. And yes, I'm touching myself too. Hand around my cock. It's so big, all because of you.

So big...and yet so far.

7,800 miles. But I feel like you're in the room with me. I can smell you. You smell like hot strawberries in the sun.

And you smell like sea spray and pirate boots.

Is that good?

So good. I think I'm going to come.

Wait. Not yet. What exactly is your hand doing? I want to know.

He closed his eyes, the better to visualize her. Even though they'd only spent a few days together, he never had a problem calling up her image. Big blue eyes, radiant smile, long legs, flirty attitude.

Hand bw my legs. Texting one-handed. So awkward.

He chuckled, because he was having the same issue. *One hand all it takes.*

Rubbing my clit. Swelling. Feels hot. Tender.

He let out a groan, then clenched his teeth to keep his sex sounds to himself. On this damn couch he felt like a thirteen-year-old boy trying to satisfy his urges without tipping off his parents. *This is killing me. I wish I was there. I want to feel for myself.*

Yeah. You close?

7,800 miles.

Don't want to laugh. I'm about to come and I can't laugh and come. My head will (exploding head emoji.)

(Laugh-cry face.) I'm close. So close. Pray my mother doesn't come out of her bedroom.

He slid his hand up and down his erection.

Oh god. I'm coming. My whole pussy's throbbing. Can you feel it?

I can almost taste it. Sweet and WILD OH YEAH

Oops, his cap lock got stuck on. But somehow it worked. A moment later he exploded into his own hand. A bunch of keys on his phone got hit with some part of his body as he jerked out his orgasm. When he finally checked it again, he saw that he hadn't sent his string of "weutirprotht[oiwJERPOWKE R."

So he sent it.

Same, she texted back a moment later. *Unless that was a stroke instead of an orgasm.*

O all the way, babe. You?

Oh yes. Amazing. I'm really good in bed with myself.

(Laughing face emoji) You're a sexy sexy woman. It turns me on thinking of you making yourself come.

Aw. You're so easy.

That's right I am. All it takes is a lil bit o Lulu.

(Smirky face emoji)

Bathroom. Cleanup. BRB, he texted.

He rolled out of the sofa bed and padded to the bathroom,

keeping a wary eye on his mother's closed door. It would be great if she would knock when she was going to come out, but she never remembered to do it. And he didn't have the heart to insist, so he just accepted that he never really had any privacy here.

He cleaned up in the bathroom, then gave himself a stern look in the mirror. "Don't mess this up, Del Rey. It's too good."

"*Tristán? Esta bien?*"

He jumped at the sound of his mother's voice at the bathroom door. "*Si Mama.* I'm almost done."

"I can't sleep, *querido*. I'm going to make some goat empanadas for your father. The doctor said that's better for his heart."

He heard her footfalls click across the floor of the little condo, then looked in the mirror again. "Seventy-eight thousand miles is too fucking many."

When he got back to his phone, he saw that Lulu had sent a long paragraph of zzzzzz's. She was going to sleep, which meant no more light in the grayness. Talking with Lulu was the only thing that really distracted him from his worry. Even though his father was getting better, he still had at least a week in rehab before he could come home. And once he came home, it might be tough for him to readjust. Tristan worried that his mother wouldn't be able to handle taking care of him.

The reality was that they needed to hire someone, because he couldn't simply move here. His life was in Lost Harbor. But every time he suggested it, his mother came up with a hundred reasons why it wouldn't work.

This was probably a job for Toni, he decided. Tomorrow, he'd call her and see if she had any ideas about the situation. Toni knew how to deal with their mother from all those years of swimming in the harbor and fishing and breaking all of Mama's gender conventions.

Instead of going back to bed, he joined his mother in the kitchen. She stood at the counter with a rolling pin in one hand and a piece of notepaper in the other.

"I'm so sorry, *mi hijo*. I forgot this message," she cried. "That day you left your phone here. I picked it up because I thought it was mine. I've been so distracted. I took the message three, no, four days ago and I put it in the freezer with my empanada dough. Here." She thrust the piece of paper at him.

"It's okay, Mama. Don't cry. No harm done."

"Are you sure? I intended to make empanadas days ago. If I hadn't waited, I would have found the message before today. *And* we would have had empanadas," she added woefully.

"Mama. *Mi amor*. It's all right. What could be so important, anyway?"

Only Lulu and Toni were really that important, and possibly Lucas, who was looking after his boat. And he was in regular touch with all of them, most especially Lulu.

But when he finally looked at the message, after reassuring her with plenty of hugs, he went cold.

The message was from Raul. He'd left a number and a request to call immediately about Seb Antonov.

"I'M USING the phone you gave me. Remember? When I left the *polizia* in Alaska? You programmed your number in. I wanted to call Lulu but I didn't have her number. My mama doesn't want me to have a phone yet, even for emergencies. Doesn't that seem unfair, especially after I *had* an emergency?"

"Raul. Focus." He spoke in Spanish, since why not? He was in Chile, the boy was in Colombia, and Alaska had never seemed further away.

Full morning now, and the smell of empanadas filled the little condo. He stood on the tiny balcony overlooking the busy metropolis of Santiago. Storeowners were opening their shops, washing the sidewalks with hoses. Delivery trucks squeezed into tight alleys. Kids in backpacks made their way to school.

"The message said something about Seb Antonov."

"*Si*. He escaped from the jail."

"In Colombia?" Tristan doubted that escape was the right word. He wouldn't be surprised if a payoff was involved. An experienced criminal like him knew all the tricks.

"Yes, in Colombia."

"Be careful, kid. Go ahead and program another number into your phone. What's the emergency number in Colombia?"

"No, I'm not worried for myself. I have a bodyguard all the time. He's such a pest. I'm scared for Lulu."

Tristan froze, his hand tightening on his phone. "For Lulu? Why?"

"Because I think he might take her next."

"*Why?* Why would he do that? She's thousands of miles away." Seven-thousand eight hundred, to be exact, but right now felt even further.

"He knows she's related to the royal family of England. When she started talking to me on the cruise ship, he searched for her on the computer. He told me what he found out. Once he even said that he should forget about me and kidnap her instead. I think that's why he kept coming after us in Alaska. Because he wanted us both. Two for one."

A two-for-one special. That certainly did explain why the bastard hadn't just skipped town once Raul and Lulu had escaped from the cruise ship. It would have been well worth his time—and the risk of getting caught—to continue to pursue them both.

Or at least he'd *believed* so. Would Lulu's distant royal

connection actually produce a ransom payment? He had no idea. She'd never mentioned any wealthy family members. In fact, he'd gotten the opposite impression.

Maybe Antonov knew more than he did.

"How do you know he's going after Lulu now?"

"I don't know. But when my bodyguard told me he escaped, I wanted to warn her about it. She should have a bodyguard too."

She should. *Him.* He ought to be there to fill the role. "Thanks, Raul. You watch your back, okay?" he added in English.

"How can I watch my back? My head doesn't turn that far."

He chuckled a bit, realizing that he'd missed the boy. "Call me anytime, Raul. Take care of yourself."

After he ended the call, he stared blankly at the streets down below. If only he could transport himself instantly to Lost Harbor, to Lulu's snowy front deck, or her cozy bed. It would take him a minimum of a day to get back.

But going back was the only option. He had to be with Lulu. He'd never in his life felt such an urgent need. It screamed through his every cell. *Lulu. I need to get back to you.* Now. Now. Wryly, he wondered if this was how salmon felt when they were swimming thousands of miles to where they'd spawned. *Now. Now.*

He called her and got her voice mail. She was probably still sleeping, snuggled under her blankets while the snow gently fell around her cabin. "Lulu, call me as soon as you get this. Be careful, Antonov might be coming after you. He's out of jail. Call me. Immediately. I need to know you're okay."

Then he called Maya and filled her in on the situation. "I'm coming back as soon as possible, but in the meantime, can you send someone out to check on Lulu?"

"Yeah, I just got a call from Agent Melbourne too." She sounded harried. "I'm short-staffed again, I had to call in some help from the state troopers. As soon as I can get away from here, I'll check on her myself."

"Okay. Thanks. I've been trying to call her but I keep getting her voice mail."

"I know she's been rehearsing a lot. The Harbor Hotties, *The Nutcracker*. She might have her phone off. And Tristan, keep in mind that he doesn't want to get caught again. Why would he take the risk of boarding a plane? He's probably laying low in Colombia."

Good point. A bit of relief eased the tension in his body, but it didn't change anything. He still needed to get back as soon as possible.

He called his sister next. "Toni. I need you down here. I have to get back to Lost Harbor."

"What's going on?" He could tell she was trying to shake off her sleepiness. He explained the situation, which went a long way toward waking her up. "Mama's still a little shaky. She started crying this morning over her empanada dough. Dad's going to get released from rehab soon, but they're going to need more help. I've been trying to talk Mama into it but she insists it's not necessary and—"

"I'll take care of it." When his sister used that badass tone—the one that had kept all the fishermen in line at the Olde Salt Saloon—he could take it to the bank. "You're too sympathetic, Tristan. She starts to cry and you just want to hug her. You have to be tough. But don't worry about it, I'm on it. I'll get a ticket right away. Bash and I will spend Christmas with them, we already talked about it. I'll come right away, and as soon as he finishes this first training camp, he'll fly down."

"You're the best, Toni."

"Nah, I'm pretty sure you are. You've been down there doing everything. Are you okay?"

"It's been good." And it had been, he realized. Spending time with his father had shifted something inside him. That shadow he'd always lived under, that of a father he revered, of the threat of disappointing him, didn't feel the same anymore. It had shifted and he saw things differently. He felt strong now, ready for the future, ready to stake his claim. "But I'm ready to go home. Even if I wasn't worried about Lulu, I'd be ready."

"You don't have to worry. She's Ms. Popular around here. I swear she has more friends than I do. She's teaching classes, dancing in *The Nutcracker*, dancing burlesque, she's busy all the time."

Watching Lulu dance with the Harbor Hotties would be worth a trip back to Lost Harbor all by itself. Actually, just seeing her smile again would be worth it. The fact was, he hadn't so much as flirted with a woman since he'd been in Chile, but he didn't want to act too possessive when he was thousands of miles away. They'd never tried to define their relationship.

But he was ready for that to change. He was ready for anything and everything with Lulu.

"Thanks, Toni. Do me a favor, though. Text me if you see Lulu, okay? Like, if you get visual confirmation that she's fine and that asshole doesn't have her."

"Will do, boo."

He took a moment with his travel app to book a ticket, then went to tell his mother the news. She took it well enough, thanks to the fact that Toni was coming in his place, and that Bash would be joining them for Christmas. His parents knew Bash well, since he and Bash had been best friends as kids. But they hadn't seen him in years, and certainly not since Toni and Bash had gotten together a few months ago.

With something like that to look forward to, she accepted his departure with only a minimum of tears.

His father didn't cry at all. Tristan took a taxi to the rehab center to say goodbye, and found him at the parallel bars, working on his balance. He told him his flight was leaving in a few hours, and apologized for the last-minute departure.

"Emergency in Lost Harbor?" his father asked.

"Maybe."

He honestly didn't know what he was going to find when he got there. Hopefully, just a quiet winter scene with nothing more exciting than an amateur production of *Nutcracker*.

"Then they need you. You've done enough here. I'm grateful, Tristan. I'm proud of you."

His chest tightened. Good God, he was thirty-two years old. Why should it mean so much to have his father say he was proud of him? And yet, it did. Whether or not he deserved it. But he would, he vowed. One way or another, he would deserve that faith from his father.

"There's a woman," he began. "I haven't mentioned her, but I think she might be in danger."

His father paused, resting his bulging forearms on the parallel bars. Amazing how much muscle he still had after all this time in the hospital. "You love her?" he asked.

"I don't know about all that. Maybe." Then, finally, "Yes. I think I do. But I only spent a few days with her before—"

His father waved that off. "Got to trust yourself."

"But..."

"I know. Julie, the divorce. The accident. You learn from it, and you move forward. Trust yourself. I do." A quiet vote of confidence.

Over the parallel bars, Tristan shared a long embrace with his father. Neither of them said any more, but it was all there in the hug. He'd always looked up to his father and put him on a pedestal, but this embrace felt different from all the others. It felt almost like a hug between equals. Mutual respect. Mutual appreciation. Gratitude. Love.

He drew back, one hand still on his father's shoulder. "I'll keep checking in on you. Don't slack on the exercises or Toni will crack the whip."

To the sound of his father's chuckle, he strode out of the clinic to the taxicab waiting to take him to the Santiago International Airport, where LATAM Airlines would take him home to Alaska.

THIRTY

Lulu woke up in the dark. She blinked, blinked again. Still dark. Opened her mouth to say something. Couldn't. There was something in her mouth. She tried to scream, to move her hands to her face, but couldn't do either of those things.

Hands wouldn't move. Feet wouldn't move. She was tied up, she realized. And blindfolded. And something was over her mouth.

What the fuck?

Her heart was beating a mile a minute and fear rang in her ears. Her thoughts moved sluggishly and her brain felt filled with fuzz. She focused on her breath, which was a technique she used to control occasional stage fright. If she was breathing, she was alive. That was good. A breath in, a breath out. Even. Count the seconds. Make the breath longer. Breathe out, same count. Okay, now she could think a little better.

That taste in her mouth. It wasn't just the cloth. There was an icky residue of something chemical too. She'd been drugged. Someone had drugged her. What was the last thing she'd drunk?

She'd bought a cappuccino with a shot of hazelnut syrup at

Gretel's Café. The scene came back to her. She'd chatted with the adorable blond sprite Gretel about how she'd challenged herself to survive an entire winter in Alaska, even though she used to be a carefree party girl. Lulu had never been a party girl, but she related to the girl's whimsical lighthearted spirit.

"Honestly, the hardest part, aside from learning how to chop wood and use an outhouse, was resisting the next door neighbor, Zander. I failed at that completely. No regrets on that, though."

After that fun conversation, Lulu had walked with her take-away cup of hazelnut cappuccino to the high school auditorium, where the dress rehearsal for *The Nutcracker* was taking place. But she hadn't had a chance to take even a sip of her drink, because she kept running into people along the way.

Ruthie Malone cornered her to talk about the Lost Harbor Truth Commission, which was looking into the group of bank robbers who had founded the town. Apparently one of the rene-gades was from England, and the journal he'd left behind included some Britishisms that Ruthie wanted to run by her.

After that, Trixie Tran waved her over to join a quick convo about the flyer for the next Harbor Hotties show. Trixie was one of the lead dancers, and in fact the one who'd roped her into it. They performed a mostly family-friendly version of burlesque— no exposed naughty bits, just some fun teasing dance routines.

The flyer was adorable—it featured a photo of one of Lulu's high kicks, with a photo-shopped salmon dangling from her big toe.

"That's one of the best uses of my high kicks I've seen." Lulu had laughed, and nearly taken a sip of her drink at that point. But a boy had skateboarded past her. Dylan Boone, the son of the fire chief. He'd jostled her elbow and then stopped to apologize. He mentioned that the teen rec center was throwing a holiday fundraiser. She and Trixie both bought tickets on the spot.

When had she finally drunk her hazelnut cappuccino? Not

until she was backstage, doing her stretching exercises. In fact, that was the last thing she remembered. She'd had one leg up on a desk to stretch her hamstring. She'd positioned her phone to take a selfie of herself to send to Tristan. But as soon as she opened a text box to send it, a sudden dizziness had struck her. She'd staggered out of the stretch and plopped onto the floor. Then nausea had seized her by the throat.

Afraid she was about to throw up, she'd crawled to her feet and stumbled out of the auditorium by way of the back exit. The fresh air had helped, but she was still dizzy. No one was around, and she remembered being relieved that she could vomit in peace.

But then someone had appeared out of nowhere.

As she hauled in deep breaths, bent over, her hands resting on her knees, someone had come up behind her. "Are you okay?" a woman's voice had asked. "Let me help you."

By that point, she was flickering in and out of consciousness. She'd barely noticed anything about the woman except that she spoke with a slight accent. Weak, nauseous, dizzy, she hadn't resisted as the woman guided her toward the street. If it had been a man, would she have fought back? Would she have known it was a kidnapping?

A car. There had been a car idling behind the high school. A very plain and ordinary car, like a Subaru. A red Subaru, similar to a hundred other red Subarus in Lost Harbor. The woman had pushed her into the backseat. Once she was horizontal, she'd nearly blacked out.

But not before she saw a man at the steering wheel. He wore a fleece-lined hat with ear flaps and sunglasses, meaning he was almost completely unrecognizable. But not for her, not with her memory for faces.

It was Mr. Bad Guy himself. Seb Antonov.

Tristan had left her a message about him and Maya had

warned her to stay on the lookout, and even suggested that she move out of her cabin temporarily. Lulu had intended to move back to the Sweet Harbor B&B as soon as she could manage it. Never in her wildest dreams would she have anticipated that he'd show up the very next day.

"Take her phone," he'd growled to the woman.

Dimly, Lulu had realized she still had her phone in her hand from taking her selfie. There was a text box already open, and she'd tried to press send. Then realized that she should text something besides a crotch shot of her stretching. Hit a bunch of random letters because her coordination was shot. And then her phone had been ripped from her hand.

Had she managed to send a message? She had no idea. Even if she had, it was probably gibberish. Besides, Tristan was almost eight thousand miles away. A twenty-hour plane flight. She should have sent her stupid gibberish crotch shot to Maya Badger.

She clamped her teeth onto the fabric of the gag and worked it down her face. It wasn't tied so tightly that she couldn't maneuver her way out of it. The man wasn't trying to suffocate her, obviously. If he wanted her dead, she'd be dead already.

Finding that thought at least a little comforting, she tackled the ties around her hands next. Fortunately for her, the man—or the couple, since he was working with the mystery woman who had "helped" her—hadn't used zip ties. By twisting her wrists this way and that, gritting her teeth against the pain, she was able to free her hands from the bindings. They obviously hadn't counted on her being as flexible as she was. Next, the blindfold, which was easy once her hands were free.

Even without the blindfold, she could barely see anything in the darkness. How long had she been out? Was it night already? Hard to tell because she was in a room with no source of light anywhere. Even the windows seemed to be covered with blackout shades.

These days it got dark by five o'clock. The rehearsal had been scheduled for nine, and she'd made sure to be on time. Had the drugs in that drink knocked her out for an entire day?

She thought back to Gretel's Café. Obviously, Gretel hadn't messed with her drink, but the cup had sat there on the counter while they talked about surviving Alaskan winters. And actually —wow, it just came back to her.

Another woman had been ordering at the same time and their drinks had gotten switched. She'd taken the lid off and said, with a slight accent, "Excuse me, I think I have the wrong drink. I ordered tea, and this appears to be foam."

Laughing, they'd exchanged their cups and Lulu hadn't given it another thought. She called up the vague image of the woman, who she hadn't recognized. Gretel hadn't seemed to know her, either. She'd been wearing dark glasses and a wool coat and a silver pashmina, which was more of a city outfit. Lulu had made the quick assumption that she was from Anchorage, here on some kind of business.

Although she'd never seen the face of the woman who had pushed her into the Subaru, she could safely assume the two were one and the same. She must be working with Antonov, either for money or because they were partners.

Smart. She would have recognized Antonov instantly if he showed his face in public. So would Maya Badger or any of the other police officers in town. Of course they wouldn't have been looking out for an unfamiliar woman showing up in Lost Harbor in a wool coat and pashmina.

So she'd been kidnapped by Mr. Bad Guy and a female accomplice. Clearly, he'd escaped from jail and come back to grab her. But why? Revenge? Anger that she'd messed up his last kidnapping attempt?

And where on earth had he taken her?

She could at least try to answer that question.

She reached for the rope at her ankles, then realized with a snort that she still wore her *Nutcracker* costume, which was a ridiculous version of a sea slug. Dark gray tights and leotard, with black leg warmers and a black fuzzy vest. Hey, it could be worse. She could have been kidnapped in her burlesque outfit, which exposed a lot more of her skin.

She was just about to untie her ankles when footsteps sounded outside, crunching in the snow. She quickly put the blindfold and gag back in place, then settled into the same position she'd woken up in. Hopefully everything would stay in place. Maybe she'd have an edge if the kidnapper didn't know she'd mostly freed herself.

A wedge of light swept across the floor as the door opened, then closed again. Someone was here.

THIRTY-ONE

Tristan had been checking his phone ever since he got off the plane in Anchorage, but the only text he'd gotten from Lulu was some kind of weird selfie with a bunch of orgasmic-looking random letters. Nothing since then, which set off all kinds of alarm bells.

Since he and Toni were essentially switching places, she'd left her truck at the Lost Harbor airport for him. He drove right to the police station, where a number of law enforcement types had already gathered.

Maya stood at the head of the group, joined by one of her sergeants, Darius Boone, Nate Prudhoe and a few of the volunteer firefighters, and even the former mayor, Dan Shipp, who had recently joined the state troopers.

She beckoned Tristan to join them. "We're formulating a search plan now. The last time anyone saw Lulu was at the high school auditorium before the rehearsal."

"She sent me a text from there. A selfie. I haven't heard anything from her since."

"One of the kids in the show says she saw Lulu with a woman in a wool overcoat. Fancy was the word she used."

A woman? That was a surprise.

"Has anyone seen Antonov?"

"No, but that doesn't mean much. No one saw him the last time he came through. He's obviously good at staying off the radar."

"So what's the plan? We're looking for a woman in a wool coat?" Tristan rubbed his bleary eyes. The flight from Chile to Alaska took nearly an entire day, and he was exhausted.

Darius spoke up. "Me and most of my crew will fan out down the peninsula."

"The rest of us will help with police interviews, see if we can't get some more leads," added Nate Prudhoe.

"I'm on that task as well." Ethan James, the investigator, who'd been propping himself against the wall, gave Tristan a little nod.

"It's thanks to Ethan that we know about the woman in the coat," explained Maya. "We're pulling out all the stops. The Feds are monitoring the situation too."

"We're here to help too," a familiar voice called from the doorway. Tristan turned around to see Bash Rivers—his best friend and his sister's fiancé—and a gaggle of high-school-age kids. This must be his first batch of fight camp students. "Put us to work wherever you need us."

He met Tristan's gaze with a slight smile. Bash was a force in and out of the ring. With him on the hunt for Antonov, their chances just went up.

"If you ask me, it's all a waste of time." Shipp—State Trooper Shipp—scratched at his chin. "How well do we know this girl, anyway? Maybe she just up and left. She's not local. She's not even American." He was an intimidatingly large man, but even so, Tristan wanted to knock his teeth out.

"I know her," he said firmly. "She's definitely missing. No doubt about that. Maya, your plan is fine, but you left out something important."

Trooper Shipp scoffed at him as he hooked his thumbs on his belt. "You're gonna jump in and save the day, son? You couldn't even last a week in the mayor's race."

Tristan's anger flared at his patronizing tone. "We got the right mayor in the end, and that's all that matters."

The former mayor bared his teeth at that dig.

Maya ignored the back-and-forth. "What are we leaving out, Tristan?"

"The ocean."

As a ring of blank faces gazed back at him, he gestured widely with one arm, indicating Misty Bay.

"I studied up on Antonov while I was on the plane from Chile. He has a pattern. He always goes for the ocean when he's trying to hide out. That's why he was on the *Northern Princess* to start with."

"Damn *Northern Princess*," Nate complained. "Always was trouble."

The others all murmured their agreement.

Maya narrowed her eyes at Tristan. "My cruisers aren't the oceangoing kind. Do you have a plan?"

"I do."

She assessed him for another long moment, then gave him a nod. "Then go. You're in charge of the ocean search."

In charge. For a moment, he hesitated. When people followed his lead, they got hurt. Then, just as quickly, his doubt evaporated. Lulu needed him. That was what mattered right now. "On it," he said crisply.

"Let me know what you need, and stay in touch. No confrontations with Antonov. That goes for everyone except law enforcement. Got it?"

"Got it."

"Everyone else, get to work."

Tristan strode out of the station and fired off a text, then another and another, to everyone on his harbor phone list. *Urgent meeting at the Olde Salt in fifteen minutes.*

Half an hour later, the entire Lost Harbor fishing fleet had assembled in the weather-beaten old saloon. About twenty-five boat captains, four times that many crew members, and a fair number of "harbor rats," the workers who kept the boardwalk running in the summer and had lots of time on their hands in the winter.

Tristan rang the old bell that hung over the bar. In the old days, when someone rang the bell it meant drinks for everyone in the place. Celebrations, extra-big catches, lost bets, that kind of thing. His sister had ended that practice after too many young fishermen had spent their entire payout on one round of drinks.

But the heavy bronze bell still brought back memories of the wild old days.

"We have a missing person to find," he told the group. "This is Lost Harbor, and we don't let people disappear on us. She's someone you might not know, but she's someone I care for. She risked her life for a little boy and she needs our help. Are you with me?"

Pedro Davila, one of the most old-timey of the old-timers, spoke up. "Who's missing?"

"Lulu. The woman from the cruise ship."

"*Lulu?* Damn, we know Lulu. Helluva dancer. Good kid. Where'd she go?" asked Davila.

"That's the part I don't know. But I know something's wrong."

Should he mention her text? It was nothing but a bunch of letters that didn't make sense, but it started with an "h" and that was enough for him—combined with Raul's warning and the fact that she'd vanished. And that selfie looked like something she'd probably retake if she had time.

He scanned the motley collection of weathered, stoic faces before him. Most were men, but there were some women in the group as well. They were experienced, skilled, self-reliant, gutsy, hardworking people. And right now they were looking back at him with expressions ranging from expectant to reserved.

And he realized that he couldn't ask anything of anyone until he got something out of the way first.

"I need to say something to you all. I'm sorry I dumped out of the mayor's race. My heart wasn't in it, but I need to be accountable. I should have given you all a heads up first."

"Why'd you run if you didn't want to?" Deke Armstrong crossed his arms over his chest.

"Make my father proud," he said after a moment. "Live up to the legend."

"Victor always stood up for us," Pedro grumbled.

Ouch. "I know he did. But this town didn't need me for mayor. We needed Malcolm."

Old Crow, who didn't fish anymore but was still an essential part of the community—and Malcolm's cousin—nodded along. "He's right. Give Malcolm a chance. There's more than just fishermen in this town."

With that support, Tristan gained even more confidence. "I dropped out because I thought it was the right thing for me and for Lost Harbor. But I'll always stand up for the fishing fleet. You all know me. You know where my heart is. Right here, in this harbor, this town, this room. That's the whole reason I let you talk me into running for mayor. I mean, before I came to my senses."

Laughter broke out and he knew they were coming back around to him.

"I love my dad," he continued. "I've always looked up to him. But I'm my own person."

"You gotta be your own man," Yakov agreed. "That's why I switched from salmon to crab-fishing. Nearly broke my papa's heart."

Others in the group murmured their agreement. Tristan felt like laughing. What was this, a fishermen's meeting or a group therapy session? Sometimes they weren't too far apart, especially when you added in enough rum.

A sense of love swelled his heart. He knew these guys—and women—so well. They'd seen each other through all kinds of hell —divorces, deaths, drinking problems, any kind of drama you could think of. Feuds, brawls, the occasional bar knifing...the stories went on.

And of course it worked both ways. They'd watched him grow up. Even the younger ones had seen him go from carefree harbor kid to driven fishing boat captain to the man he was today. Older and wiser and ready to get back in the game.

All the games.

He cleared his voice and stood even taller. "I might not be mayor, but I'm not going anywhere. You can count on that. But right now, we're needed out there on the water. Lulu's missing and she needs us. Are you with me?"

THIRTY-TWO

The intruder paused and Lulu felt eyes on her. Probably checking to see if she was awake.

She groaned, as if she was just waking up. Footfalls approached her, and hands came behind her head to untie the gag. She thought about biting the hand but that conflicted with her "find out what's going on" strategy. "Where...what...what happened?"

Good thing she had performance experience. She sounded just as weak and scared as a kidnapping victim ought to.

For some reason, she didn't *actually* feel scared. She wasn't sure why not. Maybe it was because she'd been through so much in the past couple of years. This didn't even rate on her tragedy Richter scale—although of course that depended on Antonov's ultimate plans for her.

"I'm not going to hurt you," said a man's raspy voice. "Though I wouldn't mind it, so behave."

"Who...what...where am I? Who are you?"

"You know who I am."

She sighed. "Seb. It's been too long. What on earth are you doing back in Alaska?"

"I had something to come back for. You're going to make me some money."

"I barely make enough money for myself. How am I going to do that?"

"You should work on your self-esteem." The man's voice had a touch of an accent, and she remembered Maya saying that he was a Romanian national. But borders seemed to mean nothing to him.

"Thanks for the tip, Kidnapper. As soon as you let me go, I'll book a session with a therapist. You might want to do the same, because if you're thinking ransom, you've gone off the deep end."

"Louise Spencer-Bennington. Fifty-third in line for the British throne."

"Are you planning to off fifty-two people? Because that's a very complicated plan. Besides, my mother was fifty-third in line. I'm nothing."

"I'm not going to off anyone. I'm not a killer."

"That's good to know."

"Unless someone irritates me," he added menacingly.

"Same, man. Same."

He snorted out a laugh, which gave her a weird boost of confidence. Despite being drugged and kidnapped, she still had the ability to make a person laugh. "In case you didn't know, both my parents are dead. My closest relatives are like, second cousins and so forth. My grandparents cut me off long ago. They won't care what happens to me."

"Maybe not. But they'll care about their good name. They did a good job erasing all mention of your mother after she fucked that postman. Now your grandfather is being considered for a big post in the new government."

"Is that right? I should really follow the news more."

She knew that Richard Spencer-Bennington was a political mover and shaker, but that was where her interest ended.

"You should. He could be named Minister of the Interior. But if it comes out that they abandoned your poor sick mother and ignored you, there will be a scandal. I'm surprised you didn't think of this yourself. Blackmail material is just as good as gold."

Her stomach twisted at the idea of her mother's life story being used to harm her grandparents. Mama had always insisted that she was in charge of all the decisions in her life. She'd *chosen* to break with her parents. She'd chosen to raise Lulu far outside the usual lifestyle of a Spencer-Bennington.

At the end, she'd reached out to her parents to let them know she was dying. A conversation had happened, but Lulu hadn't been part of it. All her mother had said afterwards was that she was at peace now, and so were they.

Ironic that after all the work to keep Lulu out of the Spencer-Bennington orbit, the kidnapper was dragging her right into it.

"What can I say? I guess I don't have your knack for crime."

"I'm going to take your blindfold off now so I can take some pictures. And there's this."

With no other warning, he socked her on the side of her face, just below her cheekbone. The shocking pain slammed through her.

"It's really just for show," he said, indifferently. "But don't forget that I can do this again whenever I want."

She fought the impulse to put her hand to her cheek. Everything in her wanted to do so, but that would tip him off that her hands were free. It took all her willpower to keep her hands behind her back as if they were still tied together. Her cheekbone throbbed and she felt her eye swell up.

"The show must go on," she managed.

He untied the blindfold and she blinked up at him. He wore a bandana over his face, which pissed her off because it made her think of Tristan. She hated him. For the terror he'd caused Raul, for blowing up Tristan's truck, for punching her...and for stomping all over her mother's memory with his nasty schemes.

She didn't care much about her grandfather's ministry position, or whether he'd have to come up with half a million dollars. But the idea that her mother's life would be reduced to blackmail material bothered her. A lot.

"Look scared," he ordered her.

She obliged him, putting on a terrified expression.

"That's too much. It looks fake."

It wasn't the first time she'd gotten that feedback. Apparently she had one of those faces that were *too* expressive. "So you're a director now?"

"Just do it again."

This time she channeled the pain radiating from the bruise on her cheek. That satisfied him, and he put away his camera. She wondered why he wasn't using a phone, then realized that it might be possible to trace the location of the photo that way. Maybe the old-school camera didn't collect metadata like that.

He turned to go, and as much as she loathed him, she felt panic at the thought of being left alone again.

"Where's the woman you're working with? Shouldn't someone be here keeping an eye on me?"

Antonov snorted. "She's keeping warm at a hotel. My fault for choosing a spoiled rich bitch."

"That explains the expensive pashmina." Lulu twisted her face and winced. Antonov strode toward the door.

"Wait. Where are we? What if I have to go to the bathroom?"

"Do you?"

"Not yet, but I'm sure I will soon. Don't tell me you didn't come up with a plan for that."

"I'll be back in an hour and you can go outside. Can you wait an hour?"

"Yes."

An hour. She could do a lot with an hour. She wondered where her phone was. Maybe they'd left it close by somewhere and she could send a text to someone. Maya Badger or Toni. If she could let someone know where she was, maybe they could find her before Antonov did too much damage.

Her kidnapper put the blindfold back in place, but he left off the gag.

"You know, maybe it makes more sense to work together," she said. "Like you said, I have no real loyalty to the Spencer-Benningtons. I'm definitely not a spoiled rich bitch. Why don't you let me go free and we'll figure this out?"

"How about this. You do exactly what I say, behave yourself, and I'll think about it."

She heard the patronizing tone in his voice, and smiled to herself. He didn't take her seriously, and that was exactly what she wanted. He believed he could use the possibility of working together as a carrot. That would make him assume he had control of the situation, and maybe relax his guard.

That was her hope, anyway.

"Yes sir. I'll behave, as long as you consider it. I can bring a lot to the table."

"Like what?"

"I'm not sure exactly, but I'll do some brainstorming. It's not like I have anything else to do."

He chuckled. "You do that. This will be good."

In the darkness behind the blindfold, she heard him walk away. The door opened and closed. She stayed very still, listening to the crunch of snow and ice, then a short time later heard the sound of a diesel engine. He must have a truck instead of that red Subaru.

She waited until the sound vanished, then waited some more. Tuning into the sounds from outside, she heard the occasional chirp of a winter chickadee, and the croak of a raven. A remote cabin in the woods? Was she in Lost Souls Wilderness? After a time, she made out the quiet hiss of waves on rocks.

She was near the ocean.

That seemed like a clue, although with the extensive coastline around here, probably not much of one.

When she was absolutely sure that no other human sounds were to be heard, she sprang into action. She pulled off the blindfold, untied her ankles, and scrambled to her feet. First up, a thorough search of the space where she was being held. It was an old cabin with no sign of kitchen or bathroom facilities—what they called a dry cabin. A hunter's cabin? Old homestead? The only thing she found that could help identify it was a weathered wooden sign dangling from a nail in the wall.

Fishermen Reel Them In, the words painted over a buxom fifties pinup.

Other than that, the place had been cleaned out, and her things were nowhere to be seen. Of course it had been too much to hope that they would have left her phone within reach.

She drew back the blackout shade and looked at the expanse of snow and trees outside. At least it was still day and not night. The shoreline must be somewhere past the trees, out of sight. Nothing gave her any clues about where she was. She could be miles from the nearest settlement of any kind.

Her heart sank, since that information didn't offer much chance of escape. It would be crazy to leave here in nothing more than a sea slug costume with no idea what direction to head in.

It would probably be better to take her chances with the kidnapper. Maybe when he let her out to pee, she could spring a high-kick on him. Then take his vehicle and drive to the nearest road. Or use his phone and call Maya Badger.

Or Tristan.

Even though he was so far away, thinking of Tristan calmed

her. If he got that last-minute text, he'd know something was wrong. He would alert the authorities—Maya or the FBI.

But she couldn't rely only on Tristan grasping that she was in trouble. She had to come up with a plan.

Maybe her best bet was to run down to the shoreline and hope there were rocks where she could hide out, like the breakwater in Lost Harbor. But what if there weren't any? Tristan had told her about the enormous tides in Misty Bay. She didn't fancy getting drowned when the tide came in. Also, her footprints would be visible in the snow. It would be easy for the kidnapper to follow her.

Just as it would be easy for her to follow the kidnapper.

Yes! That was it. She could use his footsteps to walk to where he'd parked his vehicle. Then she could climb a tree and lie in wait like a panther. A sea slug panther. As soon as he got to the cabin, she'd climb down and take his truck.

Except that she'd be hanging out in a tree in the middle of winter, not to mention the snow she'd disturb while climbing the tree.

Damn it. She had no idea how much time had elapsed since the kidnapper left. For now, best to resume her position and keep thinking. Maybe the perfect moment for escape would appear. Maybe Tristan would properly interpret her text.

She went back to her corner, then realized that she'd left footprints in the dust. They blended in with the kidnapper's footprints, but it was still possible that he might notice them. Crap.

Oh well, she'd just have to take her chances. She didn't want to make more footprints while trying to erase the first batch. *Make sure to keep his attention*, she told herself. *Don't let him look at the floor.*

She settled back into her spot and pulled the blindfold back into place.

Then immediately burst into nearly uncontrollable laughter.

Well, Mama, I'm really living now. Just like you wanted. I'm a kidnapping victim! Blindfolded and held for ransom in a remote cabin in Alaska. How about that? In your wildest dreams, did you ever imagine?

In that moment, she could so clearly see her mother that she might as well have been there, right in front of her, laughing along with her.

Her laughter shifted to tears. Long gushing sobs that had nothing to do with being kidnapped, and everything to do with grieving for her mother.

She hadn't really cried at first. It wasn't the family way. Tears made her mother uncomfortable. Instead, she'd run. All the way around the world on a cruise ship. Then she'd stopped running and stayed in one place, filling up her time with rehearsals and classes and sexting with Tristan.

Now, unable to run, all alone, the grief washed over her and through her and wrung her heart inside and out.

When she was done, she lay breathless and exhausted on the floor.

You finished? She could practically hear her mother's brisk voice.

Yes. I think I am.

Beyond the grief, life beckoned to her, an enticing shimmer like sunlight on the bay. There was joy and hope and wonder in the world.

And then something struck her...pieces falling into place. What Antonov had said: *My fault for working with a spoiled rich bitch.* And the woman's accent. It was a very light accent, a mere hint of one, just like...Raul's.

Her gears started turning a mile a minute. Was it Raul's mother? Had she been working with Antonov all along? That would explain so much. Why it had been so easy to kidnap Raul.

Why his grandparents had never gone public. Why Antonov had been so protective of Raul and never done anything to hurt him.

Wow. Poor Raul. She needed to get out of here and make sure he was okay. She had to tell Tristan how she felt. Outside of this cabin, everything awaited her. Life. Love. All she had to do was claim it.

Well, and get out of here.

THIRTY-THREE

"Fuck it, Del Rey, you know you can count on us." Ralphie Reed spoke up from one of the stools, on which he swiveled back and forth like a kid. He was the ladykiller of the bunch, and Tristan had once come to blows with him when he'd ghosted Stacy, one of his deckhands. "We're just giving you a hard time, bruh. Where do you need us? What's your plan?"

Before answering, Tristan scanned the rest of the faces. "Does Ralphie speak for everyone?"

"Until you start speaking for us, I guess we're stuck with him," Pedro joked.

Even Ralphie laughed good-naturedly at that.

"Let me start by saying this guy, Seb Antonov, might be dangerous. He, or someone he hired, followed us across the bay to Lost Souls Wilderness in September. He fired a sniper rifle at the *Desperado*. He also blew up my truck. So I'm asking that you don't get close to him or try to engage in any way. Those are Maya's orders for all of us. We just want to know where he is. The police will take it from there. Everyone understand?"

There was some grumbling, but nothing serious. Boats and guns were a scary combination, and no one wanted to founder in the winter seas of Alaska.

"So you think he's got her in Lost Souls?" asked Ralphie. "Damn, I hate going out there in the winter. It's bleak AF."

"Then you're in luck. I don't think he took her there. It didn't work out for him last time, and like you said, it's hard out there in the winter. But on this side, there's a whole shoreline of places to hide out around here. Little getaway cabins closed down for the winter. Hunter's cabins. Ocean-view lodges, you name it."

"That's a lot of territory, Tristan." Deke Armstrong shoved his hands in the pockets of his canvas bomber jacket. He wore a black Grundens baseball cap, with his gray hair flowing in waves to his shoulders. He'd given up cutting his hair one year for Lent, then decided he liked letting it go free.

"Don't I know it. What do you think you all are here for? The free drinks?"

Through the scattered calls of "oh yeah" and "that's what I'm talking about," he added quickly, "Afterwards. Don't want to get Judy on my ass."

Judy Rand, who'd recently taken over as the manager in place of his sister, gave him a nod from behind the bar, where she and Old Crow were tidying up. She'd been listening closely as she wiped glasses with a bar towel. The ship's lanterns over the bar gave her brown skin a rich glow.

"I saw a boat leave out of the visitor tie-up when I was taking out the trash earlier," she said. "Didn't look familiar."

"What kind of boat?"

"Most boats look about the same to me. But it wasn't a fishing boat like what you all have. It was more of a..." She sketched an outline in the air. "Like a speedboat, I suppose."

Tristan glanced at Lucas Holt. "Harbormaster, anything you can do to figure out the mystery speed boat would be helpful."

"I know about it." Boris Clancy poked his head from behind one of the Russian fishermen and raised his hand. Tristan noted that he held his chicken in his arms—and that he was trying to hide it from Judy. Toni would have thrown him out on his ass for bringing his pet chicken inside. Maybe Judy would be more accommodating, but probably not. Was there an exception for emotional support chickens?

"Did you see it, Boris?"

"Yah. I sure did. Came in this morning and left a couple hours later. Was a man and a woman onboard. She wore one of them fancy scarves."

"Did you talk to them?"

"Oh no. No no no." Boris shuddered, every skinny limb shaking. "I don't like strangers. Or bad people."

Everyone knew Boris was "different," though no one really put a label to it. He was more sensitive than most people, but a person would be a fool to dismiss him. He often picked up on things that other people missed.

The Russian fisherman shifted so he could squeeze Boris' shoulder. "Was he a bad person, Boris? Did he hurt you?"

That was the other thing about Boris. Every single person in this harbor would defend him fiercely if someone tried to hurt him. Or his chicken, for that matter.

"No, but I got on my bike so he couldn't see me. He looked mean."

Judy leaned her hands on the bar and peered at Boris. "Is that a damn chicken in my bar?"

With a squawk of his own, Boris scuttled backwards toward the door.

"Wait," Tristan called after him. "What kind of boat was it?"

"Hewescraft twenty-five footer with twin engines. Black and silver with a white canopy." Another thing about Boris: he knew his boats.

"Horsepower on the engines?"

"Two-fifty each." With that, he flung open the door and fled to the boardwalk, where his chicken was always welcome.

"Judy, ma'am." Deke Armstrong raised his hand. "Maybe we should relax the rules about poultry coming in here, since we nearly had a rooster for mayor."

A murmur of agreement rose from the others.

Judy tossed her bar towel over her shoulder and shook her head at them all. "I've got half a mind to let in the chickens and keep the fishermen out."

"Nooo....we'll be good...shut up, Deke," chorused the fishermen.

Under normal circumstances, Tristan might find all this pretty entertaining. The back-and-forth between the fishermen also brought him great joy. But right now, he could have strangled them all. He lifted his voice to cut through the din. "We got our description, guys. That's progress."

"I'll look into it," said Lucas, joining him in his attempt to get things back on track. "If I learn anything more about this boat or its occupants, I'll let you all know. Keep your radios tuned to the storm frequency."

"Good idea," said Tristan. "Took the words out of my mouth."

From past experience navigating the wild storms that swept through Misty Bay, the fleet had designated a special channel for emergency situations. Outsiders didn't know about it, although of course they might stumble upon it. The kidnapper would be unlikely to do that, though, since he'd probably be monitoring the official police channels.

"So where you want us to start?" said Old Crow from behind the bar. "You're not going, are you?" Startled, Tristan cocked his head at the old fisherman. He'd recently retired and shifted into bartending. "We need someone here to hold down the fort."

"Find someone else for that. The *Ravenwing* always was a good hunter."

"All right. Well, thanks, Old Crow. That's above and beyond. I have some ideas about how to do this."

He laid out his plan. He'd divided the shoreline into sections, and assigned two boats to each section. They'd used the buddy system, except with fishing boats. "North of Deep Gulch, that's Deke and Pedro. Deep Gulch to Kimlik, Jacob and Erica." He kept going, using the familiar landmarks they all know so well. "Look out for anything out of place. A cabin that ought to be empty, a boat with a white canopy, lights where there shouldn't be any. Not just on shore, but on the water. He could have switched boats. He could be anchored somewhere. Anything you notice, let me know. I'm going to be onshore."

"Can I take the *Desperado*?" Ralphie asked right away. Although Ralphie was one of the most experienced deckhands in Lost Harbor, he'd never owned his own fishing boat. He'd never wanted the responsibility, he claimed.

"No," Tristan said automatically.

"It's one more boat out there looking for her," he pointed out.

Damn. The guy was right. Tristan ground his teeth at the thought of someone else driving his boat. The only time he allowed that to happen was when he needed some sleep. He only trusted a few of his crew members to take the wheel of his beloved boat. And Ralphie wasn't generally one of them.

But they needed all hands on deck, and all decks on the water. What was more important in the end, Lulu or the *Desperado*?

Sorry, Desp. You know I love you. But I have to go with Lulu here. I know you understand. You want her back too, right?

Weird that even though his boat was hundreds of yards away, floating peacefully at slip forty-two, he sensed the *Desperado's* silent agreement. *Bring back Lulu. That's what matters most.*

"Fine," he finally told Ralphie. "But take someone with you."

"There's that cute blond over at the art store, I was thinking—"

"Not a date," Tristan gritted. "Another experienced hand. See if Alicia's up for it. I trust her."

Ralphie's face fell. Alicia Watts had swatted down every play he'd made for her. She was a no-nonsense, hard-working hand who'd made enough money fishing to open a bookstore on the boardwalk. She certainly had no interest in a playboy like Ralphie.

"I'll text her," Ralphie grumbled.

"Everyone ready? Got your assignments? Let's go!" Tristan clapped his hands. "Remember to call me with anything you see. I'll be on the storm channel *and* I'll have my cell phone with me. I'll be in constant contact with Maya. Let's find Lulu and bring her home."

A cheer went up.

"Even if it isn't technically her home," he added under his breath. Only Old Crow heard that part from his spot behind the bar.

"Man, where've you been? This is Lulu's home, all right. Maybe she don't know it yet, but it is." Old Crow grinned at him, his weathered face creased in lines of amusement. "Never seen anyone make so many friends so fast. Everyone loves Lulu."

Everyone loves Lulu. Of course they did. Because she was a spark of light and joy and empathy and fun. And he'd do anything and everything in his power to make sure she was okay.

No, he was going to do more than that. He was going to make sure he had a chance to tell her what he'd only just realized himself. That he'd fallen helplessly, urgently in love with Lulu. He didn't want to just rescue her. After that, he wanted to tell her he loved her, and that he believed they were meant for each other, that strange, magnificent destiny had thrown them into each other's paths for a reason.

If that sounded superstitious, too bad. He was a fisherman after all.

THIRTY-FOUR

The next time Antonov came back, he took Lulu outside so she could relieve herself. The trickiest moment came when he reached behind her to untie her hands. She kept talking the entire time to distract him from the fact that her hands came loose so easily. It seemed to work, and she made a show of rubbing her wrists after he hauled her to her feet.

As he pulled her outside, she kept talking. Maybe she could pry something more out of him. The one topic she avoided was Raul's mother. Better to keep that knowledge as a hidden card up her sleeve, just in case.

"I still don't understand why you had to come all the way back to Alaska to find a kidnapping victim. Wasn't there someone closer to home? Not that I want you to kidnap anyone," she added quickly. "You should really find another line of work."

"Mind your business," was the only response she got.

They stopped in front of an outhouse that was practically rotting into the ground, tilting to one side.

"I'm supposed to go in *there*?"

"Unless you want me to watch you piss under a tree."

She definitely didn't want that. Squaring her shoulders, she gingerly pushed open the door and stepped inside. It smelled of must and dampness, but only faintly of feces. No one had pooped in here for a very long time.

And at least the kidnapper couldn't see her in here. Maybe there was something she could do while she was out of sight.

She squatted inside the frozen outhouse, squinting to block out the reality of the rough plywood structure and the toilet seat carved from driftwood. "How did you even know I'd still be here in Alaska?" she called to the man outside.

"Took a guess. Seemed you had something going with the fisherman. Tracked you on Instagram so I'd know if you left."

"I post there about once a month."

"Yeah. Nice photo of you in your costume. Helped me figure out where to grab you."

God, she was an idiot. Her own social media posts had helped him kidnap her? Great. She needed to be smarter than that.

Being smart meant she had to take action. She couldn't count on anyone finding her in this isolated spot. There had to be something she could do to help herself.

As she hovered above the toilet seat that she refused to touch, she ran through her options.

High kick to the throat. But if she missed, he'd make sure she paid for it. And he was well aware of her kicking prowess. He'd be ready.

Run for the vehicle. He probably had the key with him, so that wouldn't gain her anything.

Knock over the outhouse. She started to laugh, then stopped. That wasn't a bad idea. In fact...with her eyes now entirely adjusted to the dimness inside the outhouse, she carefully scanned every inch of it. There wasn't much. An empty basket to hold the used toilet paper. A piece of driftwood sitting next to an ancient roll of toilet paper. And there, hiding behind the toilet paper, something that might actually help her.

A Bic lighter.

Of course it might be empty after all this time. Out of lighter fluid. Just plain dead. But it was worth slipping into her bra.

"Time's up!" The kidnapper banged on the rickety door of the outhouse. "Come on out of there."

"Are we on a deadline?" She quickly pulled up her pants. She hadn't even peed; her body simply had no interest in this decrepit little shack. Didn't matter. She planned to escape soon enough anyway. That lighter snuggled under her left boob was going to get her out of here.

She preceded him back to the house, surreptitiously scanning the area for helpful details. The house was on a little rise, with the outhouse farther up the slope. Its view of the ocean was even better than the cabin's. The sun was low on the horizon to her left. That meant that she was probably not in Lost Souls Wilderness but on the peninsula side of the bay. Which meant she'd be able to access a road.

And then she realized something else. *She couldn't see a vehicle.* Bollocks, how long had it taken her to put that together? The outhouse must have traumatized the common sense out of her.

He hadn't been driving a car here. He'd been coming *by boat.* That was why it had sounded like a truck with a diesel engine. Maybe they'd ditched the car because someone might have seen her getting pushed into it. They'd transferred her to a boat, which meant this cabin probably had a little cove or a dock of some kind.

Inside the cabin, he retied her hands, but left her feet loose. He didn't bother with the gag or the blindfold, which she appreciated. "You know, it's silly to tie my hands up when there's nowhere to run to," she said.

"You're right. There's nowhere to run to. But I'm still tying you up, so get used to it."

She made a show of disappointment, although she felt confident she could get her hands free again. "When are you coming back? I'm hungry."

He plopped a bag of Lay's potato chips next to her, then a bottle of water. "Snacks. Water."

"How am I supposed to get those open?"

"You have teeth, don't you?"

"You're not a very agreeable kidnapper. Have you heard anything from my grandparents yet?"

He didn't answer, which she took as a *no*.

"I told you they don't care about me. You came all the way back to Alaska for nothing."

"You'd better hope that's not true, because if I don't get an answer by the end of today I'm getting out of this damn place and leaving you here."

Oh hell. He meant it. He wouldn't mind ditching her here to freeze to death. She couldn't count on her grandparents coming through for her. They never had before.

She had to get out.

As soon as he was gone—and she heard the faint sound of the engine that she now was sure belonged to a boat—she worked on freeing her hands again. It took longer this time. Her hands were cold from that trip to the outhouse, and he'd tied her even tighter.

When the ties finally fell away from her hands, she sat up and scrabbled inside her bra.

Please, little lighter of mine. Please still work. The first click did nothing, and her heart plummeted. The next one created a tiny spark. Biting her lip, chanting a prayer, she tried again. A small flame flared to life. *Thank God.*

Following the rough plan that she'd formed in the outhouse, she dashed outside and hurried back to the little structure. Dusk was falling fast, and pretty soon it would be too dark to see anything. Her only chance was now.

She crumpled all the toilet paper into loose balls and piled it in the driest looking corner of the outhouse. The toilet seat went in next—after she cracked it into splinters under her knee.

Then, after praying the old Bic had one more spark in it, she lit it all on fire.

After waiting for the flames to catch, she backed out of the outhouse and ran back to the cabin. Her hope was that someone would spot this beacon and come investigate. All she had to do was wait inside for a fire engine, or just a random passerby who spotted the smoke.

Every few seconds, she peered out of the cabin and checked on the smoke billowing from the top of the outhouse. She could feel waves of heat from the fire, but there was enough distance so that the cabin wasn't in any jeopardy. Neither were the surrounding trees, whose branches were laden with snow. The last thing she wanted to do was touch off a forest fire, after all.

The outhouse burned like a torch in the still air. Smoke spiraled upwards, taking with it all her hopes for a rescue. *Come on, come on*, she muttered out loud.

The roof of the outhouse caved in and the little structure collapsed in on itself. The smoke grew blacker and thicker—more visible? Or less visible, because it was almost night now? *Come on, come on.*

IT DROVE Tristan crazy to be patrolling the roads instead of the sea. His natural habitat was the ocean; that was where he felt the most confident. But someone had to be available onshore to investigate possible sightings.

Lucas had offered up his truck, which had a short-band radio that could be tuned to the fleet's storm channel. If someone spotted something on the shoreline, but couldn't tie up to check it out—which was very likely, given the bluffs and low tides and lack of easy landing—he could try to access it from the other direction.

Lucas also insisted on coming with him, and Tristan didn't argue. The buddy system was important. Since he knew his truck best, he drove while Tristan sat in the passenger seat with his cell phone and a detailed map spread out on his lap.

In the back of the truck, they'd loaded up snowshoes, skis, a rifle, a spotting scope, lights, a backpack full of protein bars, water, and first-aid supplies. Bethany Morrison and Nate Prudhoe—a doctor and a paramedic—had helped them pack everything they might need. They were waiting back in Lost Harbor, ready to spring into action if they were needed.

This was Lost Harbor at its best, Tristan thought. Not squabbling over cruise ships and tattoo parlors and roosters running for mayor. Actually pulling together to help someone.

A few false sightings wasted most of their daylight. The darker it got, the more Tristan's tension grew. He and Lucas didn't talk much, choosing to keep alert to their surroundings.

So it took Tristan by surprise when Lucas said, "Been wanting to tell you, I heard a rumor through the harbormaster grapevine."

"What rumor?"

"The president of APFA is stepping down. You should put in for it. You'd get a lot of support." APFA was the Aurora Bay Fishermen's Association, one of the most powerful industry groups in this part of Alaska. The president did things like attend state legislature meetings in Juneau, and lobby the federal government. Tristan had seen many clips of the president of APFA talking to the news media. The current president was a woman from Sitka who'd won high marks from just about everyone.

"Hard shoes to fill," said Tristan.

"You're used to that."

"Huh?"

"Any son of Victor Gammelgaard has hard shoes to fill. And any son of Victor has the means to do it."

Tristan's heart warmed at the respect Lucas obviously had for his father.

"Scratch that. *You* have the means to do it."

Tristan had to admit he was honored that Lucas thought that highly of him. And the job did appeal to him. He was just starting to say, "I'll think about it," when Ralphie Reed's voice came over the radio.

"Spotted a fire near Spruce Bay. About a quarter mile south of it. Want me to check it out?"

Tristan aimed his head lamp at the map on his lap. "Looks like there's an old pier in that area from coal-mining days."

His adrenaline surged. Maybe this was it. Two things worked in its favor—a place for a boat to tie up, and an unusual fire. "We'll go, Ralphie. You stay close."

"Ten-four."

Lucas located a turnoff that hadn't been plowed in days. Good thing the truck had plenty of clearance. After rattling toward the shore a ways, they too spotted the smoke. A thin trail of it drifted toward the sky—the tail end of a fire soon to expire. It was nearly invisible against the darkening sky.

"Probably nothing," Lucas murmured. "Burn barrel."

Tristan said nothing. His nerves felt stretched to the limit. Night was here, and if they didn't find something soon, they'd have to wait until tomorrow. What if Lulu was out in the wilderness somewhere? What if he was wrong and the kidnapper had taken her into Lost Souls? Or driven her up the coast to the damn airport?

But he didn't believe so, simply because the further away he took her, the more chance she'd have to make a fuss and escape.

And Mr. Bad Guy knew, more than anyone, how resourceful Lulu was. He wouldn't take a chance like that.

They made their way down a bumpy two-track drive that hadn't seen a plow in weeks. When they reached a turnoff where a massive spruce tree had fallen across the other fork, they continued on, forging through the half foot of snow. The shadowy forest closed in around them. It seemed to take forever.

What if it was just another false lead? They'd be stuck here at the end of a two-track road in the middle of the forest with no idea where Lulu might be. What if he'd made one wrong decision after another? What if harm came to Lulu because of him?

Got to trust yourself.

He drew in a long breath, shoved his doubts aside, and focused on helping Lucas navigate the icy road.

THIRTY-FIVE

Shit. No one was coming. Despair made Lulu slump against the wall. Maybe there was no one around to see the smoke. Maybe seeing smoke in the winter wasn't unusual. People had burn barrels, after all. Smokehouses. Why would anyone go out of their way to investigate a fire this small? A fire that had burned hot and bright, but was already going out.

Plan B. She needed a Plan B, desperately. She couldn't stay in the cabin any longer because the kidnapper would know she set the outhouse fire. Maybe she should make her way to the shoreline and steal his boat after he tied up. *Yes.*

She did a quick search of the cabin for anything that would help keep her warm out there, but there was nothing. Her sea slug costume would have to do. Steeling herself, she stepped into the clearing.

Smoke stung her eyes and for a moment she thought she was hallucinating. Someone *had* seen the smoke. In the shadows at the edge of the clearing stood a young girl, about thirteen or so. Her white snowsuit and pink knit cap with a pompom make her easy to spot in the darkness. Lulu felt a moment of envy for her warm winter clothes.

But the girl looked off...ill, even. Her eyes were swollen and her nose red. A rash covered her face.

"Hullo there," Lulu called to her. "I'm Lulu. What's your name? Do you live around here?"

The girl coughed, then said, "Iris," in a hoarse voice. "I'm sick. Everyone's sick. We don't know what it is. Our generator died and we can't charge our phones. We need help. I tried to drive to Grantview but a tree fell across the road. I saw your fire..." She stopped to cough again. "Can you call for help?"

Lulu's heart turned over. She was in such dire straits herself, how could she be of any use to this girl? Of all moments to run into someone even worse off than her. She'd just have to do whatever she could. "I don't have a phone. But I'll help any way I can. Maybe together we can get the tree off the road. Lead the way, Iris."

She bounded across the clearing, wondering if she should try to mask her footsteps from the kidnapper. On the other hand, if rescue came, she'd want them to follow her. So she decided to take her chances. If Iris had seen the fire, surely someone else had too.

"How far do you live?" she asked as she followed the girl through the woods. Iris had a headlamp, luckily. That single beam of light provided their only illumination. Lulu didn't have snow boots like the girl did, so she aimed for the deep footprints Iris left.

"I don't know. A mile maybe."

A mile of walking in the snow in black neoprene wetsuit footies. At least they were waterproof. And at least she was free...for now.

"You said your whole family's sick? How many?"

"Thirty."

"*Thirty?*"

"It's several families. There's a longhouse and a farm and we all live together. We're homeschooled. First my dad got sick, then everyone else did too. Everyone's in bed and can hardly move. I couldn't even get up at first, but then I felt a little better so I got out of bed and brought water to everyone. My dad told me to get help any way I could. But I couldn't." She gave a sob and a shiver.

"Hey, hey. You came and got me, didn't you?"

"Are you a nurse or a doctor?"

"No. But I have a lot of experience with sick people. And maybe I can get that tree off the road for you. There's got to be something I can do."

Iris paused to catch her breath. She glanced over her shoulder at Lulu and gestured at her neck. "You should put that on."

Lulu touched her neck, realizing that her blindfold was still there, knotted around her neck. "Oh, this is a blindfold...long story, I'll tell you some time."

Apparently too ill to be intrigued, Iris just shook her head. "Over your nose," she explained. "So you don't get sick too."

"Of course. Right." *Thank you, Seb Antonov,* she thought as she settled the black cloth over both her mouth and her nose, then tightened the knot at the back. *If I don't get sick, I guess I owe you one.*

"Do you ever think that things happen for a reason?" she asked Iris, her voice muffled by the dense fabric.

"What?"

"Never mind." She gestured for the girl to continue on. Using Iris' bootsteps, she followed after her, blocking out the cold seeping in around the edges of her dance costume. Each step crunched on the icy snow. Silent trees watched from all sides. The darkness intensified along with the cold. A winter night in the wilds of Alaska.

I'm really living now, Mum. I'm tromping through the snowy woods in a sea slug costume using my kidnapper's blindfold as a mask so I don't get a mysterious disease. How about that?

And then it occurred to her that she might get sick. Or she might actually freeze in these woods before she'd walked that mile. Or...or...or...

Tristan. She wanted to see Tristan again. Just one more time, she wanted to touch him and kiss him. If she got the chance, she'd drop the jokes and the teasing and the flirting and tell him the truth. She loved him.

AFTER AN ENDLESS RATTLING DRIVE, Lucas and Tristan finally reached a small clearing lit by the last embers of a small structure fire. Beyond the fire sat a rough abandoned cabin.

Leaving his headlights on, Tristan swung out of the truck. He snapped on his headlamp so he could scan the rest of the area. "Hello?" he called.

No answer. He heard the sound of the driver's door closing, then joined Lucas at the pile of charred wood that used to be...

"Looks like an outhouse burned down," said Lucas. "That's odd."

"Then someone burned it down. No reason it would just spontaneously catch on fire." Tristan played his headlamp across the snow. "Footprints. Lots of them."

"Let's check the cabin."

Stepping around the existing footprints, just in case, they made their way into the cabin. Empty. Goddamn it. Tristan breathed deep, smothered in disappointment, and smelled...strawberries.

"She was here," he said with absolute certainty.

Lucas didn't argue. "Think she set the outhouse on fire and then ran? Why?"

"No idea. Let's see if we can find her trail."

They went outside and searched the clearing for any signs of Lulu's footprints. The area between the fire and the cabin was filled with a jumble of prints. Another overlapping set of prints led to a path that clearly went toward the shoreline. Tristan followed it, spotted an old concrete pile of pier blocks at the water, and the running lights of the *Desperado* just offshore.

He set his headlamp to a flashing pattern and called Ralphie. "Do you see us?"

"Sure thing. Is Lulu there?"

"She was. We're on the right track. Can you stick around here and give me a call if that Hewescraft shows up?"

"Aye, Captain."

"Found something," Lucas called. Tristan jogged back up the path and found the other man crouching over a set of footprints to the south of the clearing. "I see two sets here, but then they kind of meld into one. And one of them...looks small. Like a kid. Does Lulu have small feet?"

"Not especially, no."

"Well, what do you think?"

It only took Tristan a micro-second to decide. He had no idea why a kid was involved in this situation. Maybe Lulu hadn't been the only one kidnapped. But if there was one thing he knew for sure about Lulu, it was that she'd be making sure no harm came to that kid. "Let's follow them."

Lucas nodded. They went back to the truck and snapped on their skis, then shouldered their backpacks. Because he had no idea what they'd find, Tristan attached the ski raft straps around his hips and slung the rifle over his back. A moment later, they plunged into the dark woods.

The trail they followed wasn't an established path. Instead, it wound between trees and zigzagged past thick clusters of willows. The silence of the night was almost absolute, except for the sounds of their breathing and the swish of their skis through the snow.

"Do you remember anything about the houses nearby?" Tristan asked in a low voice.

"I think there's a compound of some kind around here. I remember hearing about a group that lives up here, they're macrobiotic or something."

"A religious group?"

"Not really. They just like growing their own food. They come down to Lost Harbor to gather seaweed and pick cranberries. They weave their own cloth and yarn, that sort of thing. Good folks, at least when I've talked to them."

"Not kidnappers or allied with kidnappers?"

"That, I couldn't say. I guess we'll find out soon enough."

Maybe. Or maybe this was a wild goose chase. Maybe he was making one bad decision after another. "Yeah," he said brusquely. His breath steamed into the cold air, with crystals of frost glittering in the beam of his headlamp. They looked like fairies dancing around him waving little frost sparklers.

Which made him think of Lulu.

"I love her," he said out loud.

"Huh?" Lucas called from behind him. Probably couldn't hear over the sound of his own skis.

He didn't answer, since he hadn't meant to say it aloud to begin with.

But it was true. He loved her. He knew in his bones that they were on her trail. Would she be alive? Hurt? Traumatized? She'd been through so much already. He had to be prepared for anything.

After about a mile of hard skiing, they rounded the last willow and caught sight of a large wooden-beamed structure the size of a cathedral. At the doorway, he saw a splash of pink and one of gray. Two people. The pink figure was small, and the black one, barely visible in the dim light shed by the automatic sensor light, tall and lanky, with legs that went forever.

"Lulu," he shouted, nearly stumbling over his skis to reach her.

"Tristan? Is that you? Oh my God!" She launched herself toward him. He kept skiing and she lurched through the snow in some kind of weird wetsuit, and then he was sweeping her off her feet and into his arms.

"You're okay. You're safe," he muttered frantically into her neck. "I was so fucking scared."

"*You* were scared. I had to set an outhouse on fire! I never want to do that again. I thought all the poop might make it explode."

He laughed, and couldn't stop from the sheer relief of hearing that lighthearted voice of hers. "God, I love you, Lulu. I'm *in* love with you. This is it. You and me. I mean, if you... me."

"*Yes*. Whatever you were going to say, yes. I love you, too. I do." She lifted her face so he could kiss her, which he did, fiercely, deeply, until she tore herself away. "But we have no time. People are sick in there. We have to help them. Iris is the only one who's mobile, and the poor girl's about to collapse. She says everyone else is in bed. Thirty people. And it's very infectious, so we have to be careful. Oh, and there's a tree blocking the road out."

"We saw the tree. It's okay. We got this." He pulled out his phone and called Ralphie. While he was waiting for the call to go through, he called to the girl in pink. "Iris. Does this place have a boat landing?"

"Just for dinghies," she answered. "You have to land on the beach."

Damn, that would make things more difficult. But not impossible.

"Yeah, Captain," Ralphie answered.

"We've got Lulu, but now there's another crisis. We need everyone to come to these GPS coordinates." He sent them along in a text. "We have thirty sick people who need to get medical help. They're infectious, so I only want two per boat, and wear some kind of face covering. Can you get everyone here?"

"On it."

"Oh, and you'll have to row in to a beach. There's no landing." Hearing Ralphie's groan—no one liked rowing in the winter—he said, "It is what it is. These folks need us, and we're their best bet right now."

"Of course. I mean, yes, Captain."

THIRTY-SIX

And that was how the famous Lost Harbor Boat Lift took place. It took the fleet hours to get all the ill residents of the compound into the dinghies and onto the boats. One by one, the Lost Harbor fishermen chugged at top speed toward home, where every fire engine, ambulance, and police car awaited them, their lights flashing on the boardwalk as if a carnival had moved in.

Maya Badger ordered everyone to use the proper biohazard suits, or some homemade approximation. Lulu spotted everything from bandanas to carpenter's masks. She stuck with her blindfold, considering it good luck at this point. She gave Tristan her gag, which he scowled at with such fury that she was surprised it didn't burst into flames.

He glared even more when he saw the bruise purpling her cheek. "That bastard is going to pay..."

"Yes, my love."

"Can I kiss you? Does it hurt?"

"No, it doesn't hurt. It's mostly numb from the cold. Kiss away."

He kissed her as if he never wanted to stop, as if each kiss was their first. As if each kiss was forever.

At the Misty Bay Regional Hospital, Bethany Morrison sealed off one wing so that the infection wouldn't spread. She and the other doctors went to work treating symptoms and taking blood cultures to figure out what the group had come down with.

It was the most exciting thing Lulu had ever been part of, especially because she got to see Tristan Del Rey in "captain" mode, which was hands down the sexiest thing she'd ever witnessed. He kept his calm, came to quick, logical decisions, fired off commands that the others followed, and just generally demonstrated why everyone respected him.

When the last of the compound's residents had been loaded onto the *Desperado*, Lucas skied back through the woods to his truck, while she and Tristan rowed out to the *Desperado*. Tristan took command of his boat as Ralphie tended to their two passengers, who just happened to be young women.

Lulu joined Tristan in the wheelhouse, where he beckoned her to his side. She nestled blissfully under his arm as he stood at the wheel, steering them toward Lost Harbor.

"I have a surprise for you," he murmured. "They caught Antonov. Maya arrested him and handed him off to the FBI. They also located the woman in the wool coat. She isn't talking yet, but they're confident they have the right person."

"Mmm." Cozied under his arm, she barely cared about the kidnappers anymore, as long as they couldn't hurt anyone else. Raul was probably in for years of therapy, but he was a level-headed kid. She had faith that he'd be okay. "I have a surprise for you, too," she told Tristan.

"Yeah? What's that?"

"I've decided to settle down. I've had enough of roaming the world practicing my high kicks."

"That's very good news. If you're trying to decide where, I

have some ideas." His arm tightened around her. "One idea, really."

"Unless it begins with Lust and ends with R, I don't want to hear it."

She could sense his smile over her head. "Sometimes people like to get married when they settle down," he murmured.

A wild thrill danced through her. "I've heard something of the sort."

"I have some ideas about that, too. Well, one idea. You should marry me." The firm conviction in his voice sent electric prickles along her skin.

"I should?"

"Yes. Immediately."

"Immediately? That might be tricky, considering we're on a boat."

Even though there were three other people onboard, Lulu felt as if they were alone in the world, tucked into this wheelhouse, with wild adventure just outside. Sea spray splashed against the windows as they hit a swell. Tristan held her close so she didn't stagger. She'd never felt more alive.

"Yes, but don't forget. I can perform marriages."

He dipped his head and claimed her mouth in a kiss that held all the passion of the restless winter ocean, and then some.

"You can?"

"I am a captain, after all," he murmured wickedly. "And this is a boat. And you...you're my love."

They kissed for a long, long time. "I may want to have children," she finally said, when he'd kissed the breath out of her. "I seem to really like them."

"The sooner the better."

She detected no hesitation in his voice, no reluctance to take on the role of father. "You seem a little different since you got back," she noted.

"Yeah. I know who I am now, and what I want. I want you, babe."

She wrapped her arms around his solid chest. "Same, desperado. Same." After a moment, she added, "I also want to make sure that creep goes to prison for real this time."

"The sooner the better for that too."

"And I really, really, *really*..." She paused for effect.

"What? Anything, my love. Anything."

"Want to get out of this sea slug costume."

He threw his head back with a roar of laughter. It vibrated through her body, making her heart sing along with him. "Like I keep saying, the sooner the better."

Yeah. This was life. And this was where she belonged. With Tristan, chugging back to her new hometown...laughing.

LULU TWIRLED her way past the costumed members of the Rat King's Court toward the tall man already waiting in position. Tristan was playing the "God of Seaweed" to her Sea Slug. He wore a wig made of bunches of dried seaweed made by Zoe Bellini. The first time Lulu had seen him in it, she'd nearly peed herself laughing.

Along with the wig, he wore skintight shiny long johns and mud boots. The combination worked so well—wildly, erotically well—that every time they rehearsed, she jumped his bones the very second they were alone.

But tonight, for the grand opening night of Lost Harbor's quirky annual production of *The Nutcracker*, she had to focus on dancing instead of all the sex they were going to have afterwards.

On all sides of her, familiar faces watched and smiled. *The Nutcracker* was truly a community affair. All sorts of folks, especially young people, had been recruited to take part in the "entertain the Rat King" portion of the show.

Bo Briggs and Dylan Boone had put on a mock skateboard duel that had everyone howling.

Maggie, previously known as Spruce Grouse, had performed a knife-throwing act that brought gasps from the audience.

Her good friend Cara, the younger sister of Maya's boyfriend Rune, was playing Clara; she had real talent that Lulu had every intention of nurturing. There was even a role for Fidget, the harbormaster's old Irish Setter, whose paw Lulu had helped treat on the *Desperado*. He played Clara's dog, though he kept falling asleep at inconvenient moments.

Ruby, Megan's little girl, didn't care to perform, but she'd done something amazing for the show. She'd recorded various ocean sounds and seabird calls and offered them to the sound tech to include with the music. They added an authentic touch to the "Nutcracker at Sea" theme of the production.

It wasn't just the kids who were involved in the show. A crew of fishermen were playing sea otters; they kept popping their heads up behind the other dancers.

The Harbor Hotties burlesque group—Trixie and her friends —played sirens trying to shipwreck Clara and her boat pilot. Some of the volunteer firefighters—led by Nate Prudhoe—came to her rescue, playing orcas chasing away the sirens.

The whole show was hilarious, but also visually stunning thanks to Zoe Bellini's costuming and art direction. She'd really thrown herself into it, explaining to Lulu that she had to cram in lots of creative expression before her baby came and she got temporarily sidelined.

Padric Jeffers, her rock star husband, had written a song especially for the show. Every time Lulu heard it, it made her cry.

. . .

WHEN THE TIDE GOES OUT, no need for goodbyes
No need for tears when you're at sea
We'll meet again, my beautiful friend
And when we do, you'll see it's true
The dream goes on, and on and on,
And my heart is yours
wild as the ocean's kiss
deep as the ocean floor

PADRIC WAS GOING to perform it live for tonight's performance, and she hoped she didn't cry onstage and ruin her sea slug makeup. After the opening show, there was going to be a party backstage, catered by Alastair Dougal and Jessica Dixon from the Sweet Harbor Bakery. Her mouth was already watering just thinking of that feast.

As she twirled across the stage, she caught Tristan's eye. He winked at her, a quick flash of sea-gray, and braced himself for the lift.

As a cruise ship performer, she'd never included lifts in any of her acts. The can-can, her high-kicks, her comedy bits, none of them required a big strong man to catch her in midair. She and Tristan had rehearsed extensively, but you never really knew how something would go onstage.

Besides, every single one of their rehearsals had ended up with them naked. Something about the way his big hands guided her above his head, then held her there, supporting her pelvis as she balanced, turned her on every damn time.

"Am I ever going to be immune from wanting you?" she'd asked him after the last time, when they both lay sprawled on his living room floor, gazing up at the newly repaired ceiling.

"There's only one way. Move in with me. See if you get sick of me."

Hands interlaced, they smiled at each other, and Lulu knew there was no chance of that. They might quarrel—they did quarrel—but they managed to work it out. Tristan was damn good at listening; he claimed he'd learned how to listen from the *Desperado*, tracking all the sounds his boat made.

"So we're moving in together," she said softly. "Right here in Lust Harbor."

He let out a crow of laughter, then kissed her hand. "Yeah, the sooner the better, if you ask me." That was his mantra lately, and she didn't have any objections to that.

Now, waiting for her onstage in his seaweed wig, he mouthed it to her again.

The sooner the better. And: *I love you.*

Her mother would appreciate that mantra. The sooner the better. Live your life. Take a wild leap.

Maybe Mum hadn't meant "take a leap into the arms of a God of Seaweed while dressed as a sea slug," but Lulu had to do it her own way. And she did, hitting her mark and launching herself into the air in perfect timing with Tristan's movements.

He caught her and used her momentum to swing her over his head. He stabilized her with the oak-solid strength of his core muscles and his legs, braced as if he was on the deck of the *Desperado*. The crowd applauded wildly as she held her swan-dive pose for one breath, two breaths, three, held securely in his steady grip.

This was her life. Her unexpected life. Her seafaring love. Her newfound home.

The dream goes on, and on and on...
my heart is yours
wild as the ocean's kiss
deep as the ocean floor

THANK you so much for reading! For more Lost Harbor romance, find the entire series here.

Join Jennifer's newsletter and be the first to hear about new books, sales, and VIP giveaways. You'll receive a full-length novel download as a thank you gift!

ABOUT THE AUTHOR

Jennifer Bernard is a *USA Today* bestselling author of contemporary romance. Her books have been called "an irresistible reading experience" full of "quick wit and sizzling love scenes." A graduate of Harvard and former news promo producer, she left big city life in Los Angeles for true love in Alaska, where she now lives with her husband and stepdaughters. She still hasn't adjusted to the cold, so most often she can be found cuddling with her laptop and a cup of tea. No stranger to book success, she also writes erotic novellas under a naughty secret name that she's happy to share with the curious. You can learn more about Jennifer and her books at JenniferBernard.net. Make sure to sign up for her newsletter for new releases, fresh exclusive content, sales alerts and giveaways.

Connect with Jennifer online:
JenniferBernard.net
Jen@JenniferBernard.net

Lost Harbor, Alaska

Mine Until Moonrise

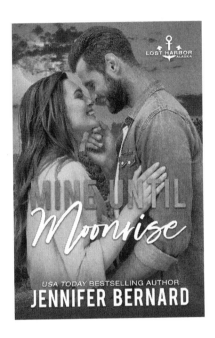

Yours Since Yesterday ～ Book 2

Seduced by Snowfall ~ Book 3

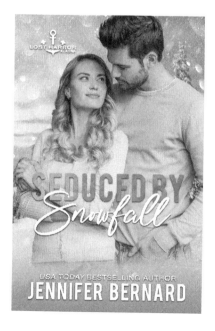

Wicked in Winter ~ Book 4

Naughty All Night ~ Book 5

Love at First Light ~ Book 6

Mischief after Midnight ~ Book 9

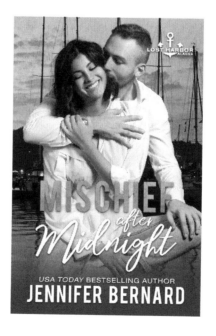

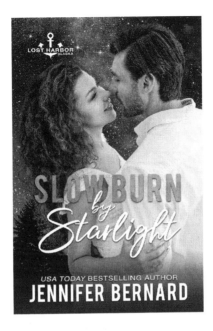

The Rockwell Legacy

The Rebel ~ Book 1

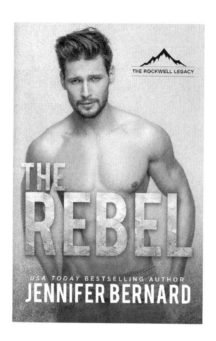

The Rogue ~ Book 2

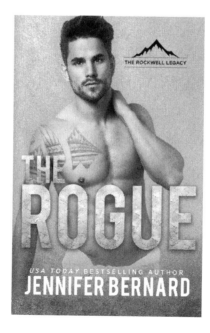

The Renegade ~ Book 3

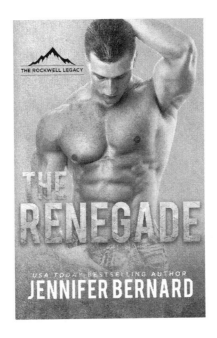

The Runaway ~ Book 4

The Rock ~ Book 5

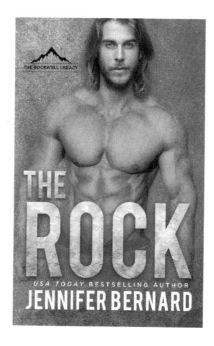

Jupiter Point ~ The Hotshots

Set the Night on Fire ~ Book 1

Burn So Bright ~ Book 2

Into the Flames ~ Book 3

Setting Off Sparks ~ Book 4

Jupiter Point ~ The Knight Brothers

Hot Pursuit ~ Book 5

Coming In Hot ~ Book 6

Hot and Bothered ~ Book 7

Too Hot to Handle ~ Book 8

One Hot Night ~ Book 9

Seeing Stars ~ Series Prequel

The Bachelor Firemen of San Gabriel Series

Love Between the Bases Series

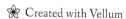

Made in the USA
Columbia, SC
23 November 2021

49660863R00190